Vision is the art of seeing
what is invisible to others.

~ Jonathan Swift
(1667 – 1745)

Also by Gwynne Hunt

Unlocking the Tin Box (Silver Bow Publishing 2019)
The Adventures of Bob & Boo (Penny a Line 2018)
Rampage; the pathology of an epidemic (Penny a Line 2011)
bruises & bad haircuts. (Penny a Line 2011)

Through My Lens

by

Gwynne Hunt

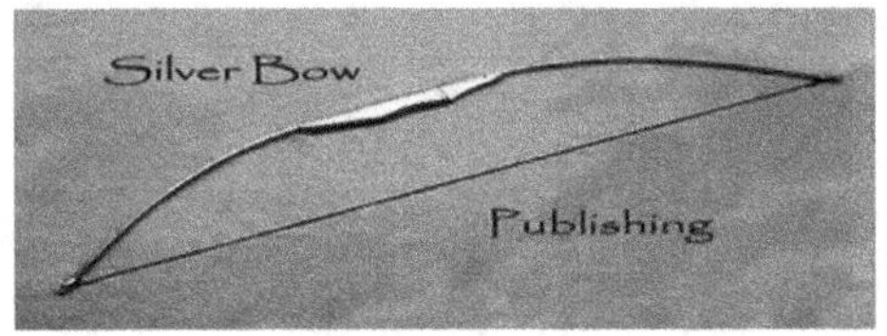

720 – Sixth Street, Box # 5
New Westminster, BC
V3C 3C5   CANADA

Title: Through My Lens
Author: Gwynne Hunt
Cover Art: "Through My Lens" art piece by Rhonda Simmons
Layout and Design: Candice James
Editor: Candice James

www.silverbowpublishing.com
info@silverbowpublishing.com
© Silver Bow Publishing 2021
isbn: 9781774031339 book
isbn: 9781774031346 e book

Library and Archives Canada Cataloguing in Publication

Title: Through my lens / by Gwynne Hunt.
Names: Hunt, Gwynne, 1949- author.
Description: Includes index.
Identifiers: Canadiana (print) 20210211652 | Canadiana (ebook) 20210216492 | ISBN 9781774031339
  (softcover) | ISBN 9781774031346 (Kindle)
Subjects: LCSH: Robinson, Ron, 1906-1973—Fiction. | LCSH: Berglund, Gunvor, 1910-1984—Fiction. |
  LCSH: Robinson, Marie, approximately 1899-1980—Fiction. | LCSH: Larsen, Harold, 1916-1983—
  Fiction.
Classification: LCC PS8615.U677 T47 2021 | DDC C813/.6—dc23

- Dedicated to my husband, Dave . . . he has been my biggest fan and offered me more support than anyone else. He has designed covers. He has been my audience of one. He has performed in my plays, sold the tickets, and even built the stages at times. He has been a big part of all the theatre productions, poetry readings and brainstorming for my books, plays, short stories and he has tirelessly worked on 'our' magazines. He has made my life as a writer possible.

- Thank you to Rhonda Simmons for allowing me to use her art piece for the cover of my book. From her show at the Harrison Art Gallery in 2010, I purchased the piece "Through My Lens".

Contents

Author's Foreword:

When I wrote my book Unlocking the Tin Box in 2019, it was an autobiography, telling the story of not only my life, but of my parents as well. I have done more genealogy research since then and have uncovered a history I was not aware of before. I decided to tell the story of my parents 'through my lens' based on my research. They are no longer here to ask how they felt or exactly what happened but there is a lot of information, memories, and family gossip to fill in the pieces.

I did not discover until I was 69 that my father Ronald Robinson was not my biological father. Despite family rumours over the years I was devastated. Ronald was English and I grew up believing I came from my Swedish mother and my English father. Ron had me convinced I descended from royalty. Through three DNA tests I found out I have no English DNA in my line but am Swedish and Danish. I found many DNA connected relatives. A new family of sorts, although nobody wanted to celebrate the birth of a new 69-year-old girl in their lives. One 2nd cousin, who I am still in touch with sent me a lot of family history. A few other cousins and a nephew provided information, but we do not keep in touch often. I understand that. I barely keep in touch with most of the relatives I grew up with.

I have had a few years now to put the story of my life in perspective and want to honour my parents; all three of them, by telling their stories. Their lives were complicated by World War I and II, the Great Depression, poverty, alcoholism, and families who did not understand them, disowned them, abused them, and abandoned them.

When I found out my biological father was Harold Larsen, I also found out some of his family members did not even know he existed. After comparing notes with the few that did know him, I discovered I knew more about him then they did. I only knew him in life as my father's best friend who my mother hated. As I said, it is complicated. They all impacted my life in profound ways, for at their core, each of them was wise, kind and loving.

Ronald Robinson   1906-1973 (father who raised me)
Gunvor Berglund   1910-1983 (mother)
Harold Larsen   1916-1983 (biological father)

Chapter One

Ron (1928 to 1931)

He was not sure where they had taken Marie. To a cell for only women was his best guess. They were in a mess. Marie could be a handful and Ron struggled to keep up with what he called her 'shenanigans'. He was only twenty-two and Marie was thirty, on an honest day. Sometimes she claimed to be twenty-five but that did not seem possible as her son Bill was fourteen. Ron knew he was going to have to marry Marie to clear up the mess they had just gotten into. Wives cannot testify against their husbands.

Ronald Robinson, known as Ron or Robby, Tiny or even sometimes Ray, had met Marie a few months earlier when he arrived in Saskatoon. He was trying to get to Winnipeg where he knew there was a bustling rum running business. He wanted to be part of it. He was fed up with what he called the bull and hypocrisy of his family. He left Nanaimo, British Columbia for points east back in April just after he turned twenty-two. His mother Elizabeth told him to get out if he was not going to live a clean and honest life. He thought the irony of that was ridiculous.

His father Thomas had died of syphilis in February, just before Ron's birthday. All Ron could think was, 'pot calling the kettle black'. His dad died from a venereal disease, but the family frowned on Ron having a pint of beer at the pub. The old man had lost his mind, ran away from home and had been found wandering the streets of Vancouver. He was incoherent and in the final stages of the terrible disease.

Ron was born in Felling, Durham County in England on March 28th, 1906. His parents: Elizabeth and Thomas were poor, hardworking folks. Elizabeth was more refined and came from a family of joiners, carpenters, and cabinet makers. Thomas came from a long line of coal miners. Both families belonged to the Anglican Church, were devout and did not believe in the 'drink'. Ron knew his dad liked a beer at the pub when he was boxing. Ron had seen the old man stagger in on more than one occasion, so that was hypocrisy number one.

During the First World War Thomas went off like many young Englishman to serve his country. He ended up in Mesopotamia; a land unlike anything he had ever seen. The hard, dry landscape was certainly nothing like jolly old England. He longed for the lush, rolling hills and the ocean he knew in Northumberland. He was in the Army and part of a crew of soldiers building roads to help the war effort. He was stationed there from 1914 until 1918 with a group known as the 'Royal Engineers'. And like most of them he came back with malaria and syphilis. It is unlikely even Thomas knew he was infected with syphilis or that the crazy thoughts, slurred words, and staggering gait were connected to the disease.

On June 21, 1922, four years after the war, Thomas left for Canada on the Empress of India to work as a farm servant on his sister's farm; Felling Farm in Redcliff, Alberta. He did not have a sister in Redcliff, but it was common to claim close relations to be allowed to come to a new country. He arrived with six pounds leaving his family behind at 10 Charles Streets, Bolden Colliery where he had been employed. He hoped, in Canada, he could work with horses and never have to go down a mine shaft again. The promised land offered rolling hills and farmland. He had been told he could get a job on Felling Farm as a stable hand. He had relatives in Gretna Green, Scotland and as a boy learned a bit about being a farrier at a blacksmith shop owned by an uncle.

Ron missed his father, who had gone to Canada first to find work and then planned to send for the rest of the family. Two years earlier Ron had completed four and a half years of school, receiving a Standard II from Bolden Colliery Council School. He was only fourteen but that was the highest level of school available for young boys at the time. There was no money for university. Most boys were down in the pit by the time they were ten. Thomas did not want that life for his son. He had to leave home at ten to work in a mine.

Bolden Colliery was a lovely little village. However, the row houses they lived in were tiny and gloomy and Elizabeth could not wait to leave and go to the new country. It took Thomas three months to send passage for her and Fred, their youngest son. Ron and his sister Freda paid their own passage.

On September 15th they left on the Montclair; Elizabeth, Freda who was eighteen, Fred who was ten and Ronald who was sixteen. Ron was listed as a 'Draper' which simply meant he was the one who draped the cloth for the seamstress to cut out the pattern in a fashion house. Freda was a tailoress. The two of them took the bus every morning to Sunderland which was six miles away; a seaport for coal and salt. It was also a booming town with lots of factories and fashion houses. Freda and Ronald were employed by a company that made men's suits.   They liked it but Canada was calling and they were eager to relocate there.

They all reunited in Redcliff with Thomas. None of them worked on a farm but lived in a rooming house; Ron and Freda in one room, with mom, dad, and Fred in another. Fred and mom did not work, Thomas had several labour jobs. Brother Ron and sister Freda worked at the Dominion Glass Factory. Ron must have admired the glass blowers as he claimed he was one of them to most people he met. In fact, he worked in the warehouse packing up orders to be shipped around North America. They specialized in milk bottles, but cups, bowls and plates were made there as well.

Redcliff was surrounded by rolling hills, farmland, and prairie. There was wide open spaces Ronald loved to explore on his days off. There was a mine Thomas found work at and they settled into a quiet life in the rooming house; every penny saved. They all dreamed of living on the West Coast of Canada as they missed the ocean and sea breezes around Newcastle. There were no pubs, no social life but they all took to the outdoors on their bicycles and made a lot of friends. They stayed in Redcliff for two years.

Along the way Thomas passed his exams for Deputy Work in the mines and that was what brought them to Nanaimo. British Columbia was booming, and Nanaimo on Vancouver Island had lots of underground mines. There was big business in shipping coal and Thomas was a coal miner at heart. Thomas never went to school, did a little boxing and was what people might call backwards. But he dressed like a proper gentleman; very dapper and grandiose. He was a member of the Sons of Temperance and worked hard. Early in January of 1928, he wandered away from his home, caught a ferry to Vancouver and disappeared. He turned up at a local hospital not knowing who he was but some identification on him led to Elizabeth, letting her know he was safe.

A few days later he escaped the hospital and was later picked up by police. They determined he was a lunatic and took him to Essondale Hospital in a suburb of Vancouver. The facility used to be called Crease Clinic after the doctor who first started the clinic. Over the years it had become a dumping ground for anyone who was 'not right'; women with postpartum depression, mentally challenged children, miners with head injuries, men who were violent and anyone who was considered criminally insane.

When Thomas arrived by police escort to Essondale he was registered as a 'Lunatic Wandering at Large' by the Province of B.C. He had sixty-five cents, a safety razor and blades, a collar stud, a shaving brush, and a broken watch. He was wearing a coat, vest, pants, braces, sox, boots, a tie, a scarf, and garters. He also had a handkerchief and a cap. He eventually suffered a seizure and died of Exhaustion of General Paresis (syphilis). He lived for seven months at the Clinic and when he died, he was forty-nine years old. He was patient number 9770.

Elizabeth was shocked when she heard he had syphilis as she never contracted the disease. She remained a good wife sending him gifts and visiting as often as she could. She even paid the exorbitant amount to have his body shipped by ferry back to Vancouver Island. She had written a letter to the Doctor at the Clinic and declared, "Had I known what his affliction was, well, I would not have been happy. God works in ways to correct mistakes."

Thomas was Ronald's hero until he learned his dad had syphilis. His mother had reported Thomas had pneumonia and was suffering amnesia from being hit on his head by a rock in the mines. On one of Ronald's visits, the Doctor sat Ronald down and explained why his father could only stagger around and had fits. Ron was furious with his mother for the betrayal and angry with his father for the shame he brought on the family. He walked out of Essondale a week before his father's death and swore he would never forgive either one of them.

All the years of the 'old man' being hard on him, strict and unforgiving left a bitter taste for Ron.   He tried to live up to his father's expectations.   He finished school with honours and began working at the age of fourteen. Even during World War I he was a pigeon keeper, helping the war effort with training homing pigeons. He was eight and worked with the birds until the war was over when he was twelve. He was the man of the house and took care of everything, after school, that this dad used to; like taking out the garbage, raking up the leaves, hammering in a nail if it was needed. After school and chores, he took care of the pigeons on the rooftop as it was getting dark; frightened by the bombers that would fly overhead.

Later he worked in men's clothing, for two years, before he left England. He was a smart, funny boy; a boy his parents could be proud of. He saved his own passage to Canada. He was a shipper in Alberta then worked at a florist shop and then Semple Shoes in Nanaimo. His mother was running a rooming house in Nanaimo and he even paid her rent; just like the young coal miners who rented rooms. In the evenings he sat down for the dinner his mother had laid out on her horsehair burgundy tablecloth. He admired the formal candlesticks, the linen napkins, and the beautiful china she brought with her from England. And all those years even though he had contrary beliefs he went to church with his parents and abstained from drinking.

Nobody talked about the thousands of men who came back to Britain with malaria and syphilis. Even if they had, Ron believed his father was a better man than that. He found it impossible to comprehend his father could not abstain from sex and be true to his wife for four years. That was not the man he knew. It was a rainy day when Thomas was laid to rest in the Nanaimo cemetery. Freda had married and was living close by her mother. Fred was training to be a cabinet maker. They had made a lot of friends in the area in the four years they lived there. They stood, shoulder to shoulder, in the rain under umbrellas and listened to a rousing memorial praising Thomas. None of them knew he had died from syphilis except Ronald, Freda, and their mother.

Ron felt his father betrayed him. Ron started drinking, he started rebelling and then he left. He had a friend who was driving to Saskatoon, so he quit his job at the shoe store and left. The day he arrived in Saskatoon, he went into an underground drinking establishment and there she was, the most vivacious woman he had ever seen. He was cocky and sure of himself so he approached her and asked her if he could buy her a beer.

Marie winked at him and said, "One beer won't be enough honey, you better have a lot of money on you."

She was like something out of a movie with her long black hair, pale complexion, and pouty red lips. She had a very Burlesque look with two little dots high on her cheekbones. She was curvy and provocative in a fringed, red silk dress. He was in love long before he realized she was a prostitute and a scammer. It was not long before they were a team. She reeled them in with promises while he waited in the shadows for his chance to relieve the 'John' of his money. They made a good team and were bringing in enough money to buy a car, rent a nice apartment and party all they wanted. Marie, pleased with her new young boyfriend, felt safer working with a partner. She grew even bolder than she had been before Ron came into her life..

In the late eighteen hundreds, a group of Methodists left Toronto to start a temperance town and in 1903 they founded Saskatoon. The only thing that kept the city alive was wheat. By

1928 the first Beer Parlours were opened on the Prairies and drew folks to the city in the evenings and on weekends. Ron and Marie however did not go to the beer parlours, women were not allowed. There were underground `speakeasies` or private clubs with burlesque dancers and `women of the night`. Saskatoon was still a small city and only boasted two such clubs. Marie craved the brighter lights of Winnipeg.

Marie had family in Winnipeg and so they often went there to eat Polish food in the family café located in the North End on Selkirk Avenue. It was called Café Polska, painted in bright, sunny colours. It was a few doors down from her cousin's shoe store and a block from another cousin's theatre. A lot of Ukrainians and Poles were big into classical theatre, the arts, and live productions. Theatre houses were abundant and produced the classics and vaudeville, and even burlesque.

Marie's son went to school, living with the family who did not approve of her lifestyle. Her son Billy was a good kid; fourteen but he was hanging out with some tough boys who were into petty crime. His last name was Dick as Marie had married briefly at fourteen to an Englishman, who was the father. Her maiden name was a long Polish name, she claimed to not remember and had shortened it to Hoick.

It was a different life for Ron, and he loved it. Marie's family was eccentric, bohemian and some of them were even fortune tellers. The part they did not approve of was Marie being a prostitute. They were fine with the gypsy way of life, carnivals and caravans, fortune telling, bootlegging, and selling snake oil but they were not alright with getting paid to have sex. However, Marie did not have to do that very often. She was able to get the money and run before she had to work for her money.

Back in Saskatoon, at the Bon Ton Burlesque House, Marie was known as Bohunk Marie because she came from Poland. She liked the name because it was not girly. Many of the women were known as Flower Lily, Cherry Pie or Sassy Suzy. To Marie, Bohunk meant they knew she was a bohemian gypsy. It meant she was a proud woman who was in control of herself and her life. She did a little fortune telling; her mother taught her. She did a little bootlegging from whatever rooming house she was living in. Sometimes she sold heroin. Marie carried a little knife in her pocketbook, and she had been known to use it. She was smart, fast, and felt she was a step ahead of everyone except Ron. He was her match.

On the night of October 8th on a cold, brisk Saskatoon evening, a guy named Mike Pilawski wandered into one of the clubs with four hundred dollars in his pocket. He was working at one of the grain elevators and had been paid out because he was going back to Montreal in a few days. He and three French Canadians went to the club looking for women and found Marie. After many drinks Marie figured out which one had the money and who she and Ron would target. Marie made a date with Mike for the next night. As she was leaving, she saw Mike fighting with one of the men at his table. Marie was used to men fighting over her and kept walking.

On October 9th Mike went to the club to meet up with Marie who was accompanied by Ron who she introduced as her younger brother Ray. Mike admitted one of the guys took a round out of him because he was flirting with Marie the night before. He straightened the guy out, he told Marie and Ray. He confided to Marie, "I let them know you were mine."

The three men turned up later but did not come over to the table or even speak to them. There was a three-piece jazz ensemble playing and Marie danced a lot with Mike and her `brother`. Mike laughed and asked, `You got to dance with the baby brother so much? I might get jealous."

They drank until closing then Marie suggested a walk to sober up a bit. The three French Canadians didn't follow but watched Marie, Ron and Mike leave the club. Marie asked Mike if his friends were going to cause any trouble, but he said no, it was all good. The three walked off hand in hand, Marie in the middle. Ron was telling jokes, each one cornier than the rest. He quipped, "Where does a pirate keep his buccaneers, ha-ha, under his bucking hat."

The three of them were laughing, joke after joke. They were very jovial as they walked along the tracks. Marie wanted to get Mike to a dark area where they could grab his money and run. They had planned the route out in the afternoon. Ron knew the signal so when Marie stopped and planted a big kiss on Mike`s lips, he was ready. Mike reached down to grab Marie around the waist, Ron moved in and picked his pockets, a skill he had perfected when he was young. It was something the schoolboys had done back in England partly because Ron was a big fan of Oliver Twist. Ron loved Charles Dickens and the character, in the book, Fagin who taught homeless boys to pick pockets. Ron signalled to Marie with a head nod and said, "Marie I`m tired. Let`s go home now."

Marie pushed Mike back, laughing that kisses were for later. He stumbled on the tracks and fell. She ran after Ron, waving at Mike and yelling, "Have a good night. Thanks for the drinks."

As Mike tried to get up, he mumbled something but did not make it to his feet, Ron asked, "Did he hurt himself when he fell?"

Marie yelled, "You OK Mike?"

"Yep", he replied and laid back down as if he were going to go to sleep, take a nap on the tracks. Ron was concerned but Marie said, "He's fine. No trains running this time of night."

Marie and Ron walked around the corner of the club and saw the three French Canadian men hanging around the door. One of them asked where Mike was, and Marie motioned that he was behind the club by the tracks. Marie thought it odd they were still there and thought maybe they had a plan to beat up her and Ron. Something didn`t seem right and Marie whispered to Ron, "We better run."

As they ran off one of the men hollered at them, "What the hell did you do to Mike?"

That was the last they saw of Mike or his three friends. They got back to their apartment and Ron counted out three hundred dollars. That was a huge amount of money for them. Marie poured him some whiskey and they were celebrating, clinking their glasses. Not long after, they heard cop sirens from their apartment window, and they figured they better lay low. Ron pulled the string on the lightbulb and the apartment went black.

The street did not settle down that night; cop cars, an ambulance, people milling about behind the club. Marie was snoring but Ron could not sleep. Ron finally left the apartment and went to see what was going on. He got to the corner as the ambulance drivers were loading up a body. He did not know why but he knew it was Mike. He went back to the apartment. He woke Marie up with a jab to the ribs, "We gotta get out of here."

She rolled over and asked, "What the hell for?"

"He's dead," He answered in a flat tone.

"Not from us," she declared and jumped out of bed.

Ron and Marie loaded up their few belongings and left in the car he had just bought a weeks earlier. It was a 1920 Ford Model T he had picked up for two hundred dollars from a guy who was losing money fast on the stock market. It was the prettiest and best thing he had ever owned. They drove to Winnipeg in the middle of the night and checked into Fort Garry Hotel. They decided they may as well live large and spend the money before they got arrested.

At the front desk, Marie said, "Do you feel okay about all that happened?"

Ron laughed, "I feel like a gangster."

The clerk asked, "Is that Mr. and Mrs?"

A few days later they heard about Mike`s death and as money was getting tight, moved into a cheaper place. That's where they were when Detective Brown came from Saskatoon to arrest them on suspicion of murder.

They had seen the circular put out by the RCMP looking for Marie Hoick sometimes known as Dyck or Bohunk Marie and Roland Robinson. Her name was Dick, not Dyck and he was Ronald not Roland. The circular mentioned three unknown French Canadians but the suspicion for the murder was placed on Marie and Roland as the papers stated that Robinson was the last person seen with Mike. Detective Brown brought them back to Saskatoon for questioning and then said they would be held in the cells until he could check out their stories.

Ron had a lot of time in jail to think about what might have happened. He knew Marie did not kill Mike when he fell. The papers said Mike was found brutally beaten with a severe head wound. His head was on a big stack of blood-soaked newspapers. They had not seen a stack of newspapers anywhere near where Mike fell. Ron knew it had nothing to do with them and was waiting for the Detective from Saskatoon to come and tell him his story was the same as Marie's. He wished he could talk to her; get their stories straight. They only had about a hundred dollars left but he had stashed it very well in the Model T.

On the morning of November 6th after the detective had questioned Marie and Ron, they were brought to the courthouse three days after their arrest. Ron was not sure what he was being charged with and was anxious until he saw Marie waltz in with the biggest smile he had ever seen. She winked at him as she came up to the lawyer`s table. She was wearing a white suit with a little matching hat he had never seen, while he was in his rumpled clothes from three days ago. She tapped the little hat and grinned, "Nothing to worry about," she whispered.

The Magistrate came in and took the bench and announced that the two of them were going to be charged with registering at a hotel as man and wife when they were not married. It was illegal to do that.

"As you know", he bellowed, "that is a crime. I sentence you to time served and a ten-dollar fine . . . each."

He slammed down the gavel and they were free to go. Ron could not believe they were not being charged with murder. The Detective had been, as he told Marie, a prick when he questioned him. Marie looked at Ron and said, "Detective Brown? I've known him for a long time, honey. He believed everything I said."

She poked him in the ribs, "he was just jealous of you. That is why he treated you so bad. He really is a good cop."

Ron did not even feel jealous he was so relieved. The cop believed their story because it was the truth. The other three men were the ones under suspicion now and it was them who tried to cast shadow on him and Marie. Problem was the three men left

Saskatoon before the police could arrest them. Nobody knew their names. Ron and Marie paid their twenty-dollar fine and left the Courthouse. He never did find out how she got new clean clothes in jail.

That afternoon they went back to Winnipeg and Ron rented a new two-bedroom apartment fully furnished for them. Marie`s son moved in with them. He was a tall, gangly kid who was handsome and smart. He did not like Ron much. Three days later Ron and Marie went to City Hall and got married. Marie insisted they had to get married and he agreed. Once married they could not testify against one another if the case ever came to trial. So far, nobody knew they'd stolen three hundred dollars, and it was going to stay that way. Ron phoned his mom and told her he was a married man with a fourteen-year-old son and Elizabeth replied, "Well, you`ve made your bed and now you are going to have to sleep in it."

Ron was sad because he loved his mom. He wanted her approval. He was not going back to BC until he had a lot of money and then she would forgive him. First, he had to get a job and in Winnipeg in 1928 it was not that hard to find a job if you were OK with breaking the law. While Canada had opened with beer parlours, the United States had remained locked down for the legal purchase of alcohol. Ron met a guy who knew a guy and within a few days he was driving his Model T across the border with booze hidden in the back. While the United States Government was pressuring Canada to sign an agreement to stop the illegal traffic Ron figured he had at least a year to make some real money.

Marie told Ron she was not going to prostitute herself anymore. She wanted to make a real home for her son Bill, and he was going to be making so much money she should not have to work so hard. Ron agreed. He did not like sharing his wife. He did not want to get syphilis like his dad. She went to the Hurdy Gurdy Burlesque Theatre not far from their new apartment in Winnipeg and as they say, a star was born. One of her cousins owned the building and leased it to a Theatre Company for rehearsals and plays four times a year. In between times, they had to make money and the Hurdy Gurdy was a huge money maker. During off-season weekends seven or eight girls danced each night sharing the stage with comics doing skits.

Marie's reputation from Saskatoon, as being a tough broad, followed her. Nobody messed with Marie. She was a small woman with a big reputation. Soon her young, short, English boyfriend was given the respect she received. If Marie thought he was alright, then he was. It was a fast-paced life, and they seemed to be connected to almost everything considered illegal.

Chapter Two

Ron & Marie (1932 to 1940)

Ron and Marie never settled into a happily married life. The two of them never settled into anything. There was always a new scheme, a new con and the necessity to make money. Winnipeg, like all the big cities, was struggling to feed the people, keep them working and keep them from dying on the streets. Crime was on the rise, which was perfect for Ron and Marie as they were dyed in the wool petty criminals. It was mostly small stuff in the beginning, picking pockets, robbing grocery stores. Sometimes they would find a 'mark' sitting on a park bench, often a young woman. Marie would wander up and start chatting and while the 'mark' was distracted, Ron grabbed her purse and was gone. Marie would be concerned and helpful but then would have an appointment and could not 'stick around until the cops came'.

"Sorry sweetie, gotta run but the best of luck to ya honey. I'm going to miss my bus," Marie would holler as she ran off.

One Sunday afternoon, Marie and her girlfriend, Anne Boyer went on a joy ride with their husbands searching for something to do. Two days later, they ended up in Perdue, Saskatchewan, tipsy on whiskey. They left their husbands in the car and went to get soft drinks. Ann strolled into a local Chinese restaurant and struck up a conversation with the cook. She managed to pick his pocket and ran out with twenty-seven dollars. Marie, at the same time was across the street at a garage and stole a minimal amount of money she found on the counter. It was not enough for the two couples; so, while Marie and Ron sat in the front seat of the car, the other two went back into the King George Restaurant and ordered some soft drinks. Ann was going to cause a distraction and her husband would rob the till. However, the cook saw Ann and rushed out of the kitchen yelling, "She take my money."

The cashier said, "Ma'am did you do that?"

"No way," she claimed and grabbed the soft drinks and said to her husband, "How rude. Let's get out of here."

The four escaped with the soft drinks and sped down a back road. There was a police chase. They were not hard to find in the small town, the only sedan with Winnipeg, Manitoba plates. The four of them got to finish their soft drinks before they were placed in a cell for the night. As Marie would say, we had a lot of 'shits and giggles' in those days. Justice was swift in the small town. Marie got a five-dollar fine and Ann had to pay ten. Ann's husband who had taken a few law classes at night school defended the two wives, claiming as well, that he and Ron had no idea what hijinks the women were up to. They laughed about it all the way back to Winnipeg which was an eight-hour drive. Even the Judge agreed it was a long drive for a Sunday. The two couples were over a hundred dollars richer and the crime spree had paid for the trip.

It was 1932, hard times. The four of them had been on a whisky drunk for days, travelling all over Saskatchewan as the little towns were easy pickings. Ron always felt that if you robbed a store or a restaurant, they were an establishment and that meant they were established. They had money and he did not. He felt in these tough times that a restaurant owner should be giving out free food to those in need.

"Robbing from the rich to pay to the poor," he would say.

Marie would chuck him under the chin and claim, "You're a regular little Robin Hood."

When they were not travelling around committing petty crimes, Ron joined Marie at the Hurdy Gurdy Burlesque House in Winnipeg as the opening act. He had a bathtub scene that was vulgar and hilarious. Some of the dancers started to complain that he was stealing the show. Ron had a variety of funny 'bits' he performed. They were both so talented they drank free most nights. Plus, they got paid five dollars an act; each. Ron had a flair for theatre and when friends hung around at drinking parties; he always ad-libbed some funny 'bits'.

The theatre itself was beautiful; gilded everything. It sparkled in gold tones and the sets were elaborate items like park benches that looked like they were wrought iron, huge papier mache flowers for the dancers and brocade screens. Ron's bathtub was a real claw foot tub on wheels the stagehands rolled out. There was a brake on the tub so Ron would not roll off the stage. Even the claw feet were painted gold. He looked naked but he was wearing brown bathing trunks, fake bubbles filled the tub, and he sported a pink bathing cap. It was a bit all about losing your soap in the tub.

Towards the end of 1933 Ron had been running booze to the States for a few years. Sometimes he smuggled heroin or morphine in special shoes Marie's cousin made for him. It was too easy. The shoes had false heels with an empty pocket inside the heel that hid what he needed to. He also had a suitcase with more shoes and would wink at the Border Crossing Guard and say, "I'm a fancy dresser, a pair of shoes for every suit and see the special heels on my shoes? Makes me look an inch taller."

He was so brazen, he would point out the unusual higher heel and say, "Short guys like me need an advantage."

Ron never felt guilty. Part of that was because he was using opiates. By the 1930s, users spent more and more time travelling around the country in search of a 'fix,' resorting to crime more frequently to finance their habit. There were few jobs for men around. They often became caught in a cycle of imprisonment. Three squares and a bed became a way of life.

Four years after they got married Ron and Marie broke up. Ron was dabbling in the narcotics he was smuggling far too much. It was not that Marie was worried about his drug use, she used as much as he did. She was worried about him getting caught tasting the product. He was as he would say, 'on the lam'. They didn't have a huge fight or disagreement, Marie just said to him one day, "Ron, you're in too deep, pal. Too much booze, too many drugs. I don't want the heat on me."

Ron started travelling with the carnivals. The drug trafficking was drying up. Nobody could afford the narcotics anymore. Most Americans were getting their booze from stills up in the mountains and were not looking for Canadians to bring drugs to Chicago. But it had been a good time for Ronald, as he was calling himself in 1933. Most of his carny and con friends called him Tiny. Change of name, change of scenery. He was in too deep. He even knew some Mob types well known to the F.B.I. like Baby Face Nelson. Baby Face was a short little guy with a young-looking face about two years younger than Ron. He became famous for helping John Dillinger escape from prison and he was gaining a reputation as a killer. Ron was hanging out with him too much when he was in the States. He liked the gangsters. So, for Marie, it was not so much that they split up it was more of a 'see you later when things cool off'.

Eventually, Ron figured he knew too much, and he decided to try Edmonton; run some drugs there. He was mostly getting prescriptions for opiates from doctors; some legal and some not. He paid guys on the streets to get the prescription. A few doctors were willing to write a prescription for money. They had families to feed as well. Ron left the car for Marie and went to Edmonton. He rode the rails like all the bums were doing in those days. He was probably the only homeless guy in a suit, but he liked his suits. He also liked other people he saw as disadvantaged like him, like Chinese people. He had an affinity for 'the Chinese' as they were called in the thirties. The Chinese were not well liked in the thirties and believed to be the opiate pushers and the pimps for prostitution. Ronald had no prejudice against any race, or anybody. He accepted everyone at face value and trusted a lot of people. That was probably his downfall. He would meet someone in a bar and become instant friends. Things were rough. Eventually, even the carnivals stopped running.

The Depression was in full swing and nobody had money. Ron struggled to stay warm, dry and fed. The four Western Provinces were the hardest hit, British Columbia, Alberta, Manitoba, and Saskatchewan. They were bankrupt. Ron had to rely on picking pockets, stealing and the odd poker game. He was a good talker, had nice suits and could talk himself into game rooms. Nobody knew he was sleeping under a bridge sometimes. He was also able to get a few jobs because he had a good resume for such a young guy. He could read and write, he claimed he had a university education and could talk like that could be true. He would work for a day or two unloading a freight car, or once he got on at the T. Eaton Co. warehouse as a shipper, receiver but that only lasted two days.

He had no idea how Marie was doing as he just drifted for a couple of years. He did not really care. He was heading west and hoping he could get back to see his mom in Nanaimo. BC. He reasoned that once he got home, he could lay low, get healthy and fixed up before he went back to Marie in Winnipeg. Besides, he missed his mom, a lot. He left a few months after his dad died when he was only twenty-two. He knew he had grown wiser, but he did not feel that mature, even though he was twenty-eight now.

Ronald had moved into a rooming house with Mark Sue Kwok. Although the room was rented by someone else, Kwok and Ron had been there a few nights when they were arrested. In July of 1934 at the height of the Depression he was given six months in Fort Saskatchewan Jail for Vagrancy. Several stolen items were found in the room but both men swore they did not know where the goods came from as the items were in the cupboard when they arrived. The renter had no knowledge of any of it and had allowed the two men to take over the room when he had to leave town. They were not all that sad about going to jail; three squares a day. North of Edmonton, the jail housed three hundred men who made license plates, built roads, and took care of cattle. Most of the men in the prison were happy to have food and a place to sleep. Violent encounters were minimal during the Depression.

Single men could not collect welfare but instead were put into Relief Camps that paid twenty cents a day for work like building roads. The conditions in the camps were terrible, worse than jail. In 1935 conditions at one of the Regina camps was so bad the men rioted, and an officer was killed. Ron was content stamping out license plates until the day he was released. He liked the beans and bread meals. He was fine with drinking water if he had tea in the morning. He made a lot of friends. It was an easy six months.

When Ron and Mark got out in October it was cold and they had to steal a few things to get some money. Everyone was driving around in Bennet Buggies named after Prime Minister Richard Bennett.   It was not a compliment, they blamed him for the Depression. There was no gas, so people took out the engines of their Model T's and then the windows. They hitched up their horses. And yet, despite the poverty, women could still get a 'wet comb out' for five cents or a perm for two dollars and fifty cents. Ron and Kwok ran every scam they could. A can of vegetable soup cost fifteen cents, and they had to eat.

Six months later their crimes caught up to them and they were arrested. This time Kwok swore he did not know Robinson until he met him in Edmonton and knew nothing about him, even though they had spent six months together in prison. The newspapers read that Robinson who lived in Winnipeg admitted he had a police record of theft and shoplifting but he had given up on crime and narcotics a few months earlier. The cops said that Kwok's claims of not knowing him were ridiculous as they found matching caps. They both wore the caps with Saskatoon labels and there was a note in Kwok's pocket from Saskatoon that read, 'Tiny says be careful and don't get caught'.

In a room on 98th Street in Edmonton the cops found flashlights, an electric iron, gloves, and other articles. All they were able to charge them with was theft of three sets of driving lines worth twelve dollars and sixty cents from the T. Eaton Co. warehouse. With the Bennett Buggies, driving lines or harness lines as they were also called were a hot commodity. As Robinson was the one who had worked briefly at T. Eaton Co., he was found guilty of the theft and was sent back to Fort Saskatchewan for another six months. Ronald figured he could say goodbye to his stuff that was left in the rooms; he knew he would never hear from Kwok again. Ronald was annoyed with Kwok. The electric iron was his, he stole it so he could keep his limited supply of suits ironed.

It was March of 1936 when Ronald got out. He was able to pick up a few things he left with a woman he knew but she had a new boyfriend, and he could not stay there. He struggled for a few weeks trying to find food to eat; he slept under a bridge and hung around the nicer parts of town so he could steal purses and pick pockets. He was sleeping under the bridge one night when the cops came out in force and rounded them all up. One guy said, "Finally, room and board coming up."

Ron was charged with vagrancy again. The magistrate this time said, "You're not a bad guy and I don't want to send you to jail again. You have forty-eight hours to get out of Edmonton."

Ron sent a telegram to Marie because a nice law clerk gave him a few bucks. Marie came to take him back to Winnipeg. She had a job for him; one that would put them on Easy Street. The Red River was high and muddy, but he could see as they pulled into Winnipeg that the red-light district was busy and he knew right away where he could get into a high stakes' poker game, if Marie would float him some cash. She was still driving his car and by all appearances was not starving or in trouble of any kind. Her and Billy were getting welfare, she said, and she was running a few deals. He knew she was hooking again. She was even wearing a fur coat.

She told him on the ride to Manitoba that she knew some guys who were friends of her son's. Billy had been hanging out with these guys and pulled a few stunts, but this job was too big for the Kid as she called him. The morphine or brown heroin as it was sometimes called, was already in capsules and tucked away in several pairs of Tiny's shoes her cousin made for him. All he had to do was get on a train to Vancouver and put the suitcases in a locker at the station.

Once he had successfully obtained the money and turned it over to one of the brothers, Billy's friends, Marie would be given a thousand dollars. She and Billy would get on the next train and meet Ron in Vancouver. He did want Marie back. He was tired of drifting and ending up in jail. He figured at least with Marie complicit in the trafficking he could count on her to have his back and she did. And it was worth the risk, but he told Marie this was the last time he would deal in drugs.

And it was. Job over, and living in a rooming house in Vancouver, they were hanging out at the Niagara Hotel one night and Ron met a lawyer who had not found his way home from work yet. He hired Ron as a Barrister's Clerk in Vancouver and he put the drug money away in his name. The idea was to give the money to Ron and Marie slowly so as not to raise suspicion.

The lawyer had a lot of scam jobs for Ron to do. One of the easiest was to set up husbands for wives who wanted a divorce. Infidelity was the only reason for a divorce, so Ron and Marie would get the 'mark' drunk and then Marie would pose in compromising positions with the guy. The lawyer went to court with the pictures and the woman was given her divorce. Charity work is how Ron saw it. He convinced himself that the 'poor' woman was being beaten or abused in some way and he needed to help her. Sometimes the woman was just a gold digger, but Ron overlooked those cases when he retold friends about his social work on the job.

"Just helping out the little ladies," he would say and grin.

Vancouver was more laid back than Winnipeg and he and Marie, along with Billy and his girlfriend, Helen, found a great place on East Hastings; two bedrooms and a bath with a big kitchen for use by all the boarders. By 1937 the four of them were trying to take small amounts of drugs to the States but often were turned back at the border because of Ron's Criminal Record. Their ages and ethnicity changed on the forms with regularity; sometimes Marie was Ukrainian, sometimes Polish and her age ranged from thirty-five to thirty-seven. She was the mother of a twenty-one-year-old. Marie was thirty-seven, Ron was thirty-one. Sometimes they were not allowed across and were barred. It did not stop them from trying again and again.

They were living in the heart of Japan town, a thriving community full of restaurants and fish markets. Things were getting better; money was flowing again if you looked in the right places. All four of them had started working the carnivals. It was easy, legal money. Ron ran the Crown and Anchor game which had a pedal on the floor so he could 'cheat' the patrons, hard working men he called chumps. Marie hustled players to the games with her big personality and smile when she was not working the Cotton Candy machine. Billy worked an add up joint, popping balloons and Helen sold corn on the cob. Ron was only called Tiny in those days, Bohunk Marie's old man, and Billy the Kid's stepdad.

Everyone knew there was a war coming. Germany invaded Rhineland in 1937, and in 1938 Bohemia, Morovia; people could see how unsettled it was in Europe. Movie theatres were bustling with people trying to escape reality and the lingering effects of the depression. People flocked to the movies to watch shows like A Star is Born and Stage Door. Next to movies, carnivals were exciting events when they rolled into town.

They were working with a Carnival that focused on small towns in the Interior, like Kelowna, Peachland, and Kamloops. Ron still worked for the lawyer but only when there was a client, so he and Marie resorted to picking pockets and doing vaudeville at the carnival to supplement their income. The thousand-dollar drug money was tucked away with the lawyer. Compared to most people they were doing well financially.

Ron made every effort to reconnect with his mom. She was running a boarding house at ninety-nine and a half Nicol Street in downtown Nanaimo, close to the Harbour. He started taking the ferry to Nanaimo every few weeks to visit her. He never told her what he had been up to; she did not know about crimes or prison. He did not tell her he was working carnivals. She thought he worked for a lawyer. Her son was legitimate, and she was proud of him. As it was, she did not like Marie, so Ron usually visited her alone. The two of them became close once again and he turned up on Saturday nights so he could make her roast beef and Yorkshire pudding for Sunday lunch. His brother Fred was married, and he often came, his wife bringing the apple pie. They talked a lot about the first world war and how his father had served his country. Ron was very patriotic to England.

His brother Fred had married in 1938 with one of the biggest weddings in Nanaimo during the Depression with over one hundred guests. Ron was there with Marie. His sister Freda's daughter Joyce was the flower girl in a French frock of stiff yellow taffeta. The reception was at the Eagles Hall which was a stylish new building and Elizabeth hosted the buffet dinner. She planned it down to the last shrimp roll. She did not plan the wedding but was given full run for the reception and she directed it like an orchestra. It was one of the happiest nights Ron and Marie ever had together. Ron wore a new suit and Marie was beautiful in a taffeta teal suit. It was a memory to hold on to. Everyone knew there were dark times coming. War was expected.

September 1, 1939 Hitler invaded Poland and that began the Second World War. Ten days later Canada joined the war effort, but most Canadians figured it was too far away and not their problem so did not enlist at first. Ron felt a responsibility to protect England. He was itching to go to war, but his mom cautioned him. "Look what happened to your father."

Marie said, "Why ruin a good thing?"

She convinced him to stay in Canada for the time being. He did, and to become more legitimate for his mom he started working in the lawyer's office and really became a Barrister's Clerk filing and sorting mail. He was making about thirty cents an hour. He liked the warm, old building the offices were in. They had floor to ceiling windows, lots of arches and marble floors. There was even a gargoyle on the roof. It reminded him of England.

He and Marie had entered a time in their marriage where life was almost normal. She was working as a cook in one of the Japanese restaurants in the neighborhood; no burlesque, no scams, just work during the day and hanging out in the bars with Ron at night. Marie's looks were fading and she was so skinny there was not much left of her. They did not quit drinking or partying. Billy finally moved out with Helen and the two of them came over only occasionally. Ron and Marie enjoyed the social scene with lawyers, going to the Press Club to dance and reliving the crime fueled days only in private. By the end of 1940 Ron was getting bored.

Chapter Three:

Gunvor (1940 to 1942)

As she walked to the end of the driveway; the apron she made from a cotton flour bag blew a bit in the wind, flapping around her belly. She stopped at the main road and turned back to look up the rutted path that her husband Alton called the driveway. He barely got his 1924 Ford pickup tires to line up with the two tire trails. Deep grass poked up through the bits of snow on both sides of the rutted tracks. The blue truck was parked up at the barn now, out of gas since Germany invaded Poland. Many young Canadian men volunteered to support the war, lots of them seeing the pay cheque, rather than the risk. Farmers were being recruited into the armed forces. For a lot of men having gone through the Depression, war seemed like a good way to make money. The World War I song claimed, "how ya going to keep them down on the farm after they've seen Paree' and it seemed that war paid the bills.

Her thin fine hair was bleached blonde from last summer's sun. She doused her hair in vinegar after wetting it from the water pump and sat in the sun every day. It usually stayed light until Spring and it was early March. She ran her hands down her belly over the cream-coloured cotton shift dotted with lilacs. Her mother had sewn the dress extra-large for the pregnancy. This was Gunvor's eighth pregnancy in ten years. She was skinny, worn out and tired. She did not see her father Alfred walking down the road with the can of milk he was supposed to bring her, so she turned and started to walk back to the farmhouse. She hugged her thick woolen shawl over her shoulders with a whisper to the light wind, 'please let this baby live, let this one survive.'

In 1937, Gunvor gave birth to a baby girl who lived and was now sitting on the front porch waiting for the milk that grandpa was bringing. Two and a half years old and she had been walking for over a year. Wearing a knitted sweater, zippered up because it was cold, she was entertaining herself with wooden blocks her grandpa had made for her.   Gunvor smiled when she saw her tiny daughter playing on the saggy porch. Her child had defied the odds and lived. Born just under five pounds, Gunvor had the baby at home on July 31, 1937. She was born at seven months like the first six babies but this one survived because Gunvor's mother Vendla, took the tiny baby and put her in a basket made by local natives. It was stuffed with a knitted blanket. She placed the basket on the oven door of the wood stove to keep the baby warm. She told her daughter Gunvor, "The isolette helps to hatch the chicken eggs so maybe keeping her warm might hatch this little chick, eh?"

Gunvor was so relieved that her mother was there to help. She called the baby Elna Katherine Vendla; 'such a big name for such a tiny girl', her mother had whispered the first time she held her. Elna was a name that resonated back to family in Sweden. Vendla was after her mother, Katherine after her husband's mother. Her mother stayed for four days taking care of the baby, as she put it, 'so this one will live'.

The others had not. In 1930, Gunvor had a girl who lived seven hours, in 1931, a boy who lived nine hours. In 1932 she gave birth to a girl she held in her arms for the full day until she passed. The death certificate for the boy who was born in 1933 at the Red Cross Hospital in Dryden, Ontario says he lived for six hours and died of a congenital malformation of the heart. The other certificates only say that the babies were all seven months premature.   In 1935; another boy. In 1936 a girl is born who lives for eleven hours and the death certificate says she was removed for burial four days after her birth. All of them born at the end of a seven-month pregnancy.

All of them born at the Dryden Hospital where incubators were not in use.

Incubators did not come into use until the 1940s and were not widespread until the fifties, even though they were invented in 1880 in Paris. Dr. Pierre Budin published reports of the success of the incubators in 1888. Women and children were not seen as important. At the beginning of the Twentieth Century, premature babies were literally a sideshow exhibit. Visitors would pay to walk through rows of tiny babies in incubators. Hospitals had little regard for 'weaklings', as they were known.

Some desperate parents flocked to these fairs, begging them to put their child in an incubator for a chance at survival. Many babies were saved because they became sideshow exhibits. In 1936 through to 1938 Coney Island included these sideshow babies as a tourist attraction. The invention just did not catch on with hospitals. Babies continued to die.

The Dirty Thirties were not good years for premature birth either. In general, people died at a younger age because of malnutrition; pneumonia and diarrhea. In some areas food was scarce. The death rate of premature babies was higher than the earlier part of the century because of poor nutrition. Also nitrates in the soil and contaminated water leached from outhouses contributed to the mortality rate. Babies born with heart defects, were called 'blue babies.'

As Elna was the only baby to be born at home and the only one who lived, Gunvor was determined to stay at home for the birth of this next baby which was due in May. Alton believed that babies should be born in a hospital. He and Gunvor had fought about this just the night before when she argued that the only one born at home survived. Alton, who prided himself on being a modern man and not some hick farmer, yelled at her, "And what about you, you can die giving birth too. They know best at the hospital. I know Elna lived because your mother was here but how do you know she would not have lived at the hospital?"

Gunvor never raised her voice but said in her steady calm way, "Because I have already lost six babies. I don't trust the doctors. Six of our children have died, Alton. I want to have this one at home."

Gunvor never cried about the babies after the first couple died. She was stoic and calm. It was not uncommon for women to lose their babies. She did what all women did when a child died after birth or they miscarried; put the child in a wooden box. Then she got a shovel out of the woodshed and dug a hole and planted a lilac tree. The farms around Eagle River were full of lilac trees. Some of them were planted around the outhouses, as Swedes are practical, and the aroma of lilacs was as good an air freshener as any. The lilac bush had dual purpose.

Alton and Gunvor fought a lot. He was a loving husband, but he drank a lot and was not always around when she needed him. They got married in 1929 when she was nineteen and he was twenty-one. They fell in love after a Baptist Church picnic one afternoon. Not that he had ever been to church before, but he had his eye on her. One Saturday night in 1928 she snuck out after her parents went to bed. That was not hard to do. They went to bed at eight every night as they were up at the crack of dawn with the chickens.

Gunvor went to a dance in Vermillion Bay, just a fifteen-minute drive away. She caught a ride in the back of a truck driven by one of her cousins. Life felt exciting and she was taking a risk getting caught in her blue dress with a matching ribbon in her hair. She liked to party. Her strict Baptist family frowned on dances and drink.

After the party, her cousin drove her home. He turned off the headlights driving slowly to try and conceal his complicity. She jumped out of the back of the truck, exhausted from dancing. When he waved, she raised her finger to her lips to suggest he be quieter and ran smiling across the grass. She had danced with the tall, dark, handsome neighbour Alton. Even though they only lived a farm apart, she had never really spoken to him before.

She went into the outhouse to pee before bed. As she sat down, she thought she heard crunching on the gravel path and was hoping it was a racoon or something. She had encountered a bear one night and could not leave the outhouse for an hour until he left. She heard the hook on the outside of the door, that kept the door from swinging open, click into the eye that was screwed into the bleached boards of the outhouse.

She knew before he started cursing that her dad had locked her in. He had done this before. Her mother had scolded him in the morning and said it was not safe for her daughter to be locked out of the house. It was not just his two girls he liked to lock in; anyone who came home late was treated the same, even his sons. In broken English he yelled, "You're a prostitute."

Gunvor begged, "Dad please do not lock me in again. It's cold and I get scared."

He turned and went back to the house. He was an odd man with violent rages and sullen deep depressions. He had a brain injury when he was young, she knew that. 'Nobody should listen to him', she thought, but who would cross him? She could hear the screen door slam and she could hear him spit into the slop bucket by the door. For a few minutes she heard mumbled voices and knew her mother was begging him to let her out but then it was silent. Her mother would never defy him and come to help her. Gunvor spent the night staring through the cut-out moon in the door to the one up in the sky. She tried reading the catalogue they used for toilet paper, but it was too dark. She pulled her knees up under her dress and squatted to the side of the hole. Even though it was summer she hugged her thin sweater to her body and shivered. She vowed right then that the next man who flirted with her was going to be her husband. The outhouse stunk and she could hear rats scratching around in the dark.

She was not allowed to go back to any dances. Her dad put the word out and none of her relatives were brave enough to defy him. Everyone in the village knew that Alton had taken a shine to her. Alfred swore he would not let a Weberg marry his daughter. Alton was as stubborn as Gunvor's father, but even he was not brave enough to go to church with his mother and risk Alfred's glare. Alfred had helped to build the Baptist Church and guarded it like a hound dog. But everyone in the community was welcome at the church picnic.

All the picnics were at Eagle Lake, famous for walleye and lake trout to sport's fishermen. Gunvor had been fishing there many times with her brothers. Sometimes at night when they were late getting back with their fish they sat and watched the fireflies. Gunvor loved them, calling them 'a bit of magic'. Sometimes they caught them in little Mason Jars and used them like flashlights as they walked home but they always let them go before bed. They were surrounded by nature and animals. Gunvor loved the calm and peacefulness.

When Alton got to the lake a week later, about sixty church goers were sitting on blankets in the sunshine. A few men were strumming guitars, children were running around. and the women were laying the food out on the tables. He saw Gunvor sitting on a log laughing with her sister Charlotte, who got up quickly when he approached. Charlotte, or Lottie, as she was called, knew who he was. Alton and his older brother had bad boy reputations. The Weberg farm was next to the Berglund farm and the kids had all grown up together despite Alfred trying to keep the five Weberg boys off his property. He did not mind the three sisters, so Gunvor and Lottie played with them. But Alfred had his eyes on the boys at all times.

Gunvor looked up and saw the tall dark-haired man coming up to her and she decided right then that if he asked her to marry him, she would say yes. Well, he did. Not that day but within a couple of months. They got married with friends standing up for them, no family, on October 19th. They went to the Justice of the Peace in Kenora.

Alfred and Vendla did not approve of Alton Weberg. The Webergs came to Eagle River, Ontario from Minnesota in the United States after originally emigrating from Sweden. They lived next door, but they were not friendly neighbours. There was a constant stream of kids and young men in and out of the shack they called home. They were poor, getting work by selling blueberries they picked not only from their farm but wherever they could find them. They were not church people except for the mother. Alfred and Vendla had a reputation of being pious and 'holier than thou'.

In 1869 The Hudson Bay Company set up a post and trading store and attracted farmers and trappers. In 1913 Alfred and Vendla left Sweden and migrated with many Swedes who were offered cheap land in the area around Kenora and Dryden. They picked Eagle River where they received a large parcel with a creek and woodlot for little money. The farmland sat on a road that was called South Road. Many years later it was called Berglund Road, after them, of course.

Alfred and Vendla, were two of the twelve founding members of the Eagle River Baptist Church. In the beginning, 1921, it was called Svenska Forsamlingen and only Swedish was spoken. They were the church; the church was their lives. They were regarded in Eagle River as 'pillars' of the community.   They were upstanding citizens. on the surface anyway. Their four children may not have believed that, as they were the ones who were disciplined, living under strict rules. Gunvor who was not afraid to speak her mind, said more than once to others, 'Baptists! Have sex with their daughters on Saturday night and go to church on Sunday'.

Gunvor did not have a good relationship with her parents. Even though she was spoiled by farm standards. She had few chores beyond helping with the two younger children and light housekeeping. Lottie was more serious and did not run off to dances in neighboring villages. Lottie belonged to her mother's sewing circle, churned the butter, and hung the wash on the line. Gunvor did her chores, sweeping and washing dishes. She also helped her mom do the baking; she loved doing that. She was very much the favourite older daughter but that did not mean she had freedom to come and go.

She started rebelling when she was pulled from school at the age of thirteen. She snuck out at night and ran around. Then she married the bad boy, and her father was livid. Gunvor did get the dowry of linens and embroidered curtains her mother had been saving for her. It would have been a community scandal if she had not.   Charlotte complained that Gunvor got more than her. But

Gunvor felt that it was the other way around. Charlotte got everything, Gunvor mused, even a pretty name. Who called their child Gunvor? For all the pretty Swedish names available to use, she resented the ugly name they gave her at birth. She did not feel special. She was the work horse. Her and Lottie fought about it all the time.

Around the same time Gunvor married Alton, Alfred was able to purchase property in town close to the church. Farming and working everyday was hard for him because of the brain injury. He preferred to be a Local Guide and woodworker. That way he could pick the days he worked; a day when the headaches were not so bad. He wanted all his children to work the farm so he could focus on the future but being adults, he was losing control of them.

Gunvor and Alton lived on the Weberg farm in a small cabin. His brother and wife lived in the big farmhouse. His parents had moved into town with the younger kids and his older siblings had scattered. Alton took care of the chickens and pigs and shared all the food from the vast garden with family. His brother took care of the cows and helped Alton and Gunvor with the garden.

Life was hard in Eagle River; winters were harsh, and summers were so hot if there had been any sidewalks, they could have fried eggs on them. The newspaper in Winnipeg, Manitoba only a few hours away posted a picture every summer of an egg frying on the sidewalk. It was a tradition. The Lake of the Woods area was well loved by Americans who came across the border to fish, swim and boat. Even in the Depression rich Americans still came to holiday. Alfred and a lot of the men in the community made money as hunting and fishing guides. Even though Alfred did not like Alton he gave him work as a guide to help his daughter. Alfred grumbled to everyone he could, "He can't take care of a family picking blueberries."

Although during the depression people had to ration in the big cities, they did not have to ration much on the farm. The only thing they had trouble keeping in the cupboards was butter and sugar. But Gunvor churned her own butter and used honey instead of sugar. Her Engdahl cousins kept honeybees. She made up for her years of light work at home once she got married. She had to work from dawn to dusk just to keep food in the house. She began to resent feeding the Weberg family with her sweat. She started to appreciate what she had when she lived at home.

She remembered, in winter when they were kids, they would take their lunches to school in lard buckets and by the time they walked the tracks to the schoolhouse their lunches were frozen. But mom always had warm buns or cookies for them when they came home. Social life revolved around the couple of churches in the village and the General Store. She was three when they arrived in 1913. It was her home. She loved the fields, the sunshine, the flowers, and the chickens. She had a happy childhood. They had big family dinners of fish, potatoes, and vegetables with desserts of pastry and rice puddings.

Everyone in the family played a musical instrument and sang. In fact, the Berglund family made most of the instruments, guitars, violins, and ukuleles. Family gatherings were huge with many aunts, uncles, and cousins. Gunvor remembered the safe and warm feeling she felt in her childhood. It sustained her as she grew older, like a blanket to keep her safe.

She knew a bigger world was out there and she wanted it. When she was thirteen there was no more school for respite just boring work on the farm. She started running off and staying out late. Not long after she was fourteen her dad caught her one night and sent her to the barn. She expected a scolding but could not believe when her father made her bend over and pull down her pants. He spanked her hard. She fell to her knees, but she knew better than to cry out. When he was finished, he told her to keep her mouth shut. She did not. She was humiliated and furious with him. She told everyone what a monster he was. It began a bitterness in Gunvor that she never overcame.

If not for the babies dying Gunvor would have been happy with Alton, their life, and the farm routine. Alton treated her with respect. At least he did when he was sober. He had no problem drinking homemade wine with her unlike most husbands in the community who drank only with the men away from their wives.

Gunvor loved to drink. It was the only time she was happy, and she earned the nickname Gay. She had noticed with the passing of each baby she was drinking more but it seemed like harmless fun. She never drank when she was pregnant which was most of the time. She had been feeling so good with her eighth pregnancy and she was sure it was going to be fine.

Alton had been building a road for the McKenzie Dam. But that was when there was work; now he was unemployed like the rest of the country. When he was not picking blueberries, he was a local guide for hunters. More and more he was home and spent lots of time in the barn tinkering with old engines. Of course, the farm kept him busy. They had thirty chickens who laid eggs every day and six or seven pigs.

Gunvor had been feeling so good she told Alton he could go find a job, if he wanted to but he said 'no', he wanted to be able to drive her to the hospital when the time came. It came later that same day, two months before the due date. Maybe it was a premonition, but Alton had managed to buy some gas from a farmer he knew, and the truck was ready to go. Just after a dinner of macaroni and salt pork, Gunvor thought the salt pork was causing the rumbles in her stomach. Then she recognized the contractions. They grabbed Elna and climbed into the truck for the thirty-minute drive to the hospital. Once they were on the road, Gunvor had a bad feeling this one was going to die as well.

There was a skiff of snow on the roads, but it was not that bad, and they made it in quick time. They did not talk much, they never did. Sometimes Gunvor felt that Alton`s words were a waste of time. As they wheeled her away in the wheelchair, Alton sort of grunted, recognizing she was about to give birth to their eighth child. Alton sat with Elna in the waiting room. Even Elna was not a chatty child, rather quiet and subdued as she sat with her father. The doctor on duty had been around for a few of the other births but had not seen Gunvor for a while and commented, "I hear one of 'em lived a couple years back. Congratulations."

It was not a hard delivery, only a few hours and there he was, a boy . . . so tiny and wrinkled. Gunvor did not even want to hold him. She knew he was going to die. The nurse, who had been there for four other births, put him on her stomach and said, "Mrs. Weberg, you have to hold your son. He is another weak one and he isn't looking too well."

Gunvor held the baby to her heart. He was like a little kitten. His breathing was shallow. She shook him a little to try and get some colour in his cheeks. He was waxy like the other six that had died. She felt listless and sad, but the nurse told her to hold him and she did. She held him for three hours and felt the last tiny breath leave his body. After having a live birth, his passing felt unbearable. It was more than Gunvor could take and for the first time in many years she sobbed. Three days later when she was able to leave the hospital, they took the corpse home and buried him next to two of the other babies. Four of them had never been brought to the farm. The doctors had never said, "Do you want to take this child and bury it?"

Nobody questioned the doctors, ever, not then. Gunvor never said, "Can I take this baby home?"

Four times she left the hospital empty handed and never thought to ask for her dead baby. The only babies to come home with her and Alton did so because the doctor on duty when she was discharged thought to ask, "Do you want to take the child with you to bury on the farm?"

Gunvor never knew what happened to the bodies. Her and Alton never talked about it. She did not feel like a person with rights sometimes. Even at the hospital and on the death certificates they did not get her name right, not once. Gunnar Weberg, Guborg . . . but that is because nobody ever asked her what her name was. Alton took care of all the paperwork. He made the decisions. And she never asked him, 'where are my four babies buried'. She really did not want to know. A lot of the family called her seven-month live births miscarriages. Most relatives did not even know she had lost seven babies.

Alton dug a hole in the back yard and placed the baby boy in a tiny wooden box and he, Gunvor and Elna buried the boy. A neighbour had donated a lilac bush. Gunvor placed the bush in the dirt on top of the box coffin and she cried again. It seemed this time she did not want to carry on. With Elna's tiny hand in hers she kneeled in the dirt by the little lilac tree and wept for hours. Finally, Alton brought the two of them in the house as their hands were turning blue from the cold and he gave them coffee. They put sugar cubes in their mouths and sipped the coffee from a saucer as all good Swedes did, sucking the bitter coffee through the melting sugar cube. Then they went to bed and never spoke of the dead babies, ever again.

A month later Alton came to Gunvor, "I'm going to join the war."

"Who is going to make sure your family is fed?"

"You have to keep up with the chores. My brother is here to help." She gave him a steady gaze and said, "If you do join the army, I will not be here when you get back."

He turned and left the house. He loved her but no woman was going to threaten him. A few days later he drove up in his truck and parked it in the barn. A friend was waiting at the end of the driveway, engine running in his old car. Alton stood in front of her in his army uniform. He was so handsome. She barely looked at him and said, "If you go . . ."

He stopped her with a soft hand on her check, "I know, you will not be here when I get back."

Gunvor asked, "Why are you going? It is not our war."

"It is," he replied, "it is our war and I have to go fight to save our country. And the money is better than anything I have ever made."

"What about your family?"

He replied, "You will be fine. My brother will take care of you and make sure there is enough food. He will come split wood for you. It won't take long to beat the bastards."

He kissed Elna, packed a few things and left without looking back. Gunvor found a bottle of Johnny Walker under the sink. She got drunk. She probably would have stayed that way for the duration of the war but there was no money for booze. It was a lean couple of years. Gunvor kept the garden, she made butter, she knitted and she fed the chickens. Every time she got a letter from Alton, she wrote back that she was not going to be there when he got back. Their letters were friendly, almost in a joking tone. Alton did not believe she would go. She was lonely on the farm with only a small girl for company most days. Her sister left for B.C. and Gunvor only saw her mother about once a week. She left for British Columbia.

Two years after Alton left, she had saved enough money from selling blueberries and eggs from the farm. It was hard to save money under Alton's brother's stare, but she did. She packed a bag for her and one for Elna and they walked to the train stop. There was no station, only a stop and if you wanted to get on the train, you pulled the arm down with a flag on the end of it. The train always stopped. You handed the conductor the right amount of money and the train took you to Kenora where you had to get off and buy a ticket to wherever you were going. Elna ran along beside her.

The train whistled into town and Gunvor and Elna got on the train from Eagle River and as they pulled away Gunvor swore she would never live on a farm again. She was done. As the train rolled by the farm, she saw three crosses in the yard that Alton had put there for three of the babies and the lilac trees that meant death. She remembered the night her appendix burst, and she had to take Elna who was three and walk to the highway to hitch a ride to the hospital because Alton was drunk and passed out. She thought about all the nights she sat home alone. She did not feel bad. He abandoned her. That is how she saw it.

She took the train to Kamloops, BC where her sister Lottie was living. Lottie and her brothers Berndt and Alf had driven to B.C. a year earlier in a Model T. The brothers returned to Ontario, but Lottie stayed and married Waldy Munter, Alton's cousin. He was in the Army now in Quebec.

Lottie had wired Gunvor some money a few weeks earlier to help her escape Eagle River. Lottie had been working in lumber camps as a cook but was now cooking in a restaurant in town. Lottie was alone in a nice house she was renting and asked Gunvor to come and live with her.

Kamloops was nestled in hills with tumbleweed all around and had a desert like feeling to it. Gunvor knew it got hot and there were rattlesnakes in the hills around the town. Lottie wrote her and told her what a great place it was, lots of jobs and opportunities. She suggested that Gunvor could wait out the war with her until Alton returned. Gunvor could not wait to get to British Columbia. A few of their relatives had moved and everybody raved about what a land of opportunities it was. As the train pulled into Kamloops, Gunvor was struck with what a pretty town it was. Big shade trees lined the streets, there were stores and cafes and it looked like paradise. Elna, who was five years old, was jumping all around waiting for the train to stop; she could not wait.

Gunvor told her mother when she left that she would return to the farm when Alton came home but she knew she would not. Her mother knew she would not. Saying goodbye to her mom was hard. Vendla and Gunvor had been best friends since Gunvor was about ten years old. Vendla was strict but had a soft spot for her oldest female child. She begged her not to go. Elna was her only grandchild. Even Elna told her grandmother, "I want to go to the new place. Mommy says it is beautiful."

Vendla tried one more tactic, "What about your vows to honour and obey?"

Gunvor laughed, "Mom. Really? We obey while they go do whatever they want? You know I am not like that. I hate being on the farm. I am like a slave. I miss Lottie."

"You used to love the farm. You will miss me."

She agreed, "Yes I loved our farm mom, but not the Weberg farm. I will miss you, but you are the only thing I will miss about this place."

Vendla tried to change her mind. Gunvor was stubborn. She had told Alton, 'if you join the army I will not be here when you get back' and she had meant it.

Chapter Four

Ron and Marie and Gunvor (1940 to 1948)

In 1941 the Canadian Government rounded up all the Japanese, took away their property and belongings. The Vancouver City Council conducted walking tours of Japan town to prove the property in the area was worthless and the area should be declared a slum. Ron and Marie had moved into a rooming house called the Marine Rooms at 358 Powell Street in late 1940. In his normal and friendly way Ron had become best friends with the owner Mr. Nagano. Marie was working in his restaurant that was on the first floor of the three-story building. Across the alley was a cute little house that belonged to the same parcel of land where the owner and his family lived.

One night after several glasses of Japanese Saki, Mr. Nagano asked Ron if he could help him out as a friend. Ron agreed to do what he could as he thought what was happening was a terrible injustice. Yes, Japan had joined in a pact with Germany and Italy, but Ron did not see how that should be held against Canadian Japanese. When he was asked to buy the Marine Rooms at a bargain price to hang onto the property for Mr. Nagano, he agreed. Ron and Marie would give him a thousand dollars for the property and signed an agreement to sell it back to him after the war. They would make a hundred dollars and live rent free for the duration of the war. Mr. Nagano had the tax money in a bank account he transferred to Ron. That way the Custodian of Enemy Property could not sell his land to anyone else.

Ron got the thousand dollars from the lawyer and the deal was done. Mr. Nagano continued to run his business until the day the RCMP came and took him to Hastings Park where eight thousand Japanese Canadians were corralled like animals to be sent to Internment camps. Ron felt terrible for his Japanese friends. He and Marie could not believe their good fortune. Ron told Marie the property would be returned to his friend when he came back. She agreed but she had no intention of keeping that promise. She would be working at the restaurant keeping it alive and profitable once Mr. Nagano was detained.

Shortly after the deal was struck Ron walked into the recruitment office of the Royal Canadian Airforce on Robson Street and signed up, January of 1941. He was going to war. Marie, happy with her new enterprise did not care.   When Mr. Nagano was detained in September of that year, she closed the restaurant and sold off all the equipment. She had twenty-two rooms to rent out and take care of. Within time she added to her income from the rooms by becoming a Bail Bondsmen. She figured she knew a lot of criminals and she could help them out when they got arrested.

Ron signed up full of hope and anxious to see action. Within weeks he was told he could not go overseas. He had a weak heart. Ron told everyone he had a glass heart from years of blowing glass at the Dominion Glass Factory in Redcliff. He was a packer and shipper and never blew glass but watched in fascination, at the men who did. He turned every life experience into something grander than it was.

He was assigned to be a Security Guard on Base. There were several bases Brandon, Manitoba, Regina, and Coal Harbour on Vancouver Island. Eventually he was sent to the Kamloops base in 1944. By then he had qualified as a Motorcyclist and that allowed him more time off base. He spent all his leave returning home to Marie at 358 Powell Street. She informed him that the property was not going to go back to Mr. Nagano and made him sign it over to her.

That way, she said, "You are not going back on your word. You can blame it all on me."

He arrived in Kamloops in March and within a month he met Gunvor. They both fell in love. Gunvor had been in Kamloops with Elna for two years living with her sister Lottie. They were not getting along so well and Gunvor was restless. Lottie did not like to party. Gunvor did not like to work.

One of the first things she did when she got to Kamloops was call Tymich Cabs because they not only offered taxi service but bootlegged as well. Waldy, Lottie's husband used the service when he was off Base. The first time the cabbie came he got out of the car and came up to the house and Gunvor thought he was a nice-looking guy. He was smitten. She began an affair with Gil Tymich that lasted more than a year. Alton was still writing her letters from overseas. She sent him cookies and tinned goods, but she knew she was not going back to him. She was on her own, bored and one night she convinced Lottie to go to a dance at the canteen. She could have some fun for a change.

Three minutes at the canteen and she and Ron met. He was nothing like any man she had ever known. The farm boys she had been with before were serious and dour. They worked from dawn until dusk and had no time for fun. Ron was charismatic and funny. They knew nothing about each other and did not even ask. He took her home but had to leave her at the door because Lottie did not allow any 'hanky-panky' in her house. It had been the first time Gunvor had ever ridden on a motorcycle. Even though there was a bit of snow on the ground and he slid around the corners she felt safe with him. She stood at the window and waved to him. He got on his bike, cocky and grinning. Either the bike was tipsy, or he was. They both fell over. He bounced back up laughing and he drove off with her heart as corny as that sounds. She told Lottie, "This is it. My Prince Charming has arrived."

"Your Prince is overseas fighting a war," Lottie replied.

"Not my war," Gunvor said.

It was a quick romance. After a week or so Ron admitted he was married but without ties. So was she, she had replied. They were both fine with the situation. By the beginning of May she was pregnant and had moved into her own place at 28 St Paul into one room with Elna. Ron paid the rent. Alton was sending money to her as well. Gunvor never told Ron she had seven babies die at birth. She did not think he needed to know. And for his part, he never would have guessed by looking at her that she had given birth eight times. Gunvor was about one hundred pounds and did not look like a thirty-four-year-old woman. She looked like a teenager with her shoulder length sandy blonde hair. Her skin was smooth, fresh looking. She did not even have stretch marks.

Ron had loved Marie, but she was at the far end of her forties and a tough woman; there was nothing soft about her. She had been known to take her umbrella to more than a few men. She was full of spunk but Gunvor, she was beautiful and soft spoken; 'wouldn't say boo to a ghost', he liked to say. Of course, he knew nothing about what a strong woman she was and for some reason she allowed him to coddle her and acted like she was helpless. He had never seen her on the farm, pulling the tiller because the horse was lame, or swinging an axe to chop wood.

When she was five months pregnant Ron had a week's leave, so they went to the Interior and rented a small cabin on a hill overlooking Okanagan Lake. It was the only holiday Gunvor had ever had. That week Ron shot rolls of pictures of Gunvor running around the hills with army type boots on but no clothes. He rouged her cheeks with dots of lipstick, and she tried to look doll like, posed with a doll and tried to look child-like. She would never have done anything like that with Alton. She and Alton had sex in the dark while she was wearing a flannel nightgown. She doubted if Alton had ever seen her naked. Ron celebrated her and made her feel beautiful. She laughed when she told her disapproving sister Lottie about the week, "I was running around naked as a blue jay and loving it."

Lottie who was not sure about Ron and even suspected he might be giving Gunvor drugs of some kind, managed a smile and claimed, "I'm glad you have found the man for you."

Lottie was happy that her older sister would be off her hands. She had been supporting her and Elna up to that point with the exception of the bit of money from Alton. Even though she liked to laugh, there was a lot of melancholy. Gunvor carried an air of sadness with her like an old coat. She was also demanding. It was almost as if the tough years on the farm left her wanting too much. Happiness seemed to be just out of her reach. Lottie was tired of trying to please her. She had a husband and a child on the way.

Ron and Gunvor seemed to offer each other a freedom they both craved. Her nickname back home had been 'Gay' because she liked to party. She was no longer, stern, and silent Gunvor. She was no longer the farm slave who had seven babies die in her arms. She no longer had to go to church and pretend she believed in God. She did not. God would not let seven of her babies die. She was a fun girl. She and Ron rode his motorcycle everywhere. They ate in restaurants and he introduced her to Chinese food. They went to movies. They danced a lot.

But it was not all fairytales with Ron. He came home a couple of nights with a black eye and one night his face was beaten to a pulp. She knew he liked to get into fights. He was always standing up for the little guy. Gay did not know much about his crimes or jail time back east. She did know there had been 'some trouble' as he liked to call it. She believed him when he told her that Marie was the problem, the instigator, the crook. She did not find out the extent of his crimes until they had been together many years. It was about the same time she confessed to him that she had lost seven children.

She was not prepared for him to go to jail and not be there when their child was born. Just before Christmas he was asked to find some young women for a party on the base, for the Sergeant and his friends. Always wanting to be the big shot and please everyone Ron found four young women and brought them to the party. Trouble was, they were juveniles and when the party got busted, several of the men were charged.

Three of the men went to court and paid a fifty-dollar fine and all three of them vowed it was Ronald Robinson who was responsible and not them. Ron did not have the money to pay the fine and he was sentenced to three months in the Kamloops Jail and because it was a Provincial Court conviction, he was Dishonorably Discharged from the RCAF. This was a crushing blow for Ron. He gave up his life of crime to serve his country and he did not deserve this. He thought he belonged to a group of soldiers who would protect each other. At the very least, he thought one of them would lend him fifty bucks. The event changed the course of his life. It changed him from a confident, brash man to one who felt beaten by the system. He was bitter. He wrote the RCAF from jail begging them to pay him the discharge money owed to him. He was a good soldier; he had no charges against him, and he served his time well. His letter was never answered.

That was not the only letter he wrote from the Kamloops Jail. He also wrote Marie and told her she could have full ownership of the property at 358 Powell Street. He advised her that when Mr. Nagano came back from the Internment Camp that she should take his money and keep it for herself. She drove to Kamloops and confronted him. She begged him to come home with her. He told her that Gunvor was pregnant and he wanted a child. He told Marie it was over. It had been over for a long time.

Although Marie had told him it was over when she found out about Gunvor, Marie still loved Ron.   He was listed as living at the property until 1947. She was waiting for him to come to his senses and come home. She did not let go of him that easy. They were a good team. She travelled to Kamloops several more times to break up his relationship. She offered him opportunities to make money, but he turned her down. He was done with crime; he was done with her. Marie did not believe it.

Feb 9th, 1945 his daughter Gay Ronaldine Grace was born while he was sitting in Jail. Lottie was there for Gunvor. She had her own small daughter and was incredibly happy Gunvor had a healthy baby girl that she carried to term. When Ron got home at the end of March, just after his thirty-ninth birthday, he fell in love with his tiny baby who was a Robinson clear to everyone. He felt that his life was complete. And he tried, he did try to settle down as a husband and father, but it was not an easy task for Ron.

He managed to get a few jobs here and there. He found a lawyer in Kamloops, J.O.C. Kirby who loved Ron's divorce scam idea and the two of them became best friends and partners. Around that time Ron had business cards printed up declaring he was a Private Investigator for hire. He surprisingly got a lot of work. So much, he hired Waldy, Lottie's husband to help him out. Waldy had trained as a police officer but it was not for him, he was happy to use his skills to help Ron out. It was not long before Ron had a lot of influential, rich friends. He and Gunvor were living well. They were invited to all the important parties because of J.O.C. Kirby. Ron arranged for J.O.C. and his wife to adopt one of Gunvor's cousins' babies as she got pregnant out of wedlock. He did a lot of favours for his rich friends.

Ron and Gunvor went to a lot of costume balls and dinner parties. Ron became friends with Phil Gaglardi who later became the Minister of Highways of the Province and was known as Flying Phil because he was always speeding down the highways. There was a dude ranch outside of Kamloops where a lot of Hollywood stars came to play. Ron and Gunvor were there one weekend when Yvonne DeCarlo attended the Ranch. Gunvor said she was thrilled when Yvonne fell off her horse because she was attracting too much attention. As Gunvor said, "Ron was following Yvonne around like a lost puppy."

After a while, the parties were too much for Gunvor and she would stay home with a bottle of whiskey on her own. She could not keep up with Ron's 'fast life'. He seemed to have a lot of reasons to go to the Coast and see Marie and it caused problems. When Ron was away Gil delivered the booze and stayed for a while. He was just a good friend, even to Ron but Ron did not like it, any more than Gunvor did not like him seeing Marie.

Ron could not say why he agreed to help Marie one last time, but he did. The same Brothers who smuggled heroin with him ten years earlier called her up and said they had one more job for him. She summoned Ron to 358 Powell Street one more time. He promised Gunvor it would be the last time. When Marie laid out the plans Ron said he did not want to go because of his two little girls.

He said he would be the middleman and organize it all from the Vancouver end. It was Billy who would have to go collect the drugs. Ron came up with an idea that Billy would get on the train to Toronto with the ruse that they were buying a Tilt-A-Whirl for the carnival they were working for. Tiny never gave up the carnival gigs and the carnival he was working for was in search of a Tilt-A-Whirl. It was a popular ride and the old one was breaking down. He had several carnies lined up to testify that it was all legit.

John Cerniak was the back east contact and the one who put the suitcase full of drugs on the train. Billy was the innocent passenger and all he had to do was put the suitcases in a locker when he got off the train and then go back two days later and get the suitcases. Ron told Billy he just needed him to pick up some suitcases for him while he was on the trip to cost out the Tilt-A- Whirl. Billy really believed he was on a legit trip to check out the ride. Billy knew nothing about the drugs. He questioned his mom and she said not to worry, it was a legitimate trip. He did not trust Ron but he knew his mom would not lie to him.

It seemed to be a success. Billy got off the train and went home. Two days later he went back and got the suitcases from the terminal.   But someone double crossed them, and the cops got on the same train with Billy and intercepted the bags. They removed the morphine and replaced capsules in the shoes with baby powder. The shoes had contained seventy thousand dollars' worth of drugs. Some reports claimed it was eighty thousand dollars. It was the biggest drug bust the West Coast had ever seen.

When Billy picked up the suitcases to take to Ron who was going to get them to the Brothers, the cops followed him and arrested him in Stanley Park. They had already arrested Cerniak who got seven years and a thousand dollar fine. Billy got a five hundred dollar fine and five years. He never told anyone about his mother or about Ron. He took the rap for the two of them because they asked him to. Billy did not want to lie for Ron, but his mother begged him to. There did not seem any way to rat out his stepfather without implicating his mother, so he stayed silent. But he went to BC Penitentiary angry with Ron. He did not blame his mother.

Ron felt terrible; not only was there no payday but Billy went to prison. Marie blamed Ron and took his name off the land title which he had told her to do three years earlier. She had held on thinking one more deal together, one more rush and he would come home. Marie had to finally face that Ron loved Gunvor and their child. She resigned herself to the fact he would no longer be her partner in any way, and she released him from her heart, but she never released him from his obligation to her and Billy for keeping his name out of it. Marie blamed him for her son being incarcerated and she finally gave Ron the divorce he wanted. But to Marie's way of thinking, she still owned him. She knew too much about the things he had done.

Ron went back to Kamloops and tried to settle down with Gunvor and the two girls. After a few months he suggested they move to Vancouver where he could get back in with the lawyer he used to work for and make some real money. He was also moving there because Marie said he owed her for taking her son away. She had work for him to do. Ron figured maybe he could hang around for six months or so and run a couple of small scams and she would consider the debt paid off. Her never told Gunvor anything. He did not think she needed to know.

In Vancouver they moved into a little room on Davie Street, not far from the Niagara Hotel. It was the fall of 1948. Things were not going well for Ron and Gunvor. She knew about the drug bust and how Ron was involved. She also knew that Marie had a hold on him he was never going to get out of. She was also angry that he gave away a piece of property to Marie. They drove by the building one night and then he showed her the cute house across the alley that belonged with the property. Gunvor could see them living there, the girls playing in the front yard and did not understand how he could give away something as great as that. Land meant everything to her. She longed for a garden, a bit of the farm like she had known.

Ron told her the only way to get rid of Marie was to give her the property. But he never got rid of her. Marie had the goods on him, she could turn him into the police whenever she felt like. Gunvor could see the futility of the relationship she had gotten herself into. In an angry drunken fight one night, Gunvor screamed at him, "You've ruined my life. You kept promises to a woman who is a crook and what about your promises to me? We have a child together."

Ron yelled back, "You have a child with Alton too and he doesn't even send you support of any kind. I am taking care of his child and mine."

Alton did send money for support for Elna and Gunvor but only for the first year she lived with Ron. After a year, the war was over and he had no paycheck. He also did not think he had to pay her while she lived with another man. He would not give her a divorce either. She just let it go. She felt such a tremendous guilt for leaving him because he went to war. Alton loved her and they had been through a lot together; the loss of seven children, working side by side on the farm. They had eleven years together and she repaid him by taking his child away from him. Alton was a good man. She did not feel like the girl who grew up on the farm anymore, with morals and love in her heart.

Gunvor had allowed Ron to talk her into the divorce scams with him. She did not much care when she was drunk. But in her heart, she regretted crawling into bed with men, posing with her hair spread over the pillow so Ron could trick some poor guy into divorce. It was wrong. She never thought of herself as having high standards but tricking people, tampering with their lives . . . she knew it was wrong. Ron was very loose with his property, including her. His attitude was, 'easy come, easy go'. He indicated on several occasions that if she wanted to sleep with Gil that would be fine with him. Gil of course thought it was a great idea. He told Ron he would deliver free booze for six months. He was so in love with her. Gunvor said no. She hoped that she never got drunk enough to do that because she knew as much as Ron was generous, he was also vindictive.

When Ron had money, life was good but when the times were tight, he would do anything to survive. Survival far too often meant moving. It seemed like they had to leave in the middle of the night at least ten times in the four years they had been together.

Ron was always running from someone. They were always on the move from one rooming house to another. For a while they stayed with his mother Elizabeth who seemed to love the girls with all her heart. She was close to Elna treating her as if she were blood. Gunvor did not like Elizabeth too much and Elizabeth did not like Gunvor. They only thing the two of them had in common was that they both hated Marie.   Elizabeth saw Marie as the enemy and Gunvor was an insipid woman with no opinions of her own. She was loyal to Ron. The only loyalty Ron had was to Marie.

Ron and Gunvor settled into a rooming house with the two girls on a warm night in September of 1948. Elna was ten and Gay was three. Lottie and Waldy had moved to a suburb in Surrey, so her sister was close by again. She had two girls now and the two women got together often to let their kids play together. The nightmare of losing all the babies and toiling on the farm seemed a long way behind Gunvor. She was fashionable and wore make up. Lottie sewed a lot of their dresses and the two of them were picture perfect pretty moms playing in the park with their kids.

Ron started making good money as a Private Investigator, but he was often leaving town and Gunvor was alone with the girls. She did not really know what his jobs were, tailing a suspect maybe? When he was gone, she enjoyed her time with the girls. When he was home Elna babysat a lot. Ron was working for Bill Murdock who was a well-known lawyer. He felt for once he was on the right side of the law. There were a lot of shady dealings, but they were sanctioned by the high rolling lawyers and judges he knew and hung out with. Most of his new friends would have been shocked by the low life he had been living just a few years earlier.

When Ron and Gunvor were not going to parties with the 'big wigs', as he called them, they liked to go to the clubs and dance. The two of them danced well together. They were the same height. Ron in his black suit and fedora; Gunvor in her long crepe dresses decorated with sequins. They looked good together. Ron gave her a brass snake bracelet that curled up her lower arm. She had a wedding ring even though they had not married. It was Ron who went to the Woolworth's counter on Granville Street and bought her red lipstick, face powder and tortoise shell combs for her hair. He gave her Evening in Paris perfume and a little sequined black bag. It was not lavish gifting but more than she had ever known. It was enough.

The fancy dress balls, and the parties were not as often as Gunvor would have liked. Most of the time they went to a beer parlour. Elna was only ten but she always babysat Gay. They lived in a rooming house with relatives living in other rooms so she was not all alone and could get help in a minute. Ron and Gunvor went out to the pub almost every night. It was legal for Women and Escorts to go to the bar together in 1948. Their bar of choice was the Niagara Hotel. The sign out front was a neon waterfall. Gunvor told Ron the waterfall reminded her of Eagle River. She loved the modern décor of the bar but in reality she just loved to drink.

Chapter Five

Harold (1940-1948)

Harold was restless; twenty-four and restless. There was a war going on and he was stuck at home with his wife Pearl who he did not get along with and his child who was a year old. She was his little doll and he loved her, but all the young men were signing up. He had a meaningless job and wanted more money, more opportunities. Working on the family farm was what he had been doing since he was five. He was itching to join the Army and see the world, as was promised by the posters. There was an empty feeling in Harold he could not identify. He could not understand why he felt lost. He had been anything but lost, abandoned, abused, or ignored. Harold was the first son, born in 1916 to Axel and Katherine Marie Larsen.

Katherine's mother, Kristine Hedvig Hansen married to Jens Rasmussen had six babies die before they emigrated to Canada. Those babies were buried in the Elk Horn Cemetery in Iowa. The nine surviving children including Katherine moved with their parents in 1911 to Standard, Alberta; a town that Jens and Kristine helped to establish. At that time, she was forty-nine and Jens was 50. He was the third man to ask for her hand in marriage. Her other two relationships fell apart but the third one was the charm. They were very much in love, wonderful parents, and strong members of the community.

Kristine was a prolific writer, sending countless letters to her father Andreas Hansen who was in the United States while she was still in Denmark. Kristine and her younger sister, Helene were left behind in Denmark when they were twelve and ten. The younger brother Niels who was six travelled with his stepmother to join his father after a few years and the girls were left in foster care with family. Andrea`s first wife Bodil Mitgard died of consumption when the children were six, four and eighteen months. Nobody seemed to mention or know why the two girls were left behind but in her letters to her father Kristine reminded him often that she was left with strangers at a young age. She was respectful with a tinge of bitterness. She was a master at writing letters that sounded like she was understanding and wise, but they were full of guilt trips not lost on her father. He was an artist of some fame and focused on his work. His children were not as dear to him as his paintings.

Tough and resilient Kristine moved from one servant girl position to another, eventually ending up in Elk Horn, as a housekeeper at the Elk Horn Danish Folk High School where she met Jens. A 'folkskole' was a religious school seeped in Lutheran traditions where Jens was a student. They were married in 1886 and they both died in Standard, Alberta; Jens in 1947 and Kristine in 1949. They were the patriarch and matriarch of a large family; most living in Standard at the time.

Their daughter, Katherine Marie was born in 1893 in Elk Horn and was the fifth child born. She was given the name Marie after the third born child Maria Kristina who died at the age of two of diphtheria. It was considered bad luck to name one child after a dead child. Marie instead of Maria was a tribute considered safe. Like her mother Katherine was strong, opinionated, and a hard-working woman. In Standard she worked side by side with her husband who turned to farming after he purchased land from his uncle. Before that he was a well driller but they both wanted land and family together on that land.

Katherine, on horseback used to drive the cattle to the dipping vats eighteen miles from her home. To eradicate ticks, cattle were dipped in vats containing, among other things, arsenic.

The vats in Standard were a great distance from any of the farms, for while the arsenic was not strong enough to harm the cattle, it leached into the soil. Katherine and a cousin drove the cattle, walked them into the four-foot-deep vat and waited on the other side for the cattle to walk out.

Katherine and her husband Axel were founding members of the Nazareth Lutheran Church which was the focal point of their lives. Standard was a true theocracy; a church centered community. While there was a Mayor, the town was really run by the Pastor. His word would outweigh any civil orders. Katherine spent eighteen years as a pianist at the church. This is where Harold developed his love of the piano. His mother taught him to play and he became as good as she was. Family members talk about how Harold could take a piano apart on Saturday night and have it back together on Sunday morning for him to play in church. He was always a good boy, obedient, helpful, and kind. Harold came from good people who brought their children up to believe in God and to do good work. Like a lot of second-generation church children, Harold did not believe in God like his family did.

In the twenties and thirties, Standard was five blocks long. with the Canadian Pacific Railway train station at one end and the church at the other. Along with all the other kids in the community, this was Harold's world. This safe five block stretch was where he grew up. The children all knew each other because the school only had four rooms and except for a few English families like the station master, most of the Danish folk were related. There were two blacksmiths, two grocery stores, a meat market, and a bakery store. Kids frequented the bowling alley and the curling rink. There were other more forbidden places they liked to explore like the Slaughterhouse, the pool hall, and the Stockyards. If cattle were being brought into town, Harold more than anyone loved to hang around with the cowboys and talk to them about life outside his hometown.

Harold was lucky, being born into a loving home with security and caring parents; two brothers and a sister. Katherine's first child Alma died after only two days which was common. Harold was tall, with sandy blonde hair and handsome. He was always popular with the girls in town because of his good looks and his quick sense of humour. Harold had a wicked streak that led him into some troubled times like when he was caught with some other boys knocking over outhouses. The boys lifted all the outhouses back up and made sure they were on stable ground. All was forgotten with a 'boys will be boys' attitude. When the old men gathered at the store and the boys walked in, they were teased about the event, not chastised.

Mrs. Lee had a small house in town where she acted as midwife to a lot of local women as not everyone was able to go thirty miles nor could they afford to take the time away from chores.   It was a sort of secret what was going on behind closed doors at Mrs. Lee's house. Harold liked to hang around trying to look in the windows. The thick black drapes were never open, but he kept hoping for a peek. He never heard anything but on more than one occasion he was there at the birth and heard the baby cry.

Once every couple of months a Doctor from the city came to town and he would operate on small children, removing tonsils, maybe five or six a day. Mrs. Lee provided her kitchen table as an operating room table and administered the ether. Harold was caught a couple of times trying to get a better look at what was going on. Mrs. Lee chased him down the road with her broom a couple of times. Kids in Standard were afraid of her. They talked about her as if she were a witch. Harold and his siblings went to a proper doctor in the city.

Harold got into trouble more than once for breaking into an old house on the edge of town that was abandoned. The younger kids thought it was haunted, the older kids used it as a place to make-out. It was Harold's hiding place. He not only hid himself there when he was needed at home for chores, but he hid his treasures. When he was seven, he hid marbles and a baseball glove he took from his friend. He would go into the house and rub the soft leather of the glove. If he played with it everyone would know it belonged to Ralphie so after a time he gave it back. He handed it to Ralphie on the playground at school one day and said, "I found it on the road."

Harold was one of the teens who used the old house as a place to drink. There was not a lot of alcohol in Standard but somehow the kids managed to find homemade wine on the farms. A few times some of the older boys brought beer back from Calgary and sold it to the teens. When they were stuck for booze they could always go to the stockyards and buy whiskey from the cowboys. But that was a lot of money and most of them were not paid much to help on the farm. Most of them were not paid anything at all. Harold made money playing piano at weddings, funerals, and birthday parties from the age of twelve. His mother Katherine did not think he should take money, but he did, secretly behind the church.

By the time the Dirty Thirties rolled around Harold was fourteen and spent the next nine years hating prairie life. It felt like the good times were all gone. The Dirty Thirties were called dirty for a lot of reasons, but in Alberta, dirty meant the weather. There was little or no rain, crops failed, and times were tough. There was a dry wind that whipped up little pebbles that would bite into your skin. Harold could remember his mom setting the table with all the dishes turned upside down until the food was out because it was so dusty. And there was no respite when winter came, sometimes as cold as forty below. For a few years, it seemed that the only fun they had was to drive thirty miles to the Bow River to swim in the summer.

Early childhood though for Harold was fun and easy. His mother was the best cook in town; and she sewed and made their clothes and taught them right from wrong. He adored her. Axel was stern as were most fathers in Standard. There was a lot of work that needed to be done just to survive. Mother played with them on their big green front lawn in the Spring. By summer it was yellow because there was not enough water to waste. But in the Spring, she brought picnics out to them on blankets with Danish pastry and pickled 'everything'. That was the best way to preserve her garden. She even pickled the garlic.

They made a lot of hand-crafted items on the lawn like lanterns, and leather bookmarks for the bibles. Every event they had was centered around the church. His mom created an item she sold at church events, her own creation. She would decoupage glass ketchup bottles and medicine jars. She also made corn husk dolls with nuts for heads. Harold refused to make the dolls, but he fashioned a few wooden toy guns for sale. They shot elastic bands. As Harold grew older, he started to make good money for playing piano at events, even travelling to other farm communities.

After Harold got out of high school, he went to university for a couple of years in Calgary, but he did not stick it out. He had discovered it was more fun to party and being a musician he was a popular person to invite as he could play the piano to liven up the party. He met a new breed of people in Calgary; not religious, but wealthy and full of life. He was a ladies' man and had his share of girlfriends, even though Pearl who he dated all through high school was waiting for him to come home. He enrolled in an engineering program and while it was easy for him, he got bored and dropped out.

Ten years after the Dirty Thirties, Harold was married to Pearl and they had a child. He wanted to see the world. He knew there was something beyond the Grain Elevators and farming. He loved his wife, but they had married too young. He was twenty and she was eighteen but had been sweethearts all through school. They had been together since she was thirteen and he was fifteen. Everyone knew they were going to be married, settle down and farm. But even Pearl did not want to live on the farm. She was more adventurous.

There was one fateful summer when the Pastor's daughter got pregnant and left town suddenly. There were rumours that Harold was the culprit and soon to be father. Pearl said she did not believe that and stood by him through the accusations. Harold claimed the rumours were wrong and he was not the father. Although nobody ever knew as the daughter left town suddenly and never returned. She was shipped off to a home for unwed mothers. The Pastor left soon after and was replaced by a younger man with small children. Nobody in town dared to speak to Katherine about it. She was adamant that her son was a virgin and would never cheat on his girlfriend, anyway. Pearl and Harold had been sneaking off to the old, abandoned house since Pearl turned sixteen.

Two years after the scandal Harold and Pearl married. Their daughter Marlene came two years later. Those were the best two years for them. They were in love and playing house. A baby was not in their plans. They both struggled with parenthood. Pearl suffered from postpartum depression and walked out to the farm often so Katherine could take Marlene. She would just say, "Mama Katherine I am tired today."

Harold loved his child but had a hard time dealing with his wife going from sweet and shy to screaming and sad. Sometimes Harold thought there was something wrong with Pearl. After she had the baby, she was a different person. No more running in the fields, riding her bike or playing ball with him behind the store. In the beginning they were like two kids tossing a ball in the alley, going for long bike rides, picnics in the woods. Now, he came home from work at night and made supper. She claimed she was too tired or the baby had cried all day. Harold never saw Marlene cry. She was happy and full of bubbles.

The person who held him back the most from 'running' was his mother. He saw her almost every day. Harold worked on the family farm. It was not a fulfilling job and it did not pay much. Harold and Pearl struggled to make ends meet in a tiny apartment above the store in the village. He could have gone into the gas and oil industry, but it seemed every time he tried to leave the farm, Axel needed him to come back and help.

Pearl agreed it was time to leave the farm life. Sometimes if it were not for the generous handouts from his mother, they would not have had food on the table. He knew the gifts came with a price. Mom expected him to be in church every Sunday playing piano so she could show off her talented and handsome son. Even when his mom started taking old suits and coats and making clothes for needy children through the Red Cross Society, he was the one who delivered the goods. He was also devoted to helping the Salvation Army as did most members of his family. Work, wife, child, church . . .Harold wanted to leave Standard.

The wanderlust began for Harold when he was about ten and gypsy caravans used to pull into the stockyard area for vegetables and water. He watched them sharpening the farm wives' knives and farmer's saws from the farm in exchange for supplies. His mom paid them with vegetables from her garden; sometimes with jars of honey from the farm's hives. Harold would carry the goods and some of his mother's knives to the stockyard to barter a deal.

The gypsies were bright, colourful, and the language was unlike anything he heard around the church suppers. He particularly liked the women who wore long skirts that swirled around in red, yellow stripes as they walked, and the white peasant blouses sometimes fell off a shoulder. The women in Standard did not dress like that. They wore dark, heavy dresses that buttoned up to the neck and later, on the farms they wore pants and even jeans. Standard women were, as Harold like to say, just standard.

There were a lot of standard jokes in Standard. What size is that? Standard. How common is that? Standard. What time is it? Standard Time. In 1909, a delegation of Danish men including Harold's grandfather came from Iowa to the Chimney Hills district to look for farmland on the twenty-one thousand acres the CPR had set aside for this purpose. The 1910 CPR map shows the village's name as "Danaview". When CPR officials discovered they had a town bearing that name northeast of Saskatoon, they asked for a different name to avoid conflict. A meeting was held, and the Danes came up with the name "Standard" from the flag, Royal Standard of Denmark.

Harold was close to his brother Burge who was born a year after him. He loved his sister Leona who was four years younger and a brother, Vernon who was six years younger, but he was not as close to them. He and Burge were a team. But as much as he loved and was devoted to his mother, Harold felt his mother smothered him. Burge was more interested in farming then Harold and offered to hold down the farm if his older brother wanted to go off to war. After two years at university in Calgary Harold knew he did not want to settle in Standard. He thought, like a lot of young men that the war offered him opportunity.

Early in 1940 before the spring planting Harold kissed Pearl, Marlene and his mother goodbye and hitched a ride to Calgary where he signed up and was sent back out to the Bow Valley training area called the Currie Barracks. After training Harold left with the Calgary Highlanders in September of 1940 and saw action overseas. Nobody knows what really happened to him during the war. Like a lot of farm men who came back, he never spoke about it. What his family did know they read in the papers. the Regiment sailed on 27 August 1940, from Halifax to Gourouck, Scotland, on the SS Pasteur. They arrived on September 4, for three years of training in Great Britain.

On 19 August 1942, twenty-two of the Calgary Highlanders landed on the shores of Dieppe for the unforgettable Raid. They were to be supported by the Calgary Tanks, but the Calgary Tanks did not arrive. Impressively, however, the Highlanders did not suffer any fatal casualties, and all returned safely to England. After landing at Normandy on D-Day, the Calgary Highlanders moved on to France and later returned to England in 1945. They departed for home on November 24 and paraded triumphantly through the streets of Calgary. The Calgary Highlanders were disbanded on 15 December 1945.

They knew Harold saw 'action'. They never knew if he was one of the twenty-two men who landed at Dieppe or where he saw 'action' but when he got back, he was different. Based in England they were sometimes involved in skirmishes on French soil. For Harold, Standard did not feel the same. Harold could not get out of bed in the morning because he had nightmares and sweats. He would turn up on the farm, bleary eyed and hung over. The war was harsh. Burge tried to stand up for Harold.

He explained to his father, "Dad, the war changed our boys. They saw things over there they were never meant to see. I know Harold saw men shot in front of him. I know that, father."

"Then he should be happy to be here with his family, safe. He should bend his knee to God." replied Axel.

Harold could not stay sober enough to keep his family happy. He had a key to the church and some nights he would go in and play piano until the sun came up. Then he could go home, and little Marlene would lay on the bed with him and play. Then he could go to sleep listening to her sweet voice singing. Nobody understood what was going on with Harold. Harold did not know what was going on with him. He knew that after the war his heart felt like it had been shot full of holes. The inhumanity he witnessed made him question Faith even more. How could anyone go to war and come back and believe in God? His faith had always been on again, off again but now it did not exist.

Because Pearl loved him, she agreed to go to the west coast. She had moved in with Harold's parents when Harold went to war. Katherine took care of Marlene and Pearl who lapsed into moodiness. She suffered bouts of endless weeping. She perked up when Harold returned but he was not the man she once knew. She thought a move might bring back the spark in their marriage. But he had to go first and get a job. When he returned to Standard they had moved into the apartment above the store and he was stocking shelves at the store. It was not much more than a pity job to keep him busy. He got the apartment for free and enough for groceries.

In 1947, two years after the war, Harold said goodbye to his family and caught the train to Vancouver, BC. He had stayed a few nights on the coast when he got back from England and he liked it. It was more laid back than Calgary and he loved the rain, the mild temperatures. It was a melting pot of all races and people did not seem to care as much where you came from and where you had been.

He got a job as a janitor and Pearl left Standard, with Marlene in tow and came to be with him. Katherine never forgave Harold for leaving but he knew he could not be the same son he had been before the war. He did not want his mother to see the shadow of the man he had become. That is what haunted him every day. He felt like a shadow. He sat in dark corners with his back to the wall. He was afraid of what might be behind him. When he drank, he could forget and sometimes even laugh a bit.

Harold started drinking even more than he had been in Standard. He made it to work and did his job because pushing a broom was easy after farm work. It was a lot easier than being in the Army. Without the stability of church life and family, he was lost. He and Pearl started fighting. They had been living in a one room studio apartment in an apartment complex on Broadway Street called the Julian. They got the room for free because Harold went to his day janitor job at the New Fountain Hotel and came home at night and was the night janitor at the apartment building. It did not leave him much time for sleep, but he did not like to sleep.

After about six months they found a new apartment called the Pandora on twelfth street. They were offered free rent for light chores. He suggested to Pearl that if she took on the small chores at the apartment like vacuuming, he could take care of the big jobs on the weekend. All he had to do was mop floors and clean windows. The two of them made sure the garbage that went down the indoor chute was taken to the big dumpster at the back.

It seemed like a good idea because then he was able to take on a night desk clerk job at the Niagara Hotel. He felt more successful working on the front desk. At least he was able to use his skills like reading, writing and being friendly. It was good for him because he was interacting with people, making eye contact. He loved working at the Niagara with its' big flashing waterfall on the sign. The new apartment had two bedrooms and a balcony, and he liked that. Pearl liked it because she made a new friend Marion, who lived on the second floor, the first day she moved in.

Sadly, Harold made the same new friend and started sleeping with her. Strangely enough, Marion looked a lot like Pearl. They were both small boned women with dark, thick hair. They were both pretty but forgettable. Pearl was content to be a mom and she was a quiet woman who did not like to drink. Marion was outgoing, she had been working and living on her own from the age of sixteen. She was in Housekeeping at the big Vancouver General Hospital. It was one of the better paying jobs a woman could have just after the war. She liked Harold and she liked to spend her money on Harold.

Pearl kicked him out and took over the caretaking so she and Marlene could continue to live there. Harold moved into a room at the Niagara Hotel. Being on unsure ground with Pearl and not in a solid relationship with Marion, Harold was left to fend financially for himself. He had never been good at that. He had always been the guy who picked up the change off the bar table and he forgot to pay back friends, but he had never been dishonest before. Alcohol and the need for it can make people do strange things. He started making 'mistakes' when he made change at the front desk. It was so easy, a nickel here and a dime there. Nobody noticed.

Harold asked to meet Pearl and Marlene at Second Beach one sunny afternoon. While they were playing in the sand Harold excused himself to go to the washroom. He grabbed Pearl's purse off the blanket and hid Pearl's purse in the men's room in the tank of a toilet. When she came back to the blanket and could not find her purse, she had a fit and flagged down a police officer. He had not expected that. He had to sit in the hot sun for an hour while she filled out a report and he was questioned as to what he saw. Finally, Pearl took Marlene and left, and the cop looked at him with a raised eyebrow and asked, "You have anything to do with this?'

"No," Harold insisted.

The cop said, "You look like a man who could use a drink, just asking."

After the cop left, Harold rushed into the men's washroom and fished the purse out of the toilet tank. Inside he found Pearl's wallet and twenty-five dollars. He put that in his pocket and stashed the purse and wallet in the garbage at the door on the way out. He felt a tremendous amount of guilt, but it did not last long. He took money out of Marion's purse less than a week later. Both times he used the money to buy beer after work.

Pearl suspected Harold took her purse, but she did not want to get him into trouble. He was not the man she had married but she still loved him. Finally, after years of trying to keep up with an alcoholic Pearl asked for a divorce. Pearl took Marlene who was nine and went to manage a different apartment building. She could not bear to live in the same building as Marion and see Harold getting into the elevator night after night. Marion had apologized but Pearl could not forgive a woman who would steal her husband.

Pearl's new apartment was free as part of her job and she got a small amount of money to buy groceries. Harold gave her a few bucks every week and she figured she could get by. Marion made good money so Harold could ease up on the long hours. It was Marion who dropped off ten dollars a week in Pearl's mailbox. Harold did not move in with her but ate all his meals with Marion. He liked sleeping in a room at the Niagara. He closed the bar most nights and it was a short stagger up the stairs to room 204. He got up late in the morning and went to Marion's for an early supper and then to work. He saw Marlene about every second weekend.

He tried for about a minute to make things up with Pearl. It was not a serious attempt at reconciliation. He missed Marlene and he wanted them to be a family, but he did not miss the responsibility. Besides Pearl was already dating one of Harold's good friends from his university days and said there was no chance of getting together. When Harold got over the fact that Bill one of his engineering buddies from university was with his wife, he and Marion dropped in occasionally for a game of cards with the two of them.

Harold realized that he needed to make more money than he was. Harold did what he was good at. He cleaned up, bought a new suit. He pitched the idea to the manager of the hotel with his idea. He said he would play piano in the bar after work at night, free of charge. He just wanted to keep the tips. His boss had heard him play a few times and figured it was a good idea, so he said 'Okay'. Harold started working days on the front desk, having a quick bite with Marion at five and then started drinking and playing piano at seven. For the first time in years, he was happy.

After work one night he was sitting at the piano playing Bing Crosby's Swinging on a Star when he saw a beautiful, slight, girl-like woman with blonde hair walk in. His heart tripped a bit. He had never seen such a pretty little thing, he was thinking, when the man with her came over to the piano and asked, "Can you play Boogie Woogie Bugle Boy?"

He placed twenty dollars into the tip jar. Harold only made that kind of tips in a week. He was used to a quarter or sometimes a dollar. He grinned at the short guy in the black suit and slouch hat and smiled, "For that kind of money I can play anything you want."

Ron smiled back and said, "Come over and join my wife, Gay and I for a drink when you take a break."

Ron touched the tip of his hat and then he winked at him. Harold did not know what the wink was about but could not wait to find out. He was interested in meeting a woman called Gay. It sounded like fun. He took a drink of his beer and started to play. He watched the man walk back to the table and sit down. He saw the pretty blonde listen to something the guy said and then she turned and looked at him and smiled. Harold felt a surge of joy in his heart he had not felt for a long time.

Chapter Six

Harold, Ron, Gunvor and Marie (1948 to 1952)

What began that night at the Niagara Hotel would shape the rest of their lives. Harold and Ron became instant friends. The same things made them both laugh. They enjoyed ironic situations. They believed whatever they did was not wrong.   On the plus side both men grew up with strong mothers who defined them and both men felt love and respect for all people. Neither of them carried prejudice. They judged a man on his behavior not his status or colour. Harold was the perfect side-kick for Ron. Not that Ron was smarter than him or dominated him, but Ron was the one who came up with the grand ideas. Harold was willing to help him act out his crazy plans.

Gunvor loved Harold too. He was witty without being cruel, he was kind to the girls, and he was very handsome. Tall and lanky, he always wore suits, just like Ron. Although where Ron was neat and ironed to perfection, Harold was unkempt and always looked like he slept in his suits. He was respectful to Gunvor. He poured her coffee every morning when he dropped in. Occasionally, he turned up with flowers. They had much in common; they both came from Scandinavian families who were strict about religion and proud of their faith. Harold did not mind the life as much as Gunvor had but he did not have her bitter past of being abused in the name of God.

One afternoon sitting in a park she told him, "It was common for daughters to fill in for mom when mom got worn out."

Harold nodded, "Of course, help out around the house . . ."

"No," she said, "more than that. Help out with dad's needs."

Harold paused and said, "I don't think anyone in my family had to help out with dad's needs, if you are talking sexually, I mean."

"Well, it was common in Eagle River."

"Did the mothers know?" he asked.

"Well, we all lived in small houses with two to four kids in a room. How could any mother not be aware?"

Harold was stunned, "I never heard of that in Standard. I somehow can't see that being common practice in our families. In fact, I know it wasn't."

Gunvor replied, "Probably not. I shouldn't have brought it up. Sorry."

Harold shrugged, "It's fine. You can talk to me about anything you want."

But Harold did not want her talking to him about incest. Gunvor had received the signal and knew he was not someone she could talk to about private things. It made him uncomfortable. He could not fathom a man doing that to his child. He liked her but he did not want to know her secrets. Harold kept his secrets in the dark corners of his mind like everyone should, he thought. He hoped she was not going to be one of those women who wanted to tell you everything. They were not alone very often so there was no need to worry about more disclosures. Ron kept a tight rein on Gunvor. He had gone back to calling her that. He did not like other people calling her Gay either.

Harold felt an attraction to her. She was not brunette or outspoken. She was petite, shy, and quiet. Sometimes she got the giggles but only if she had been drinking quite a bit. He knew there was no future for them and less information from her the better. He did not want to get tangled up in her problems or cross Ron. Harold was still dating Marion who worked long hours. She did not like Ron or Gunvor so most of the time he was with them on his own time. And most of that time was in the bar. The three of them became close. Harold liked the fun stuff they were doing but he did care about Gunvor. He cared about her a lot.

Ron conned Harold into doing some detective work with him for divorce cases and Harold, who needed the money, was happy to snap pictures and set men up for divorce. Gunvor did not think it was so wrong once Harold got involved. He made it seem like a prank and not a serious offense of tampering with evidence for a court case. Not that Gunvor or Harold ever had to testify, they were just the actors, the props. Sometimes Harold introduced Gunvor to the 'mark', "Hey, this is my friend Gay."

She would smile and ask, "Do you want to buy me a drink?"

None of the men ever said no, she was just too good looking. Once Gunvor was settled at the table with a drink Harold was out of the picture. She drank, flirted and when the 'mark' was drunk enough, Ron stepped in with the keys to the rooming house. He would give the keys to Gunvor telling her he had to go do something and he would see her later, much later. Then he would pick up his camera and head around to the back of the rooming house. Gunvor took the guy to the room and Ron snapped the pictures from the window. By that time Harold was back home with Marion or in his room at the Niagara. It was just a game.

Ron went to court on several occasions and testified that he 'saw' the man go into the hotel room with a hooker. Sometimes there were pictures of Gunvor with the man, hair covering her face and Ron had no problem saying she was a hooker he had seen earlier that night in the bar. He had no problem lying on the stand. Harold said, "Hey, don't ever put me on the stand. I can't tell a lie with a straight face."

Ron assured him, "No reason for you to ever get that involved. I never identify my accomplices."

One night, Harold stuck around because he did not like the looks of the guy Gunvor was sitting with. Ron told him he was a boxer, and his wife was leaving him because he beat her up. He remarked to Harold, "From now on maybe he will keep the fighting to the ring. This will be a lesson for him."

Ron was not an excessively big guy and Harold figured he should stick around for this one, just in case. When the boxer got drunk Gunvor whispered in his ear and they went down the street to a rooming house where she said she had a room. It was a room Ron had rented a couple of hours earlier on the ground floor with a window facing the alley out of sight.

Ron and Harold scooted into the alley and Ron was able to get on a box by the dumpster and see in the room. Harold was tall enough to see in and leaned against a fence across the alley. Gunvor got the guy into the room and into the bed. She made them a drink and slipped a mickey into his drink. It was a mild sedative. It only took about three minutes until the guy passed out. For three minutes Harold watched in uncomfortable silence in the alley with Ron as the guy pawed at Gunvor and pulled her slip down over her breast. Ron never saw that rescuing 'damsels in distress' was abusing his wife.

He whispered to Ron, "Doesn't that bug you?"

Ron put his finger to his lips and replied, "It's work, nothing more."

Harold felt uneasy and did not want to watch so he walked to the end of the alley. He looked back at Ron on the box snapping pictures through the window. A few minutes later Gunvor came around the corner of the building with her coat on over her slip and said to Ron, "That was the shits. Don't ever leave me in a position like that again.'

Harold did not ask what happened. He had quit watching. Ron asked him to go into the room and wipe it down, clean the glasses and give the key back to the guy at the front. Harold went in and the boxer was passed out naked on the bed. He washed the two glasses and put them above the sink where the other glasses were. Then he went to the front desk and gave the guy the key and said, "Ron said to drop this off with you."

The clerk said, "Where's my money?"

Harold shrugged and replied, "I don't know."

"Twenty bucks or I tell the guy when he wakes up who rented the room and why."

Harold gave the clerk a twenty and went back outside. Ron and Gunvor were gone. Harold was mad at first. He knew that this part of the detective game was not to his liking. Ron stuck him with the twenty-dollar bribe and risk of getting beat up if the boxer had woken up. Then the little shit did not even stick around to have a drink. But he liked Ron and Gunvor. They were the best friends he had ever had. And they were good for lots of laughs and laughter was what kept him going. He was tired of drinking alone. He needed them.

That fall every time Ron left town, he asked his new best friend Harold to take care of his wife and kids. Harold had no problem with that. Pearl was still angry how he took up with Marion and was not letting him see Marlene all that often. Pearl was more of an advisor to Harold when she did see him. When she heard about his new friends, she gave him advice, "I don't like Ron and I don't trust him. You should stay away from him. And his wife? Well, watch out for that one, that is all I am going to say buddy."

Both women in his life advised him against hanging out with Ron and Gunvor. Harold figured they were the most fun couple he had ever known. He liked the kids too; Elna was a year older than Marlene and she reminded him a lot of his daughter and the little girl, Gay, was as cute as a button as he often told her. There were family times with them, good food and laughs. They went to Third Beach together. Gunvor made ham sandwiches and potato salad. He missed the family stuff he used to do with Pearl and Marlene. Marion worked so many hours that their time was spent sleeping. She sure did not make up picnic lunches with a smile on her face.

Marie was having trouble with some guys she and Ron had worked with in the past. They were talking around town that she ripped them off. She said she did not, but that would not stop any retaliation. With Billy in jail, she did not feel safe, not even with her chihuahuas. They barked a lot but would not protect her, she told Ron. She asked Ron to come to 358 Powell Street for a few days. She said to him, "Look, if those buggers think you are living here maybe they will leave me alone."

Ron knew Marie was just trying to get him back but he did owe her. Her son was serving five years in jail because of him.   He lied to Gunvor saying, "I have to run up to Kamloops for a few days. J.O.C. has a guy who is being charged with theft and I need to go find out if he did it or not. Some hot shot married to a Lady of some kind from England. Can you beat that?"

Gunvor was fine with him going away for a few days if she had everything she needed in the house. Gunvor never left the house except to go to the park with the girls, on her own. She never got on a bus, went to the grocery store or a bank. She did not even go to the laundromat on her own. Ron took her everywhere or ran the errands himself. He used to joke that he did not know why she carried such a big purse for a tube of lipstick. She never had money in her wallet, or even keys to the apartment. It baffled him but he put it down to her living on the farm all those years. She was uncomfortable around people unless she was drunk.

He asked Harold to keep an eye on her and maybe take her to the grocery store if he was not back in two days. The day he left his mother Elizabeth sent a cab for the girls because she had asked Gunvor a week earlier if she could have them for a couple of days. Ron did not know that. Gunvor had forgot. She packed a bag for Elna and Gay and popped them into the cab. When the girls left, Gunvor felt blue and called Harold asking him to drop by after work with some whiskey. Ron had left her with only a drop or two and without the girls home she felt she could use a bit more than that.

Harold was quick to say yes.   Ron had already asked him to take care of her. He did not know the girls were not home when he turned up around midnight, booze in hand. It seemed odd at first the two of them, alone, drinking. But it was not awkward. He felt at ease with her, and she with him. He asked her about the night with the boxer and what went wrong, and she replied, "He was just too big, and the pill didn't kick in very fast and I had to put up with that bugger touching my breasts before he passed out."

"Does stuff like that happen often?"

"No. One time I almost got raped but Ron got in through the window and threw a punch at the guy. Blew our cover. We lost money on that one."

"I felt uncomfortable," Harold said.

She touched his cheek and said, "Well, that is normal. I wish Ron felt uncomfortable, but he doesn't. I think he gets a kick out of seeing me scared."

"Really?" he responded then added, "that seems odd. He should want to protect you not endanger you."

"Tell him that," she laughed, and they clinked glasses.

They talked for a bit more and she explained how the front desk clerks worked. Ron had two or three rooming houses or cheaper hotels who cooperated with him. The desk clerk would lie to the 'mark' when they asked how they got into the room. They all said the same thing, "Sir, you came in here with a lady and asked for a room. You paid with cash."

Gunvor always took whatever cash the man had before she left the room. She removed the mickey with the sleeping pills in the bottle. The desk clerks never gave out any information to the guy asking. And the mark was usually hung over, feeling the effects from the mickey and was confused. Ron usually paid the desk clerk a twenty before the event though. She said she did not believe Ron was sticking Harold with the bribe the night he was there. It was just a greedy clerk trying to make more money. She said they never got caught, that is just how it was. She said, Ron and the lawyer he was working for were making lots of money from getting the divorces through that way. She laughed about it but said, "All those years on the farm taking bible lessons, I never thought I would end up like this."

"Me either. If my mom could see me now, she would be horrified."

They clinked their glasses together again. They talked about other things like growing up on farms, favourite songs and family back home. They laughed a lot. It was the first time they had been together with no concerns over whether Ron might come back. She even said she thought Ron was gone to see Marie. He agreed with her as he had been suspicious as hell.

"Does it bother you that he might have gone to see Marie?

"Of course, it does," she said, "but what choice do I have?"

It did not take long until the two of them were drunk and in bed together. As Harold told Ron later, "It was inevitable man. I'm sorry."

Ron who had slept with Marie when he was on his fake trip to Kamloops, just smiled and replied, "Don't worry about it. As long as the two of you had a good time."

"Oh, we did, "Harold laughed, "we sure did."

Harold, did not, of course tell Ron that he was in love with Gunvor. And Gunvor, of course did not tell Ron that she was in love with Harold. They both thought he was a great guy; even if they knew that he was still having a relationship with Marie. Ron was honest to some degree, but he never felt what he did on his own time had anything to do with his family. Gunvor would have been furious had she had proof that instead of being in Kamloops, Ron was across town at Marie's for two nights eating perogies and playing poker. Thinking it might be true was one thing, knowing it would have been unbearable. Ron had enjoyed his two days with Marie. She was a lot of laughs.

Harold and Gunvor grew serious that fall about each other. Whenever they had a chance, they were together. He confided in her, told her things that he had never told other women. She told him about her dead babies. She told him she was not sure of her life with Ron; it felt empty. She felt empty. Harold could not comprehend having lost seven children. He knew women in his family had still births and early child deaths in their lives, but not like that.

Harold knew Ron used narcotics. Cocaine, maybe. He was not sure. He did know Ron gave Gunvor cocaine sometimes. Harold was not interested in drugs. He never did anything but drink, but he did a lot of that. He knew that Ron and Gunvor were doing drugs. Lottie told Harold one night when she was in town that she was concerned because she felt that Ron was keeping Gunvor in a kind of stupor. That seemed obvious. When Gunvor started drinking she took to her bed for days. She kept a bottle of whiskey under her pillow and woke up and sipped on that barely eating. As an alcoholic himself he found it odd that a few sips of booze would be enough for her to stay in bed for a week or two.

Harold even had a suspicion that Ron took advantage of Gunvor in other ways. He believed that Ron may have even pimped her to men like Gil Tymich. Ron made a comment once that she had been with Gil before, so why not make money from it? One night, Ron had suggested to Harold that if he had a few bucks he would go for a walk, 'wink, wink'. That was before he and Gunvor got together. It was unsettling. He was not sure what the winking meant. He did not act on it in any way because he sometimes got lost in Ron's schemes and did not always understand what he wanted. He did not want to bring it up with Gunvor. He might have been wrong. He felt a loyalty to Ron he had never felt with a man before. He believed that Ron would do anything for him, and he felt the same way about Ron. Gunvor was collateral damage.

Soon, the drug question was no longer an issue. Gunvor was pregnant. As she and Ron had not had relations for some time and Harold was the only one who had been around, she knew the baby was his. She would be forty when the baby was born. Forty and she had been pregnant ten times. That night at the bar she was drinking a cola and Harold teased her about it. When Ron went to the washroom, she told Harold, "Yes, I'm pregnant and it's yours."

"How do you know?" he responded.

She gave him what he would have called a withering glance and said, "I have only been with you. Ron and I have not been getting along so well in that department. I have been pregnant nine times before. I think I know."

What the hell are we going to do. Ron will kill me?"

"No, he won't," she said, "he won't care. He doesn't care about me. He only cares about his daughter Gay."

"So, you think we should tell him?"

"I don't know," she said, "do you want me to be with you? With our new baby?"

"Would Ron let you take Gay?"

She saw Ron coming back to the table and picked up her glass for a sip. Best that Ron did not see them having an intense conversation. Gunvor realized in that moment that Harold was right, Ron would never let her take Gay and she was not going to go without her. She had hoped that Harold would stand up for her, maybe suggest he become a dad to her three kids; one of which was going to be his, but she looked at him and saw he did not have it in him. He could not even be a decent father to his daughter Marlene.

Harold was a drunk. Sure, they all drank. Ron drank everyday but he never got drunk. She had seen Harold fall down the stairs he was so drunk. He missed work because of drinking. He left his daughter behind because of drinking. He spent so much time in the drunk tank, the cops had a cot they called, 'Harold's bed'. She took a sip of her cola and told him. "No, things would not work out with us. You have a family now that you don't take care of," she patted his hand, "it's okay. I will tell Ron about us and that the baby is yours and see what he says."

"You don't think he will kill me?" he asked.

"No. But what we have between us is going to have to be over."

Harold nodded. He was not ready to stand up for her and three kids. He barely saw Marlene. He rarely paid Pearl child support. He would not be able to pay his rent if his new girlfriend Marion did not take care of him and bail him out every rent day. He was only thirty-four and a lot had happened to him in the past ten years. A marriage, a child, four years of war, a new girlfriend and now this. It was too much. He looked at her and sighed, "I'm sorry."

"I know," she said.

She did not see Harold for a long time. When she told Ron, he was angry and said she could never see Harold again. They were not drinking, and she was staying home because she was pregnant. He did not offer to drive her anywhere, not for weeks. He went to Harold and threatened to beat him to a pulp, but nothing came of it. Harold stood up, towering over him, and responded, "Really? What are ya gonna do climb up on me to get a punch in?"

It worked. Ron laughed. "Just stay away from her from now on. She is my wife."

He liked Harold too much and they had a scam they were running that brought in a fair bit of cash. Ron had printed up business cards that read, 'Chimney Cricket, we clean your chimneys so clean that Santa will never get stuck again'. There was a picture of a cricket wearing a stove pipe hat on the card. They hung out at bars around town, the two of them handing out their cards. They got a laugh and they got business. A potential customer paid ten bucks up front and the pair said they would be there at 8 o'clock in the morning. The customer was supposed to pay the ten-dollar balance when the job was done. Neither of them had ever stood on a roof, let alone cleaned a chimney. They would get about a dozen potential customers a night and then they would move on to another bar.

Harold had been picked up for drunk and disorderly conduct many times. He complained to Ron that the sad thing was, when he was in jail, he was bored. They decided what the local Vancouver lock up needed was a piano so Harold could play piano when he went to jail for a few nights. Even the cops had said it would be great if they had a piano so Harold could entertain them. Ron hatched the plan a couple of weeks after he knew Gunvor was pregnant. She was no longer drinking so he and Harold had a lot of time on their hands. He had already decided he was taking her back to Kamloops, away from Harold. May as well leave the guy a parting gift.

On a Friday morning in early 1949 Harold and Ron walked into The Hudson Bay downtown wearing coveralls that read. 'we can move you'. Harold had engineered a bill of sale that was identical to the Bay sales slip for a piano. He had a piano from the Bay, as Marion had bought him one for Christmas. He was able to modify that bill to look like a current one. He knew about cheque washing by using alcohol to remove the ink and discovered it worked well on bills of sale too. They waltzed in up to the second floor where the pianos were and presented the bill. They were a couple of fast talkers and that piano was in the elevator and in the truck they had rented before anyone knew what happened. They put the piano in a storage unit for a few months.

Ron found a guy at the bar one night who was as tall as Harold and would fit into the moving man's uniform. The two of them went to the storage the next morning and loaded the piano into another rental truck and took it to the local lock up. Harold could not go as the cops would recognize him. Ron went in with the piano and a letter confirming that an anonymous donor was donating the piano. The cops gathered around in awe, one cop even said, "Hope we pick up the piano guy for drunk and disorderly soon."

"Is there a full moon coming up?" asked another, then laughed, "if there is, we will be picking Harold up at the Niagara Hotel around midnight."

In May Ron, Gunvor, Elna, and Gay moved back to Kamloops. Ron went back to work for J.O.C. Kirby. The Lady story was not a lie. He was working on her divorce case with Kirby. She had lots of money and was willing to freely spend it to get out of her bad marriage. Gunvor wanted to be close to the Royal Inland Hospital, as they were so great with her when Gay was born. They could not have been much closer; Ron found a place on Sixth Street about a two-block walk. It was a little white house with a big back yard.

Harold stayed sober for a while but eventually he was picked up. He got to play the piano in early August. He got really drunk that night because his daughter was born August 1, 1949. He had not seen Gunvor since Ron took her back to Kamloops in May. He celebrated by getting so drunk he was picked up for indecent exposure while pissing on a car. A woman passing by claimed, "He waved that thing at me."

Harold told the arresting officer he was just shaking it off. He spent two nights in jail because it was a Saturday and could not see a magistrate until Monday morning. He played the piano while the cops had coffee and doughnuts Sunday morning. Then he played hymns all afternoon and drew a crowd. Monday, he got up again and played while waiting for court. After a round of applause, they took him before the Judge who said, "free to go".

He walked home feeling down. He wanted to go see his new baby girl. He borrowed Marion's car and went to Kamloops to see his daughter who was about a week old. He proudly held her blanket wrapped body in the air while Gunvor and Elna smiled in the background. Ron took the picture. Gunvor had waited to name their daughter until Harold arrived. Ron was fine with the baby, and loving, but he did not seem interested in giving her a name.

When Harold arrived, they had a drink of whiskey and she asked him if he had a name for her. Harold had played with a girl in Standard whose father worked at the railway station. They were English. Her name was Gwynneth. He had always loved that name. It was not a standard name for Standard children. He asked Gunvor if they could name her Gwynneth.

They settled on Gwynne. It was a Welsh name and Ron liked that. Ron and Gunvor called her Gwynne Elizabeth. Of course, nobody ever told her who her father was, and she grew up believing it was Ron. Harold sent money from time to time and saw her occasionally. When she was seven or eight, she asked her mom where her name came from and Gunvor said, "I was reading a Harlequin Romance and the girl in the story was from Wales and her name was Gwynne. I just liked it."

Gwynne asked her dad, Ron who said, "Well, we couldn't call you Queen Elizabeth."

Gwynne was always suspicious. Elna was Elna Katherine Vendla after a host of relatives and Gay was Gay Ronaldine Grace after mom, dad, and a grandmother. Sure, her grandmother was Elizabeth, but she never saw her. In fact, Gwynne only met her once when she was five and all she remembered was an old lady who did not smile and gave her a bitter candy. It seems Grandmother Elizabeth who she was named after cut ties with her parents, after she was born. And that was the truth although the kids were never told that her birth was the reason. The story was that Grandma Elizabeth belonged to the high Anglican Church and because Ron and Gunvor were not married, they were living in sin. It just was not true. She had accepted them living together for five years.

But Elizabeth was so upset with Gunvor having a child with another man she never spoke to her again. Once Ron brought his cute little girl to see her. Elizabeth scowled at her and remarked that she hoped he was happy with his bastard child. Ron had hoped seeing Gwynne would mellow her out, but she was not interested in forgiveness. She gave Ron the old Sunday dinner horsehair tablecloth she used to use for their roast beef dinners as a parting gift. He never saw her again.

Gunvor did not understand how Ron's mom could blame her and be angry. She knew Elna was not Ron's child and she loved her. And why did she not want to see Gay? She spoiled her and spent a lot of time with her. Gunvor could see now why Ron always said of his mother, 'she would cut off her nose to spite her face'.

Ron explained, "You did not know me when Elna was born. But with Gwynne, you cheated."

"Then why did you tell her, Ron?" she asked, "why did you tell her that this child was not yours?"

"I didn't," he replied, "it was Marie."

Gunvor knew there was something else tied to the story. She was positive that Ron stole from Elizabeth or something. He did not see his brother Fred either. The only person who still was loving to him was his sister Freda who lived in California. He got over the loss of his family, he had his own family to take care of. He was welcomed by Gunvor's sisters, brothers, cousins, uncles . . . he did not need his own family. They moved around so much the older girls did not question why they never saw grandma again. Family members came and went. In the first two years of Gwynne's life, they moved three times in Kamloops.

By 1951 they had moved to Penticton. They moved that time because Ron got all caught up with Marie again and she had started to drive up to Kamloops with every little problem. When she needed him, she expected him to come on a run. Kamloops was only a six-hour drive through the Fraser Canyon. She summoned Ron every chance she got. In late 1949 when Mr. Nagano was released from the Prison Work Camp up north, he made his way back to Japan town. He asked Marie for his property back and showed her the contract he had with Ron. He had saved every penny cooking in the camps and had the thousand dollars plus the hundred-dollar bonus.

Marie showed Mr. Nagano the property was in her name and Ron had nothing to do with it anymore. Ron had already moved to Kamloops but went to Vancouver to talk to Mr. Nagano and the two of them drank beer at the Niagara Hotel, as friends. He knew Ron would never have done this to him. But he still wanted him to go talk to Marie and get her to give him his property back. Ron knew it was a waste of time, but he tried. Marie refused. She had all the rooms rented out and it was a safe building. There had been murders and thefts there when Mr. Nagano ran the rooming house, but Marie ran a clean house.

In early 1950 Marie asked Ron to get a French-Fried popcorn machine for her from one of the carnivals because Billy was getting out of jail soon and she wanted to give it to him so he could have a job at a carnival as soon as he was released. He still had a couple of years to go but Ron obtained the machine for her. It cost a thousand dollars. She had it in a shed in her back yard until late November and then she claimed, "I was robbed."

Although she had a fairly good story about how it cost $1,600 and at one point, she agreed to let Mr. Fumano take it and use it to make money, but she had changed her mind. She said, contrary to her new plans, he went ahead and removed the popcorn machine from her shed. She took him to court, but he was acquitted for benefit of the doubt. She blamed the all-male jury for not liking her, but it really was a thin case of her word against his. Marie did not instill a lot of trust in people; she was brash, loud, and obnoxious. Mr. Fumano who was an acquaintance of hers was just more credible. She backed out of the deal and tried to claim theft.

Ron went to testify the cost was more than it was but never had to take the stand. While he was there, he dropped off at the Niagara Hotel to see Harold. He was not working at the front desk anymore but still played piano for tips. During the day he was a Watkin's salesman selling spices and ointments. He did rather well because, as he admitted, 'I have the gift of the gab'. He had just been charged with driving while drunk and had been in a car accident. Harold laughed and said, "Still playing piano at the jail."

Harold gave Ron a hundred dollars for Gwynne. He had only seen her twice in two years, but he had only seen Marlene a dozen times and she lived a few blocks from his place on Broadway. He was proud of Marlene. He taught her to play piano. He was happy that Pearl sent Marlene to Standard every summer because he wanted his daughter to grow up with the influence of his family. He felt bad that Gwynne would never get to know his mom and she would never get to nurture his second child. She did not even know he had a second child. He could have had a third child if the story about the Pastor's daughter was true. It was true but Harold did not know if he was the one who got her pregnant. She was a wild one.

Shortly after the visit, Ron got into a bit of trouble with that divorce trial. J.O.C. Kirby defended a client for theft, an Alvin Dyson. Through dealing with him, Ron met his wife who was quite a lady. In fact, she was Lady Lavender Millicent Dyson, the daughter of the Duke of Cornwall and Lady Ashcroft. Why she had come to Canada and married a truck driver never became clear through their many conversations. But after Alvin went to Oakalla Prison for theft he dropped Kirby as his lawyer. Kirby became the lawyer for Lavender who was desperate to divorce, 'the cad', as she called him.

Ron was called in to set that divorce up. It began earlier when he was still living in Kamloops in 1947. Ron found a 'quarter breed Indian woman' as she was called by the court, to follow Mr. Dyson into the stables at a Summer Fair in Kamloops. Although nothing happened; the woman testified they were intimate. Ron testified he saw them going into the stables. Of course, he lied, as did she. Unlike most marks Alvin Dyson did not accept he was being framed.

A couple of years later while still representing Lavender, J.O.C. Kirby and Ron visited Dyson in prison and bribed him thirty dollars to complete the divorce proceedings. The scam did not work this time and J.O.C. and Ron were called into court numerous times to testify. Each time they perjured themselves; as Ron would say, 'in for a penny, in for a pound'. They stuck to their stories that the money was a deposit on money Dyson owed from when Kirby defended him for theft. Lavender had since found another attorney to complete her divorce and Ron and J. O.C. were on shaky ground. If not for the woman who stated she had intercourse with Alvin Dyson, the case would have fallen apart.

They were close to being charged with perjury but a woman they barely knew stuck to her story and the judge could not find evidence they were trying to bribe Mr. Dyson. All they had given the woman three years earlier was ten dollars to say she was intimate with Alvin Dyson. They owed her. Nothing much happened, except Lavender finally got her divorce and never spoke to the two of them again.

Gunvor was furious with Ron because as she said, "You fell for that women hook, line and sinker and look where it got you?"

Ron claimed, "She did not mean anything to me."

Gunvor replied, "Yes, she did. She was the daughter of royalty and we all know how you feel about royalty."

When it was all over, Ron put the court papers in his tin box for safe keeping. That was where he had the naked pictures of Gunvor and the drawing of a naked woman on a horse that he had received from Sylvia. Sylvia was one of his bootleggers and she drew a naked picture of herself and gave it to him. There were other pictures of other women. When Gwynne was twelve and Lottie's second daughter Sharon was fourteen the two of them picked the lock to the black box with a hairpin. Inside they found a picture of Ron and Lottie being intimate. At least that is what they thought. The faces were not visible. For years Gwynne used to go to bed at night and pray to God that her mom would never open the tin box as she and Sharon had. The picture was a secret Gwynne and Sharon shared. Gwynne suggested to Sharon once that it was probably Lady Millicent. It did not matter, Gunvor did not need to see any pictures. Ron had several girlfriends since they had been together. Gunvor had only been with Harold and once, and as a favour to Ron, she was with Gil. She was regretting her decision to stay with him.

Chapter Seven

Marie (1950 to 1954)

After Marie lost a thousand dollars in 1950 on a bail jumper, she vowed to be more careful. She had divorced Ron and was happily living alone with her three chihuahuas. Ron had moved so many times she was not sure where he was anymore. She kept the retail units rented out to long term tenants so she was able to focus on running her Rooming House at 358 Powell Street. She and Ron had bought it as the Marine Rooms and she still called it that.

Built in 1907 for its Japanese Canadian owner, Jinshiro Nakayama, the building reflected the early desire for Japanese Canadians to settle down with their families. It had beautiful Edwardian-Commercial, bay-windows and was a three-story building. It was typical of other retail areas at the time in Vancouver. The Japan town neighbourhood was proud of the Hotel Yebisuya. Not really a hotel, it was a rooming house for seasonal workers while the retail spaces had Japanese run businesses such as the Ikeda barbershop, Nabata shoemaker, cafés, restaurants, a meat shop, and a tailor. By the late 1920s it was the Toyo Rooms and then the Marine Rooms in the early thirties.

By 1949, few Japanese Canadians were in a position, or had the interest, to return to Vancouver. When Mr. Nagano returned from the Internment camp, Marie refused to sell his property back to him, contrary to the agreement he had made with Ron. The economic base of Powell Street and the surrounding neighbourhood had been dramatically eroded by wartime conditions. Vacancy rates in the area remained high and buildings continued to deteriorate. Marie however was able to keep the rooms full and to take care of the upkeep on the building. She was a feisty, hard-working woman known on the street as the Big Boss.

In the 1950s, some stores selling ethnic Japanese groceries and goods reappeared, as did some restaurants and even a gambling club on the main floor of the Lion Hotel at 316 Powell Street. A few major cultural institutions also re-opened, including the Vancouver Japanese Language School. Japanese Hall, and the Vancouver Buddhist Temple. Marie rented to a few students but mostly older men. As fast as one boarder moved out, a new one moved in. There were sixteen rooms, eight on each floor with four facing the alley and four with a great view of Powell Street from the bay windows. If they doubled up in the rooms she could have as many as thirty-two people staying there. There was only one bathroom per floor.

Marie lived in the house across the alley which was a small two- bedroom stucco home on a nice piece of property that also held a large shed. She stored carnival equipment in there for various people she knew. She had put up a fence so her three dogs could run around outside. There was not anyone in the area who did not know Marie and her dogs.

She was approached by what she could only describe as mobsters, in the summer of 1950. Ron was in the process of moving from Kamloops to Penticton and not around to give her advice. Maybe if he had been, she would not have risked her home and business. The two men from Winnipeg were representing two boys Billy had gone to school with and had an offer she could not refuse. It seemed like a family type thing to do. George and John Mallock were accused of selling heroin to an undercover U.S. narcotic bureau supervisor. She was guaranteed a quick return of her money and a bonus if she put up a ten-thousand-dollar bail.

Some people were putting up money and she felt it was a safe bet. Harry Erickson on Adanac Street, Emily Rice on Kingsway, and Stella Cushman on Cornwall Street each put up ten thousand dollars. Marie took out a five-thousand-dollar mortgage and put up her house. She added that to the five she had in the bank. It was a lot, but instead of earning a few dollars on a small bond she would be earning a five-thousand-dollar profit.

She was still annoyed about James Budd, fleecing her for a thousand dollars; but more annoyed by the newspaper headlines, 'Bye-Bye Male, Bye-Bye Bail'. Attention grabbing headlines at her expense had never seemed right to her. It was her livelihood. Any unease she felt about the bail was eased by the promises of the mobsters who approached her. She also felt better about it as Harry Erickson was an old and trusted friend. She did not know the other two women and only knew they came from Winnipeg so had ties with the brothers as well. Billy vouched for them from his prison cell. At least he was putting his time to good use while incarcerated learning to cook and run a kitchen in the Big House.

Despite the promises made, in January of 1951, the Judge issued a bench warrant for the two brothers who did not show up for court. An application was heard for the forfeiture of the forty thousand dollars bail. Mr. Dohm, lawyer for the brothers said he heard George had suffered a heart attack, but they were still getting on a plane on Monday night. However, he checked and did not see that they had made reservations and they did not show up. RCMP officers stayed at the airport for several hours watching incoming planes but no Mallock brothers.

In February, Stella Cushman flew to Winnipeg to find the two men and beg them to come back to Vancouver with her. She visited their mother, Mrs. Mallock, who was in fact the one who had the heart attack and was dying. She could not help Stella as she did not know where her boys had gone. Stella came back and called a meeting. She met with Marie, Harry, and Emily. Emily and Stella cried off and on through the meeting, but Marie had no time for that. The four of them put up five hundred dollars each for a total of two thousand dollars for information on the whereabouts of the brothers. They mailed hundreds of flyers to Winnipeg and put the word out through everyone they knew.

Marie went home minus five hundred dollars, sick and worried. This began a stressful two years for Marie as she knew it was only a matter of time until the court would order the sale of her home, her livelihood, and her business. She tried to get hold of Ron because he knew people, lawyers, judges, and investigators. She finally tracked him down and he told her on the phone, "I can't help you Marie. I'm laying low. Cooking, and working in camps."

"What do you mean?" she snapped, "laying low from what? I am about to lose our home."

"Your home," he reminded her, "I gave it to you."

"You know you can always come back. What the hell are you doing cooking in camps? What happened to your Private Investigation business?"

"That is why I am laying low," he laughed, "I got into a bit of trouble over a divorce case. Kirby and I came this close to being charged with perjury. And that jerk Dyson is out of jail and threatening to harm my family."

"You mean Lady Millicent Lavender's ex?"

"Yep. I guess I got suckered in because I thought she had some class. She dumped Kirby as her lawyer and then we ended up in court defending our actions. The hubby claims we tried to bribe him into getting a divorce. Then he gets out from serving his time for robbery and told everyone he was out to get me."

"Why not Kirby?"

"He's a lawyer, he's well known. I guess I am just the little private dick who screwed him over."

"Well. You said it, not me," and then she asked, "So what are you doing these days?"

"Cooking, I just told ya. I got a job with my sister-in-law Lottie cooking in a logging camp in Prince George . . .way out in the bush. I went back to Kamloops for awhile, but I am about to head back to work on the Bonnet Farm up there. In the cook house for the cowboys."

"Staying out of trouble, I guess."

"I've got three daughters ya know. I have to take care of my family."

"What about Gunvor, she work?"

He replied, "No, you know she never works."

Marie snorted, "Not like me. I work every damn day of my life!"

Before Ron hung up, he advised her, "Get your money secured somehow. And dealing with those guys, I would get insurance on the place."

Marie asked, "Why? They gonna burn my place down?"

Ron said, "Marie, if they feel like you have crossed them in any way, they will come after you and your property."

They said their goodbyes and Marie figured that would be the last time she heard from Ron. Marie thought about what Ron had told her more than once and got insurance on her property. Around that time Billy got out of prison and moved back in with her. It was nice to have her son home. She caried on renting out rooms, renting out the commercial suites and taking care of Billy and her puppies. Nobody ever tried to collect the reward for the Mallock brothers. It was understood in the mob community that they were somewhere in the United States. She was never going to get her money back. They did not even surface for their mother's funeral.

Within a year, Billy was able to get the five-thousand-dollar mortgage off the place. He ran a few deals that he should not have but she was happy to be mortgage free again. After a year helping his mom out, Bill decided as he was heading into his forties, it was time to move out. He had a girlfriend Donna who was a waitress at White Spot on the west side of town and he moved in with her. Marie had been getting on his nerves; and the dogs drove him out of his mind with their barking.

Marie was uneasy from the start. Having Bill around made her feel safe. She had no idea if the Mallock brothers or their mob friends might turn up. It did not help that when Ron dropped in from one of his runs to Vancouver after he moved to Prince George, he advised her again, "I would get insurance on the place."

She did not tell him she had done that already. She did not want him to think she took his advice on anything. Ron said, "Marie, the Mallock boys and their friends are dangerous guys."

Three days later she went back to court and heard that Crown would not take their homes from them; at least not yet. The four ten-thousand-dollar bonds would act like a mortgage on the four homes. Each house would have a ten-thousand-dollar charge levied against the property. Marie did not think her property was worth that much. Crown still had the charge against the property for the bail. That hung over her head. It hung over her head for a long time. She lay awake at night trying to figure out how to pay it back.

And then the worst thing happened; in the fall of 1952 Crown proceeded with the ruling to sell the bail forfeited property to get the money back. Marie and the other three people involved got together with their lawyer and asked what they could do. His answer was a simple, 'nothing'. He did tell them not to worry too much though as it would be at least a year until the Court even put the properties up for sale and they could live in their homes until they were sold. For a long time, Marie resigned herself to the fact that she would have to move. In the meantime, she kept the place full and hoped to make as much money as she could to settle the account before they put it on the market.

Ron called Marie one night in the summer of 1953 and after some chit chat about how he was back in Kamloops said, "I know a guy who can fix a problem like that."

Just like that Marie knew what she was going to do. She found the 'guy' whose name was Guy. They sat many nights drinking whisky and talking about her problem. She had insurance on her property, and she figured a fire could take care of her problem. Not a big fire. She just needed a bit of a fire to cause a bit of damage and she could collect on that and go on living her life.

She had heaters in all the rooms. Little electric heaters that sat on the floor. People had said enough times, 'those bloody things could tip over and start a fire'. Guy suggested he replace the heater in one of the rooms on the third floor. The logic was the fire would spread up, not down. He said, "It will be a small enough fire that the person in the room will get out and alert the others. And if the fire department gets here quick you will have only damaged the top floor, ya know with smoke and then the water from the hoses. I bet you will get more than ten thousand in insurance."

Marie hesitated at first. She was worried that maybe someone might get hurt but then she thought about it and reasoned that nobody would get hurt. She would wake up because her dogs barked like crazy at a pin drop and she would run over and save everyone. She had an alarm system. She thought about it and figured the best room to have the electric fire problem was in Helen's room. Helen was young, under fifty and in good shape. She would be knocking on doors and down those stairs in a flash. Marie agreed to do it.

After a few sleepless nights she told Guy, the arsonist, "I don't want to know when it is going to be. I know my dogs will wake me and I know Helen is a light sleeper and I would rather wake up while the commotion is going on then to lay there and think about what is going to happen."

He said, "Well, we don't know when it is going to be anyway. I am going to swap out the heater with a faulty one with frayed wires. There is no telling when that will all happen," he stroked his chin, "could be days, could be weeks."

In August of 1953 he put the faulty heater in Helen's room. They waited and nothing happened. Marie was relieved. But it made sense, nobody used heat in August. She told the arsonist, "I'm not that comfortable with this whole mess. I think we need to scrap the plan."

He did not argue with her. He was not all that sure it would be deemed an accident and he may not get any insurance money. He did not really trust Marie, nobody did. He was annoyed and left the house in a huff. He left it up to her to get the faulty heater out of the room. She procrastinated. It was early September nobody would turn the heat on until October. As Helen often did, she was having a cup of tea with Marie in her little house on the afternoon of September 12, 1953. When Helen left to see her husband off to work for a night shift on the docks, Marie turned to her dogs and said, "Damn I gotta get that heater out of her room soon."

By the time Marie went to bed that night she was busy with people coming and going, walking the dogs, feeding them, and just running around. She settled down and went to sleep. It had been a long, hard day. She often woke up two or three times a night but this night she slept heavy. Around three in the morning she heard her dogs barking. She rubbed her eyes, foggy at first and then she smelled it, smoke. She shot out of bed and ran to her window.

The tenement building across the alley was in flames. She could see the top floor already had smoke billowing out the windows. All she could think was, 'this is not my fault', and then she ran barefoot across the alley and up to the second floor where sixteen Chinese tenants lived in the four rooms. She ran around banging on doors screaming there was a fire and then as they started to rush out of the rooms, she hollered for the people on the third floor to get out. She heard a man yell back, "Yep. We're coming."

Marie pulled the alarm on the main floor and it started clanging. Marie ran back across the alley into her house and called the fire department. She scooped up her dogs and ran into the street. She was not sure how long it would take the fire to jump the roadway. She had never been so afraid. She could hear people yelling, and then screaming. She stood on the sidewalk, her three dogs yelping and growling in her arms and wept. She did not believe this could be her fault.

It was daylight before the fire was out. She had no idea how much damage was done but it looked like the third floor was ruined, gone. She was taken to a motel with her dogs and told she could return the next day after her place was secured. She was advised, "There will be an investigation."

Marie did not know until later that day that Helen perished on the third floor. Helen was the only true friend she had. They shared tea and cookies together almost everyday. Helen was five years younger than Marie and had been the one to complain to about how tough it was to grow old. How the hell did she not wake up and get out? Marie did not sleep.

Marie went home early the next morning and convinced the fire crew on site to let her take her dogs into her house where she could settle them down and clean herself up. Marie looked out the window at the mess and wept. She got a bath; she put on fresh clothes, makeup and pulled her hair back behind her ears into a low bun. She sat on a rocking chair on her front porch and watched the clean up begin. Throughout the late afternoon and early evening her tenants came one by one to tell her the harrowing stories of how they made it out. It broke her heart.

John Wang a twenty-one-year-old student came and sat with her and told her how he got the other fifteen Chinese out of the building. Many of the men were old and disabled and John helped them see through the smoke to go down the set of stairs. He told her with a wide grin, "I got them all Boss, I got them all."

A fireman stopped and told her how when they arrived there was a man on the third floor who had pulled down the escape ladder and was hanging from it. They got him safely to the ground. There were two other men hanging out of windows. He said at one point the fire was threatening the building next door and they had to take care of it, so it did not catch. A couple of men were hanging out of windows as their rooms were filling with smoke as well. Marie was afraid to ask but did, "What about Helen?"

"Dead," he answered, "dead before we got to her. She burned up in her room, on the floor. The smoke got to her before she could get out."

Marie already knew that, but she needed to hear it from someone in charge. She found out later that two men died in the fire. Jack Roberts who was seventy-two was sprawled in the hallway outside the door to his room. A survivor claimed the sound of Jack falling to the floor was what woke him up and saved his life. Seventy-three-year-old Valentine Coccanig perished as well. All three victims were on the third floor where the fire started.

There was speculation and finger pointing but nobody was ever charged with arson. The site inspection report detailed how a faulty heater in the room Helen shared with her husband was the culprit. Everyone in the building knew that she liked to wash out her things in the shared bathroom tub and hang them to dry in her room. Even Marie knew that. Men in the building often laughed at the glimpse of stockings hanging on a line they could see through the front bay window. Helen often turned on the heater to dry her clothes at night even in warm weather.

Helen was found on the floor by the heater burned alive because she was overcome by the smoke. Marie was comforted to hear that she was gone before she burned. Rather quickly, the Fire Marshall determined it was the heater that started the fire. He added that it was hard to determine if it was the only cause to blame, adding that the house was a fire trap. An accident waiting to happen. They closed the case as quick as they could, in part because for some reason the fire department did not turn up on scene for more than an hour after the blaze started. Marie knew she called it in within minutes. The firehouse was a five-minute drive away. They must have smelled the smoke they were that close. It made Marie feel less guilty.

The three victims died within minutes of the fire starting. There was sloppy written all over the report. The place was a fire trap. It was unclear why she even was able to get insurance on such a death trap. Rumours swirled about the area. Everyone knew Marie needed the insurance money. But more anger was placed on the insurance company. What kind of business would secure a death trap with insurance, and why did it take the fire trucks so long to arrive?

Marie convinced herself that she was in no way to blame. She ran across the alley and banged on doors and pulled the alarm and called the fire department. She did everything she could. She regretted not going up to the third floor, but she had arthritis in her knees and the stairs were already thick with smoke. No doubt Helen, and the two men were dead before Marie got to the building. She would have been too late anyway.

Marie did not feel any guilt. She convinced herself she had nothing to do with it. Maybe she didn't. Nobody would ever know. She was interviewed on site about the fire and she put on a good performance. She cried to the press that she suffered a great loss and could never replace the valuable furniture and antiques she had on the third floor. The furniture was in fact cheap, second-hand stuff from the Salvation Army, and the washbowls, curtains, and knick-knack items she picked up from Flea Markets. The newspapers hinted that the fire was timely as her place was to be sold in a few months for the unpaid Bond, but the story fizzled out faster than the embers from the fire.

Marie called her insurance company and after a quick investigation she was paid ten thousand dollars in damages; most of which was used to remove the top floor from the building. It was beyond repair. It was a reminder of what had happened, and Marie wanted it gone. The rest of the money with some savings paid off the lean on the property and the debt to the Crown was satisfied. There was lingering gossip because some people believed it was too much of a coincidence. But everyone was polite and respectful to the Big Boss.

Ron was living in Kamloops but came down to help Marie sort everything out. He stayed with her for a week, lying to Gunvor because she would not understand him helping Marie through her time of mourning. He hinted one afternoon to Marie, "I guess you used the guy I sent you to help you out with your problem?"

Marie joked, "The guy named Guy?"

Ron agreed, "Ya Guy, the arsonist."

Marie wagged her finger in his face and shouted, "Don't ever say anything like that to me again. I never met up with him, not once, not ever."

Ron dropped it because he was a little afraid of Billy. Ron had seen Guy at the bar the night before and he claimed that he tried to collect money from Marie, and she said she had never seen him before. Billy and another tough looking mobster had approached him in an alley and reminded him that Marie did not know him and had never met him. They had guns, he told Ron, and he was not going to mess with Marie, her son, or the other thugs she hung out with. Ron knew better than to mess with Marie and after a few days of packing up things he could save from the burned-out rooms he went back to Kamloops.

The removal of the top floor began within a month of the fire and by November of 1953 you could not tell it had ever been anything but a two-storey building. A new roof, freshly painted walls on the second floor and a good cleaning of the business units and it was better than it had been. A new alarm was installed, wiring checked and brought up to code and she was good to go.

The Chinese men left the building. Marie fixed up the second floor with funky second-hand store finds and colourful curtains. She bought rattan mats from Chinatown and provided each room with a comforter for the bed and a stack of fresh towels. One of her new renters was a guitar player who ran guitar lessons out of his room. Another room was rented to a young couple who had just been married and were artists. With Marie's permission they painted murals in the hallways.

Marie remembered growing up in the artsy community in Winnipeg with theatres and dance halls and she kept one of the rooms as an hourly rental. For five dollars an hour you could use the space to teach a class, have a meeting or whatever you wanted. She furnished that room with a couch and a table. Three of the rooms were rented to students. She did not want to have older disabled people in the building anymore. The last vacancy, she let two young women, Fay and Margaret, take on two rooms: one for living in and one for business purposes. They were fortune tellers and children of friends from Winnipeg. She liked having young women twenty and twenty-one living there. It changed the vibe of the building. There was new life and energy there now.

A month after the Dimitri sisters moved in and hung their sign from the second-floor window Marie was a bit worried about their honesty and tactics with customers. One night they picked up an elderly man on Union Street, brought him back to read his fortune and got a bit rough with him. The felt his clothing for money and kneed him in the stomach in the process of robbing him. When they let him go, they told him to 'forget about it'. But he went to the police. Marie had to talk to the 'girls' and tell them to stop with the rough stuff or they would have to move out. It went to court, but all they got was community service.

They laughed and said they were already doing community service. Marie loved the energy the young women brought to the place. Because the four hundred dollars they stole was returned they carried on as if nothing happened. They ran their scams out of the Marine Rooms for a couple of more years. Marie was running a nice building full of young artistic, happy people. Marie entered a Bohemian phase of music, wine, and laughter.

Marie had a way of looking ten years older than she was; always in a black coat and hat. She dressed like a grandmother in cotton dresses that would have been worn on the farm, topped with a big apron because she was always cooking. She wore sturdy shoes and walked with purpose. Marie baked, cooked, and pickled things like beets and her hands always seemed to be stained with beet juice. She had a natural curl to her thick hair that had been so attractive when she was young, but now in her mid-fifties she chopped it off and slicked it back, so she looked stern. Occasionally she would giggle, or grin and the good time girl returned but not that often.

In February of 1954 George Mallock was caught and returned to Canada. When Marie heard George was being brought into court from Oakalla Prison she threw on her coat and hat and grabbed her umbrella, partly because of the rain. She was there when he got out of the police van in manacles and flashed a brief smile at her. That made her livid and she stomped down the sidewalk to the courthouse door yelling, "I'd like to scratch your eyes out George Mallock."

A reporter couldn't miss the show and asked her why and she replied, "I almost lost my home because he skipped bail. I had to borrow ten thousand from my brother to pay the court back. He owes me ten grand," she shook her umbrella and yelled, "I'll poke his eyes out with this umbrella."

Marie did not have a brother but sometimes people wondered if she did not think of Bill as her brother and not her son. She was married the first time when she was fourteen and she was pregnant with Bill when she was sixteen. Nobody knew what happened in that marriage really. He was an older English man who was very mean by all reports. By 1925 she was living on her own with the boy she called "Billie". He was ten and she was twenty-six.

She had been dancing in Burlesque shows for a couple of years to pay the bills. Her family had been fine with that. Her parents were still alive in those days.

It was a couple of years later around the time Ron entered her life that she began doing more than just tease men while she danced. That was when she moved to Saskatoon and started 'hooking' for a living. She left Bill with her sister when he was twelve and he was brought up by extended family. It was a good life for a young boy who saw life much like Marie did. He was pulling scams and stealing by the time he was eight years old.

The Mallock boys lived down the street and a lot of folks suspected the young man mentioned in newspaper reports who was a 'lookout' for the older guys, was Billy. Marie brought men home sometimes and she taught Billy to pick their pockets while their pants were hanging on the back of the chair. By the time Ron entered that picture and was introduced to the twelve-year-old, Ron was twenty-two and, in many ways, more innocent than Billy.

Marie was interviewed about the Mallock brothers and asked why she put up the bail she said, "The Mallock boys played with my kids in Winnipeg."

The only child Marie had was Billy, but she let her home become a drop in place for a lot of young men. For the short time Marie lived in Saskatchewan Billy had some stability. Then Marie was back with her new young boyfriend Ron who was not good daddy material. Ron tried, but in truth Marie treated him and Billy like they were both kids. Ron figured Marie was born tough. Marie knew that tough was beaten into her when she was fourteen and forced by her parents to marry a man twice her age.

The only two people Marie ever cared about were Ron and Billy. Ron left her and settled down with Gunvor and the three girls. It broke her heart and she never even dated after Ron. But what broke her heart even more was when Billy, at the age of thirty-nine got married. It was in the fall, November of 1954. He married Donna Humphries; no wedding party, no family; just an announcement in the newspaper. Marie who never cried, wept all afternoon.

Chapter Eight

Ron and Gunvor (1950 to 1963)

Ron had not lied to Marie when he said he had to 'lay low'. Kirby was scared he was going to lose his barrister's license. He said to Ron, "I can't let this theatrical activity we have been engaging in affect my life any longer."

Ron argued, "You didn't mind taking the money, though did you?"

Kirby said, "Look Tiny, I have had a ball working with you. When you first approached me about the idea to set men up for divorce it seemed harmless enough. But this Dyson business almost cost me my job. We are lucky we did not get charged with perjury."

Ron laughed, "We are lucky that our witness who claims to have had sex with him kept her word and lied on the stand."

"Better her than us," Kirby agreed.

Ron had been lying on the stand for Kirby for years. He had just been lucky he hadn't been caught. It was Kirby's idea to go to B.C. Pen and offer Dyson a thirty-dollar bribe. Ron had told him not to be such a cheapskate. He should have offered him a hundred bucks. The good news was they had not been sent to prison or charged with perjury or bribery. Kirby still came over and drank with Ron and they remained friends. Kirby, the great orator, loved to stand on a chair and recite dirty poetry like he was delivering a Shakespearean sonnet. Sometimes, Lottie got a bit tipsy and shoved him off the chair so she could sing Oh Promise Me. They were usually the opening act for Ron to do his famous bathtub scene,

There would be no more work for Kirby, not for a while. Ron did not want to move back to Vancouver and neither did Gunvor. Gunvor's sister Lottie heard that Prince George camps were paying big money for cooks. So, they packed up and left. Her husband Waldy went to work in camp as a logger. Lottie and Ron got jobs in the kitchen. They were a great team. They spent the next couple of years running back and forth between Kamloops and Prince George. They went back to Kamloops for one trip to pick up all the belongings they had left in storage. As usual they had enough money to get to Kamloops and no back up plan. Ron was unemployed and needed money quick.

He went to see Marie in Vancouver, but she was in a bigger mess than he was, on the verge of losing her property. So, he borrowed gas money and went back to Kamloops and took a job cooking in the kitchen at the Franklin Hotel. He got meals for the family and a free room. Two double beds and a sink to wash up in. The bathroom was down the hall. His girls were three, seven and fourteen and had to cram into one bed. Gay and Elna started school. About October it was getting cold, so Ron went to the storage unit to get their belongings. The older girls needed jackets.

When he got to the storage facility, he was told his property had been confiscated because he was two months behind on payments. The snippy woman said, "Pay the rent, get your stuff. If not, it will be sold next week."

Ron grabbed Waldy who was also unemployed and took him to the lock up after midnight. They broke in and stole all of Ron and Gunvor's stuff. They both felt it was the right thing to do. Waldy broke the locks and he and Ron grabbed as much as they could get in the two cars parked in the alley. When Ron got back to the hotel he went up to the room and laid the warm jackets on the bed for Elna and Gay.

When they woke up, he became the legendary dad who always kept his promise. He was the hero of the story, as he always was. At least in Gay's eyes. She knew stealing from a locker was wrong, but it was worse that the people who owned the lock up would not let her have her jacket. It was cold out and she had to walk to school. Elna thanked him for getting the jacket but she felt sick to her stomach knowing he committed a crime. She had witnessed far too much. She was not blind to the fact that he was a petty thief and a criminal.

After a few months, they got enough money together and they all went back to Prince George because Ron had a job on the Bonnet Farm rustling up food for the cowboys. It was a fun summer for the girls. The older girls had to take correspondence for the first half of the school year. But like most jobs, Ron did not stay long. Lottie and Waldy moved up because Waldy was building a half a house for someone and they were staying in it while he was building it. Nobody ever asked why the client only wanted half a house because it was assumed, he only had half the money needed for a whole house. It was not very warm, but they did not have to pay rent. Waldy asked Ron to give him a hand and Ron moved down the street with his family using the money. The girls missed the farm but were happy to be able to go to school again.

Gunvor was drinking a lot and Elna, now fifteen. was taking care of the kids. For some reason they got a white rabbit named Tilly with red eyes that freaked out four-year-old Gwynne. It was not just Gwynne who was afraid that winter, all the kids were. Everything was so uncertain. With Elna and an older cousin taking care of them; Gay, Gwynne, and Lottie's two girls, Linda and Sharon were on their own. The grownups were working or drinking. Occasionally, an overweight woman with wooden legs the girls called Peg Leg would come over and want to slobber kiss them all over. It was not the best of times. The five younger girls would run down the hall and hide on the shelves of a closet: smallest on the bottom. Peg Leg was the bootlegger, and the irony was not lost on the girls that she had no feet to put in shoes. Or legs, for that matter. Her wooden legs came with shoes attached which amused them greatly.

By the summer of 1953 they were back living on Yew Street in Kamloops, across the street from a park.   Ron was working for

Kirby on mostly legitimate stuff. Elna was happy to be back because Mike, the boy she loved, lived in Kamloops. They did not waste any time after they got out of grade ten to decide to get married. At first Gunvor and Ron said there was no way she was going to marry at fifteen. But she was turning sixteen July 31 and she insisted she was going to marry Mike. They liked Mike. He was a hard-working kid who always had a gas station job of some kind. He knew a lot about cars which came in handy. Mike had been in an orphanage even though he knew who his parents were. His upbringing had been as crazy as Elna's.

Gunvor wore a grey suit and she and Ron stood up for the two kids at City Hall. Elna told everyone close to her that she had to get out of 'that house'. Of course, she did not tell her mother that as she was too respectful. Elna did not care for the way Ron treated her mom. She blamed the drinking on him. The only reason she was sad to go was she knew that Gwynne depended on her. Gwynne would be five in two months and Elna reasoned she had been taking care of herself since she was five, so the little girl would be fine. When Elna and Mike drove off with the tin cans rattling on the back of Mike's old Ford. Gwynne ran after the car crying 'don't leave me'.

Elna turned around once and started to cry but Mike told her to 'knock it off' and she did. Elna wore a white suit with a tiny hat and looked like she was a child playing dress up. Mike, who was sixteen looked ridiculous in a suit, kind of like a choir boy. Elna was six weeks shy of turning sixteen. It was June 12th, just two days after they finished grade ten. Everyone who saw them could see how much in love they were. Elna was happy but prayed that mom would sober up a bit and take care of the little girl. Elna had been Gwynne's mother for four years. When Gay was little, Gunvor had been more attentive.

Elna did not go too far away. She and Mike rented an apartment in Kamloops. Across the bridge on Royal Avenue in North Kamloops, Ron, Gunvor and the two girls moved into an old manse that was still attached to the church. The church had a wall of pews. It was the best house they had lived in. There was an empty chicken coop in the yard as well. Gil Tymich's family lived across the street and he found it for them. He promised the landlord, who was a childhood friend, that they were 'good people'.

Elna came over and she often took Gwynne to stay at her apartment. It was a good thing Elna was around because Gwynne was a clumsy child and most of the time it was Elna who rescued her. When she got a button stuck up her nose, Elna got it out; when she got her legs stuck between the spindles of the chair, Elna sawed her out. Elna worried about how she would survive without her being there.

For the most part the girls were happy for the next year. The house was beautiful and there was a full yard that led down to the Thompson River. Gunvor was more active in taking care of them, making them picnic lunches, and bathing them at night. It seemed when Gunvor had to be a mother she had not forgotten how to. Maybe if Ron, Lottie and Elna made her fend for herself she would have stepped up to the job sooner. Gunvor was happier at home with Elna gone. There was less tension in the house.

Ron was working for Kirby and occasionally that work took him to Vancouver. He had to follow a guy for a couple of days who was accused of getting work benefits when it was believed he was fit for work. Gunvor was having a bad spell as they called it. She would get drunk when they were partying but when the rest of them sobered up, she took to her bed and drank as much whiskey as Ron would bring her. He gave Gunvor some whiskey and told her, "When it is gone, it is gone, so sober up."

He asked Elna to look in on Gay who was in grade five to make sure she got a lunch and went to school. Gwynne was in grade one, but Ron took her with him. He was not going to at first, but she cried and begged to go along for the ride. Sometimes it was hard to say no to her. He also felt that she was a bit young to be coming home to a big empty house, with mom in bed. Gay had friends in the area and had places she could go.

Ron took Gwynne on a stake out and the two of them had fun playing word games and telling jokes. Ron liked to tell stories about England and how they were related to royalty. He liked to talk about Lady Mary and Gwynne loved the stories about Newcastle and

Barnard Castle. At some point Barnard was a castle but when Ron grew up it was a work-house he was afraid his family would end up in. But in his stories, it was a castle where Lady Mary lived, and he and his family would take tea with her on Sundays. Gwynne would sit on the front seat with him and ask, "Does that mean that I am a princess?"

Ron grinned at her, "Yes, you are. You are my little princess."

***

When the suspect was at therapy, Ron went into reception and asked how long he would be. At least three hours he was told. They took a break. Ron took Gwynne to see Harold. Harold was still with Marion living on West Twelfth working odd jobs and drinking. He told Ron he had not been arrested for impaired or anything for a long time. He was happy to see his daughter. He gave Ron a hundred dollars, made them peanut butter and jelly sandwiches for the stake out and when they left Harold got super drunk. She was a sweet little girl. She reminded him of Marlene when she was little. Now Marlene was sixteen and had attitude. She had a boyfriend, and they were getting married as soon as they graduated.

The second day of the stake out Ron declared the guy was not ripping anyone off. He was in fact going to therapy and not faking an injury. He called Kirby and said he was on his way back. He took Gwynne to meet Marie. It did not go as he expected. He thought Marie would love to see his girl, but she did not. She offered him whiskey and suggested he take Gwynne to see the Gypsy sisters so they could have a few drinks without his little bastard child in the room. He did as he was told. He walked her across the alley and Fay came out and took her hand, "Hey sweetie do you want to see my tarot cards and my crystal ball?"

"Can we play catch?" she asked.

Fay laughed, "Not with this ball honey. It is special. C'mon I will show you."

Marie wanted to bitch to Ron about Bill and how he ran off and got married. Ron pointed out to Marie that he did not run off as he had already been living with Donna and that he was almost forty years old. She glared at Ron and replied, "Well, he lost the best years of his life in prison, thanks to you."   He noticed that she seemed run down and it did not look like she was taking care of herself, in fact she looked like hell and he told her so.

Marie said, "I work hard every day. I do not have a man to lean on like Gunvor. Nobody takes care of me."

"Nobody ever took care of you Marie," he replied.

She stared into her whiskey glass and agreed, "You got that right. Nobody was ever there for me," she took a sip and added, "well, you were. You were there for me."

They clinked there glasses together and smiled at each other. They had a lot of good times together. They had a lot of memories. But there did not seem to be much of a connection between them anymore. He did not stay long. He collected his daughter from the gypsies, and they drove through the night back to Kamloops. He told Gwynne not to tell mom, but he did not have to worry about that. Gunvor was drunk in bed for at least another week and Gwynne forgot. Marie did tell Ron that the lawyer, Bill Murdoch was asking after him. That resulted in a phone call to Bill who said if Ron came back to Vancouver, he could throw some work his way.

Just before Christmas they packed everything up and moved to Heather Street in Vancouver into a big brownstone. Gay said the wide stairs leading to the front door were like the kind you would find on a mansion. She confided to Gwynne that they were living in a mansion. The girls loved it even though they had a two bedroom flat on the main floor and not the run of the whole place. They went to a school called Model School and while it had nothing to do with models the two of them pretended they were models when they walked the halls. Even though Gay was four and a half years older than Gwynne when she saw her in the hall at school, she would do the model walk. Gwynne would put her hand on her hip and do the same. It was a sister thing.

The brownstone was a few blocks from Vancouver General Hospital and close to Harold and Marion's place. That Christmas Harold turned up with a beautiful doll with curly blonde hair and with arms and legs that bent. The doll was wearing a red taffeta dress and Gwynne fell in love right away, calling her Cindy. It was the only nice gift she had ever received. Gay pouted a bit and wondered why Harold gave her little sister a gift and not her but as was typical of the girls, they never asked questions. They just buried their pain and confusion. Gwynne did tease her sister with the taunt, "I'm just cuter than you."

Gay acted out by being mean to Gwynne. She tied her to a bus stop one day and left her there for thirty minutes while she went to play. She took her to a birthday party and did not stick around to see it was the right party. Seven- year-old Gwynne pretended everything was fine until the birthday boy opened his gift from her that she had wrapped in the funny papers. It was a cheap skipping rope and all the kids laughed. It had started out as such a good day. Gwynne in a freshly ironed blue chiffon dress. Elna, who had moved to Vancouver a few weeks behind them, had curled her hair with sugar water and hairpins. She looked adorable. She knew that. The day ended with her running home across a busy street wetting her pants and hiding in the closet. Gay didn't got in trouble. She never did.

The work did not come in from Bill Murdoch. Ron had to get a job picking up dirty laundry for Peerless Laundry who used the slogan, 'we do your clothes white'. It was probably the longest stretch of normal work he had ever had. When Mike and Elna moved into the two-bedroom suite with them they had a baby girl named Holly. The older girls had friends and spending money. There was food on the table every night and life seemed normal for over a year. Whenever Elna was around life was better.

Then for no reason they packed everything up and left for Kenora, Ontario. The only person who knew the reason was Ron. It was simple. He and Harold ran a scam offering to do a job, collecting the money up front and never turned up to do the job. As Harold had not given his name out and had been more in the background, Ron was the one who would be fingered by the guy. He also owed another guy a lot of money for a gambling debt. As they drove out of town in the old Packard Ron owned, both girls were sad. Gunvor was happy because she was going to be near her family in Eagle

River and she had not seen her mother since she left in 1947 ten years ago.

Of course, reunions are not always what you expect. Gunvor's parents Vendla and Alfred did not like Ron. The visit in Eagle River was short. Alfred told Gunvor she was not welcome in his home with Ron. He reminded her Alton was still legally her husband. Alton and Alfred had become close after he got back from the war. Alton confided to Alfred that he paid child support to Gunvor for a year after she started living with Ron. Both men agreed Elna should have become Ron's responsibility once he moved in with her mother.

Ron drove back to Kenora and set up a tent in a campground. They lived there for two months before school started and then they got an apartment in town across the street from Central Park. Gwynne went to Central School for grade three and four. Gay had to go to a middle school a little farther away as she was in grade seven and eight. It was the longest time they ever lived anywhere. For the girls they were the happiest days of their childhood. Like clockwork, Elna and Mike turned up although it was almost a year later. Elna had another baby called Shelley as well as Holly who was going on three.

Weekends and summers were spent in Eagle River with cousins. The kids milked cows and gathered clover to feed the chickens. They stayed with different cousins. Most of the relatives played instruments. In the evenings, there were sing-a-longs and laughter. It was a magical time for the girls. Fresh food from the garden and dad drove a bread truck so there was lots of bread. It seemed they were always outside running around in the sunshine whether they were visiting the farm or at home in their apartment right next to Central Park. About fifty children gathered in the park to play hide and seek every night.

Gunvor was more sober than she had been in years. She never drank around her relatives. The first year and a half was great. But it did not last. Ron lost the bread truck delivery job and was driving taxi. They barely had food on the table some nights. They had to move from the nice apartment and ended up living in a three-room converted garage in an alleyway. It was new and clean. For some reason they had a new lime green couch with a pull-out drawer. They had never owned anything new before. Gay confided to Gwynne that someone must have liked dad so much they gave it to him. Gwynne raised an eyebrow and replied, "He probably stole it."

Ron came in one night from driving cab and woke Gay and Gwynne up as they were sleeping on the couch. He made them get up so he could put twenty-seven blankets in the pull-out drawer. They were thin, more like throw blankets or for children but they were pretty. Soft with red and blue lines across the top. The girls used them to make forts, but every night mom told them they had to put them back under the couch.

It was not long until the cops came looking for Ron. He was driving cab. Gunvor told the girls to go jump on the couch and make a lot of noise. That was unusual for her. It was always, 'be quiet'. But they did it. Mom opened the door and the two police officers crammed into the hallway by the door, their shoulders touching the walls. There was nothing to see but two unruly girls jumping on a lime green couch screaming. They left. Gunvor said, "Pipe down."

It did not matter that the cops did not find the blankets, Ron was charged with theft and got three months in the Provincial Jail because he was sorry and told a good story about how they needed blankets for the children. He also said that his nephew Kenny stole them, but he would take the rap for him. He did not want his favourite nephew going to jail. The Judge did not believe him and gave him a sentence of three months served during the week. He could go home on weekends to drive cab to help support his family. It was really a sentence of sixty days, not ninety.

Ron was in a huge dorm with about twenty men. They were free to play poker, listen to music and wander the huge compound. He worked in the Jail kitchen during the week. He was able to throw cans of food over the fence. When they checked him at the gate he was not carrying anything. On Friday he went home with cans of ham and soups he picked up by the edge of the woods after he got out of the yard.

One weekend he just came home, and they packed everything up and left. He had twenty days left to serve but he did not want to. As they drove out of town, he told Gunvor, "I will never be able to come back to Ontario. There is going to be a warrant out for my arrest."

"No kidding," she said but she did not mind that they were skipping out. She was tired of taking care of the girls by herself during the week. They had no car, very little money and she told him every Friday, "Life is no picnic."

Gay was sulky and upset they were leaving as she had a lot of good friends. Gwynne was just annoyed and said loudly so her parents could hear,
"It figures the first nice thing we have gets left behind."

Ron said, "Stop being upset about the couch. You got a bunch of nice new blankets to sit on don't ya?"

They drove for days but they eventually arrived in Edmonton and pulled into the yard of a huge three-story house. It was a monster and looked haunted. Sitting in the middle of bungalows on a pretty tree lined street, it looked out of place, as did their beat-up car. The girls were surprised when Elna ran out of the house with Holly and Shelley. They had gone to Kenora for a short while but left a month earlier. Elna was pregnant again. The girls were never told anything. They had not even known that Elna and Mike left Ontario.

Edmonton proved to be a stressful year for the adults and for the kids. Mike and Ron were driving bakery trucks. The old house was cold and there was a lot of fighting. Elna had a baby boy named Mike. Holly ended up in hospital with peritonitis. After one bad fight Gunvor and Ron moved out and took the girls to the outskirts of Edmonton, called Wintergreen where they had a cute little house . . . for a while. Gay graduated from grade nine and Gwynne finished grade five. That summer they moved back to Kamloops. They moved into an ugly farmhouse in the middle of a dry dusty field with Elna and Mike.

They heard a rumour that Mike had to leave Vancouver three years earlier because he was involved in a hit and run. He went to Ontario and changed the spelling of his name and got a new license in the new name. Gwynne and Gay got all their information from cousins. Like when they were in Eagle River one summer their uncle pulled his truck into a yard and a bunch of kids ran out of the house. One of their cousins told the girls, 'those are your brothers and sisters'.

The information was not right. Gunvor's first and only legal husband, Alton was living with a woman and she had a bunch of kids. They were not even Elna's half brothers and sisters, as Alton was not the father. Elna was his only child. Gwynne and Gay did not even know that Elna was a half-sister until they were in their teens. Nobody ever told them anything. Life was uncertain and there were very few people they could trust. Like the generation of women before them, they encountered the family creeps. By the time Gwynne was eight she knew a cousin whose father tied her to a washing machine and raped her.

Life in Kamloops always seemed to be better. Because Gay was going into grade ten Ron promised to stay for three years so she could graduate there. She became one of the school's star performers winning Best Actress Awards in Theatre. And why not? She had been playing the part of a healthy, happy girl all her life. Both girls got good grades and sometimes honour roll standing. Which was amazing as by the time they landed back in Kamloops Gay had been to fourteen or fifteen schools. Gwynne was in grade six and in seven schools.

They did not stay long at the farmhouse because there was a bloody fight between Ron and Mike. Mike had cheated on Elna and Ron got into the middle of the fight. He took a swing at Mike, but the much younger, bigger man beat Ron to the floor. There was blood everywhere. Gay came in and started screaming and Ron got off the floor and slapped her across the face. Gunvor went to her bedroom and Gwynne ran out to the tire swing in the backyard and cried.

For the first time in their married lives, Elna and Mike moved away from her parents and went to Hope, a small town nestled in the mountains on the way to Vancouver. Mike liked to joke, "We ran out of gas and money before we got beyond hope."

Ron could not afford the big house on his own. They moved into town to a little house on McGowan Avenue. It came with a converted garage where Gay lived with Cousin Linda. Sharon bunked in with Gwynne most nights even though Lottie and Waldy had an apartment above the restaurant they were running. For some time, Ron and Lottie ran the restaurant called the New Day Café. Waldy worked in logging camps and Gunvor barely got out of bed that year. Gay and Linda worked at the café for a few weeks, but they were not getting paid enough so the two of them worked at a drive-in restaurant where they delivered food to cars while they were wearing roller skates. The New Day was home to a lot of bloody fights.

Waldy liked to accuse Lottie of plotting things with Ron and then he would get her on the ground and try to break her legs. One night, Gwynne and Lottie's daughter Sharon saw Ron pick up a frying pan and bash Waldy over the head. It was so routine that after Sharon made sure her dad was breathing the two girls went to the rooms upstairs and drank cokes. The two of them stared out at the lights of Kamloops and talked about all the secrets they had discovered in the tin box and had a good laugh. Gwynne's favourite was a postcard that said Merry Christmas. The letters were made up of naked bodies fornicating. She thought the artwork was awesome. She loved the irony of the sweet message being sent by what she figured were bad people.

While living on McGowan Avenue Ron received word his mother had died. It was 1961. He had not seen her since he took Gwynne to visit her six years earlier. His sister sent him a clipping of her obituary from the paper after the funeral. Ron was not notified in time to attend. It broke his heart. He had always loved his mother and respected her. Life was not great. Gunvor was more absent than ever. As he liked to say he was 'chief cook and bottle washer' as well as earning a living. They barely scraped by. Gay gave half of her earnings to her dad. She bought all of Gwynne's school clothes as well as her own from the earnings at the drive-in burger joint.

They moved into a small one-bedroom apartment on Fairview Avenue. Gay had to quit her job to stay involved with school and theatre. Ron went to the doctor and found out the pitter patter in his chest was angina and he had to go on heart medication. He suddenly felt too old for this world and at the age of fifty-six applied for welfare. Around that time universal medical was introduced in Canada and he was able to take his girls to doctors and optometrists. They found out Gwynne had a heart murmur and needed glasses. Gwynne figured her eyes were bad because Gay used to tuck Gwynne's head under her arm and poke her fingers into her eyes when she was babysitting. The doctor figured she must have had scarlet fever to get a murmur. Who would have known? She never went to a doctor until she was twelve.

They lived in Kamloops until 1963. Gay graduated and went to Summer School Theatre of the Arts at the University of British Columbia. Gwynne graduated from grade eight on the honour roll, a studious girl who belonged to the grass hockey team and the square dance club. Ron could not have been prouder and took credit for how wonderful his kids turned out. He could not have known then that his girls were actors, and the turmoil was deep inside of them.

Gunvor had been mostly sober for about a year when Gay left home. She was close to Gwynne who was fourteen going on thirty. It seemed that Gunvor's mothering skills kicked in. There was a lot of home cooked meals, baking and laughter. Gunvor started knitting. Ron only worked when he got carnival jobs which was a lot in the summers. Gwynne started working the carnivals with him. She loved it. He was trying to stay honest, but it was hard for a kleptomaniac. He put things in his pockets every time he went to a store.

Just before he left Kamloops one of Waldy's uncles passed away. Gay, back from summer school went to the funeral with her mom and dad. Gwynne stayed home. She did not like any of the uncles and refused to be around them. A room full of uncles, drinking, meant someone would try to kiss her or touch her and she had enough of that. When they got home, Gunvor took to her bed which was the couch in the living room, as she drank too much. Gay went to work, and Gwynne was the one who answered the door when several large men pounded on it. They had come to beat Ron up because he stole one of the uncle's wallets.

There was a lot of scuffling and shoving but somehow Ron ended up playing poker with them and winning their money. It was like they all forgot about the missing wallet. Gwynne went into the closet and looked in the tin box. She did not find the wallet and she prayed that this time maybe dad did not do it. But of course, he had. He had taken the forty dollars out of the wallet and thrown the wallet off the bridge on the way home from the funeral. He used the forty dollars he had stolen to play poker with the angry brothers and fleeced them for another forty.

Shortly after that incident, they packed up. Gay had an apartment in Kamloops and was waiting tables. Gunvor, Ron and Gwynne moved to Hope. Gwynne was going into grade nine. It was the summer of 1963. Elna and Mike had rented a cabin on the river out of town; no plumbing but there was running water, even if it was cold. When they moved out Ron, Gunvor and Gwynne moved in. Mike generously told them the first month's rent was on him. He was a truck driver and was making a lot of money.

The house was old but cute, set in a field of flowers and tall grass. The property slopped down to the river. Gwynne stepped out of the car and felt happy. Mom and dad seemed happy. It seemed like a fresh start. A new beginning.

Chapter Nine

Harold (1953 to 1961)

Life had been uneventful for Harold for many years. He had a routine that involved changing jobs often and moving just about as often. There were many moves but all around the hospital. Marion kept steadily working but Harold would last six months to a year and then he was fired for drinking or just not coming to work. Marion worked in housekeeping five days a week. She loved Harold and saw his brilliance more than most people did. Rather than feel annoyed that he could not keep a job she was willing to support the man she saw as a lost, creative, intelligent man.

Harold played piano for her when she came home from a hard day at work. He was funny, kind, and considerate. Except when he was drinking heavily. A couple of times his family came from Alberta and she heard the stories of how bright he was all through school and the funny jokes he liked to play on people. She felt it was her job to protect him from the world. She loved his daughter Marlene who came to stay with them at least once a month over the years. She did not live far away, and Pearl allowed Harold and Marion to be a part of Marlene's life.

Ron had been in Vancouver a few times, living there for a bit and then moving. During the last move Harold heard he went to Ontario and he knew that was where Gunvor was from so it made sense. He and Ron had pulled a scam that did not go well. They convinced a guy that they were going to gut the guy's kitchen, renovate top to bottom. They sat in the pub and went over plans. The second meeting, Ron even came in with paint chips from the hardware store. It was a thousand-dollar reno and the guy gave them five hundred dollars up front after meeting with them three times. They had a line of credit to buy supplies at a hardware store. He even drove Harold and Ron home to Ron's apartment after he gave him them five hundred dollars and joked about, "Now I know where you live."

Ron quipped, "Yup, and I'm not going anywhere."

They could not believe anyone would be stupid enough to give a couple of guys in the bar five hundred in cash. Ron had a drink with Harold with a promise to give Harold his share the next day. Harold said, "Just give me a couple of hundred now."

Ron said, "I gotta' use it to show someone I owe money to that I got the money to pay him back."

"Yer not going to give it to someone else?"

"No, "Ron assured him, "I've just got to show him the money, so he knows I got it. I've got another week to pay him. Go home, I'll see you tomorrow."

Harold asked, "What about the guy expecting the reno to start tomorrow? He knows what apartment you live in."

Ron laughed, "He knows the building, not the apartment number and anyway I got young Mikey, Elna's husband to answer the door and say he's never heard of me."

It made sense. Mike was a big guy who used a lot of profanity and seemed very tough. Nobody could push him around. The client never saw Ron's car. Harold said goodbye to Gunvor, the girls and Ron. Harold never saw them for an exceptionally long time. Harold went by Ron's place on Heather Street the next day, but they were gone. Even Mike did not answer the door. The neighbour across the hall told Harold they all left in the middle of the night, skipped out on the rent that was due the next day. Harold asked the elderly woman, "What about the girls? Didn't they have school?"

She looked at him over her glasses and said, "School got out last week. Don't you have any kids?"

"Yeah, I do." Harold replied, "And now I don't know where one of them has gone."

He left the puzzled woman at the door and went home. He was anxious at first about the guy coming after him with Ron gone. Then he calmed down.

The guy they ripped off never got Harold's last name. The card said Robinson Contractors and the name on the card was Ronald Robinson. He was only introduced as Harold. He laid low for a few weeks. He did not go back to the Niagara Hotel. For the first time in their crazy friendship, Harold was mad at Ron. Usually, the two of them ripped people off together. It hurt that Ron took the money and ran. Packed up the whole family and left in the middle of the night like Harold was the enemy.   Harold was going to miss them. What Harold would miss the most was his friend.

He had been seeing his daughter Gwynne a fair bit and he liked that. He was hoping that someday he could introduce Gwynne and Marlene but that had not happened. Once back when Gwynne was about six Ron, Gunvor, Gay and Gwynne turned up looking for a place to stay but Marlene was with Pearl, so they never met. Gwynne was curious about the piano and tried playing a tune, singing along in her squeaky voice.   Marion came over and slammed the lid shut over the keys almost smashing the little girl's fingers, saying, "This is our daughter's piano."

Harold felt bad for the child who ran and cried on her mother's lap. Gunvor shot him one of her 'if looks could kill' looks but did not say anything. It was never spoken about. Marion did not know about Gwynne, but Harold thought she suspected. Marion was abnormally mean to the little girl. Marion barely tolerated Gunvor and Ron in her home, but Harold insisted they could spend the night. For Gay and Gwynne, it was a luxury holiday in a spotless, well-furnished home with a television. They had never been in a house with a television. They watched it until after midnight when Harold came out to the living room and turned it off, saying, "Sorry girls, Marion has to get up for work in the morning."

Later that year when Ron and family moved to Heather Street, Harold bought Gwynne a doll for Christmas. He had no idea how much the doll meant to her. He knew they were living on a tight budget, but he did not know the kids rarely received gifts. What gifts they did get were cheap items like skipping ropes, marbles, and balls. The only doll Gwynne had until that year, when she was seven, was a stuffed doll with a wooden head. The doll's arms and legs had been chewed off by mice. Gunvor stitched them up but Gwynne always thought of Peg Leg when she played with the dismembered doll. It began an obsession with collecting broken dolls. She found them in closets of the many homes they moved into, in friend's houses and once in an alley. Friends were always willing to give her the doll with one arm or a crayoned face. Gwynne took them home and with her mom's help they fixed the doll up. Gunvor told Harold she had never had a new doll.

Harold went to Standard a couple of times to see his mother. His brothers Burge and Vernon came to the West Coast to see him a few times over the years and they remained close. Harold even brought Burge to Ron's once and when they left, he confided that the little girl was his. Burge was not surprised and cautioned him, "Don't ever tell mom. She has not gotten over the rumour you have a little one running around Alberta. Someone joked to her just a few years ago when we got a new minister with a cute daughter . . . good thing Harold is not here, or he would knock that one up too."

Harold laughed, "I guess I will never live that down."

The years just drifted for Harold. In 1955 Marlene married her boyfriend Ken and they moved to Kitimat. She was only seventeen but if Pearl did not care what could he do about it? Pearl was involved with his ex-best friend, Bill, who he went to university with. He was tired with the comparisons she was always making about how successful Bill was with his own marine company while Harold could not hold down a job. Harold knew he blew it. He knew he was a walking drunk who could barely do that half the time because he fell so much.

Marlene and Ken had a City Hall wedding that Harold did not attend. Bill and Pearl stood up for them. But he and Marion did meet up with everyone at a Chinese Restaurant for a celebration meal. Friends owned the place and they invited Harold to sit down at the piano. He played for about an hour. It was the happiest he had been for a long time. Marlene looked happy and Ken was a solid young man who was on his way to becoming a certified mechanic. He was a hockey player as well, so Harold figured she was in good hands.   Harold worked on a fishing boat, worked at a couple of motels as a desk clerk and sold a lot of door-to-door items. He got jobs playing piano at weddings quite a bit. Marion advertised his skills around the hospital, and it seemed there were nurses and house-keeping staff getting married about once a week. The money was good but did not amount to much more than spending money for Harold. In 1957 Marion convinced Harold to apply at the hospital as an orderly. She was as surprised as him when he got hired.   It was the first job he liked. At least for a short while.

He had to supply and empty bed pans; serve meal trays, assist patients with menu selection; weigh, lift, and turn patients. He was helping the nurses do some of the things they did not have time for or found too heavy. It was a level one entry position and he only got it because Marion had been working at Vancouver General for so long. It was fine for a short time and then he was asked to tag someone's toes one day and take them down to the morgue. That was it for Harold. He took the body down to the tunnels under the hospital and into the morgue. He felt an overwhelming panic and ran back out as fast as he could. He started shaking in the elevator and could not stop.

It seemed every couple of days he was called in to tag toes. Then he had to load the body onto the gurney and take that terrible trip to the underground morgue. The shakes were so bad he needed a drink before he could continue working. He started keeping a bottle in his locker. Staff locker rooms were right next to the morgue and easy to get to for a minute. He tried to keep the job after that experience, but he was called out one day at work for smelling like booze. He laughed it off saying it was from the night before, but he started drinking heavier at night and was unable to go to work in the morning.

Marion was furious with him. It was only a matter of time until he got fired. Harold tried to explain to her that it was from the war. It was trauma buried deep in his mind. He just could not be around sick people. Dead people gave him panic attacks. She asked him to quit the job before he humiliated her by drinking on the job, getting caught and screwing up. He went in the next day and gave notice. He lasted three months. The failure of not being able to keep that job and the memories it unlocked in his brain set him on one of the longest drunks he had ever been on.

He did not know where Ron and Gunvor had gone and it bugged him. For one they had his kid, but it was mostly because he liked hanging out with Ron. He got the idea that Ron was still in town and started looking through the phone book one afternoon. He saw a Ron Robinson living in Vancouver and it said he worked on the Canadian Pacific Railway trains as a cook. He went by the address and the woman next door said that Ron had gone to work on the late train going out that day. Harold asked her if he was a short English guy and she said yes. Harold was a little drunk and headed down to the railway station. There was a CPR train pulling out and he figured it had to be the one. He grabbed a ticket to Kamloops which was the first stop and got on the train.

He sat in the club car for a bit having more drinks and asking the waiters about the cook on the train. He was a short English guy going bald by the name of Ron. Harold figured it was his friend. Ron had been cooking in camps, it made sense he would be a cook on a train. The train was speeding along, swerving and wobbling. Harold drank for a bit then decided to look for Ron. He lurched down the aisles looking for the kitchen. He went through the club car and the dining room but when he got to the kitchen door, he was stopped by a tidy man dressed in white.

Harold politely asked, "Is Ron cooking today?"

He said, "Sir, you cannot go in there."

Harold flashed one of his old fake Private Investigator business cards and spoke. "I'm here to arrest the cook. Ron Robinson."

The man held up a hand and said, "Wait while I get some assistance."   Harold slumped down into a chair. He was too drunk to comprehend what the man meant about getting assistance. But he got impatient after a few minutes and started banging on the kitchen door, "Tiny, ya little bastard get out here."

Nobody came out of the kitchen. The man came back with a railway cop who asked him to sit down. Harold flashed his badge and said, "I'm here to arrest that little bugger in the kitchen."

The cop said, "You have no authority on this train sir."

Harold pushed the cop. The cop grabbed his arm and twisted it behind his back and walked Harold out of the dining car. He put him into a secure room he used for unruly passengers. All the while Harold kept screaming for Tiny to come out and take what was coming to him. The conductor was called in and he explained to Harold that Ron, the cook was not his friend. Eventually, the cook came into the car and said to Harold, "I have never seen you before, sir."

Harold knew that to be true because although the man was English and bald, he was also a black man. The conductor reported that the police in Hope had been alerted. Harold would be removed from the train when they stopped in Hope. Hope was not a scheduled stop on this run, but Harold had to be removed. He argued that he had a ticket to Kamloops, and he wanted to go there. It had entered his mind that if Ron were not in Vancouver, he was probably in Kamloops. But the conductor told him, "Sir, you are going to be arrested."

Harold yelled at him as the conductor left the room, "Then I want a refund on my ticket ya son of a bitch."

When the cops boarded the train and took Harold off the train he did not go willingly. They had to handcuff him and push him along to the exit. Later it was reported in the papers that 'a troublesome drunk was removed from the train. He was insisting he was a private investigator and he had to arrest the cook on the train'.

It took the RCMP a long time to convince Harold that he did not deserve a refund and what he had done was a serious offence. He was informed he could be charged with a lot more than causing a disturbance. He could be charged with impersonating an officer of the court, assault, and being impaired in public. He was put in lock up overnight to sober up. The cops sent Harold home on the bus the next day. Harold went home, hungover and annoyed at himself. Where the hell was Ron? Harold had to go to court in Vancouver the following Monday and the Judge gave him a warning and a twenty dollar fine for causing a disturbance and had to pay the costs for the bus fare from Hope to Vancouver.

Even more annoying was the way Marion reacted. She said she had enough. He was so drunk he told the cops he was thirty-six and he was forty-two. It seemed he lied so much he could not even get his age right. He mumbled something to her about the last time he was happy he was thirty-six and left the room. He was growing increasingly disruptive and depressed. Since Marlene moved to Kitimat, he seemed more lost than usual. Pearl moved there too, and he knew that Bill was replacing him as a father. Not that he had been a great father, but he was still her dad.

After Marion threatened to kick him out, he sobered up for almost a year. Marion said if he went to Alcoholics Anonymous, she would not pressure him to get a job. Harold liked AA and met some great guys there who became his friends. He liked being the house husband who did all the cooking and cleaning. If he did not drink, he did not need money. It was a win-win situation for them both.

Vernon and his wife Una came for a visit with an old family friend Nurse Hall. He and Marion acted like tour guides showing them around Stanley Park. They took them to the Capilano Suspension Bridge but while Marion, Una and Nurse would not go on the swinging bridge Marion snapped pictures of the two brothers smiling from the middle of the bridge. Marion was a pretty, petite woman who had a beautiful smile. She had been smiling a lot for the last year. She loved Harold when he was sober. The family visit was a nice break for them.

It was the first time she saw Harold proud of his family and his past. They sat around in the evenings and talked about relatives alive and gone. She heard about Grandpa Jens and Grandma Katrine whose father was a famous artist. And the great uncle Niels

Ebbesen Hansen who gained fame as an explorer and scientist. He travelled the world bringing back seeds and plants including alfalfa from Russia. His Cossack Seeds bore white flowers and he kept the seeds pure. He was responsible for all the fields of alfalfa in South Dakota, Vernon said. Niels also brought back tailless sheep from Siberia. He cultivated grape, pears from China and plums from Japan. Professor Hansen was a great adventurer and hero to his family. They were proud of their farming roots that began with this man. Harold showed love to his family, something Marion had not seen before. They even went to church when Vernon was in town. Marion was seeing a different man and it made her happy. She smiled a lot during that two-week visit.

Visit over, the sobriety did not last long. When his brother left Harold grew quiet. A year and a half after the train episode Harold was in a car accident in October of 1959. He banged his knee up and was charged with impaired driving. While he was still recovering from his painful knee injury in November, he was sentenced to three months in jail for impaired driving. He was sent to a work farm for alcohol counselling in the Fraser Valley. Harold enjoyed the three-month break and the sobriety. He loved working on the farm. He was tending to a small number of horses, feeding them, and caring for them. He got to ride them once in awhile. It was like being back home on the farm in Standard.

Harold got out in February of 1960 and took a train to Standard, sober this time, to visit his family. He stayed for a couple of weeks helping Burge and Vernon farm their land. It was a time of reflection for him. This could have been his life. He would have owned property, had a wife and children who loved him. He could have belonged to a church community, played piano on Sunday mornings. He had not felt such peace, not for many years. But then it was time to return to Vancouver. Marion had lined up a job for him as a front desk clerk at a posh apartment building.

All he had to do was sit at the desk, receive parcels and the mail, greet people, and direct them to apartments. He was not the door man. He was a desk man. It was an easy job, and he did very well at it until about the third week when he slipped a bottle under the counter of the front desk. It was not long until someone who lived in the building came home and found him passed out at the front desk. Harold apologised and begged to keep the job, but they let him go. Harold never held much of a job after that. He just worked casual jobs, a few days here and there. He could not drive as he had a two-year suspension.

He got a call from Ron. He said he was living in Edmonton but moving to Kamloops and when he got back to B.C., he would look him up. The news perked Harold up for a few days. Some of the best times he ever had were with his old friend Ron Robinson. When Ron did turn up it was about a year later and the two of them went on what you could only describe as a bender. Neither of them had much money but they went to Marie's and stayed in the room she rented by the hour. It was like old times and then it was not. Even Ron got annoyed by Harold's drinking and shouted at him while they were playing poker, "Look at you man. It's four o'clock in the afternoon and you're nodding off in the middle of a game of cards."

"Sorry," Harold muttered.

But the fun was over. Ron liked to drink but he liked to drink with people like Marie who could hold her liquor like he could. Nobody every looked at Ron and could see that he was drunk. He never staggered, drove drunk or stumbled and fell. Ron could not fathom why booze took such a hold on Harold and Gunvor. He had left Kamloops for a few days to be around some fun people. Marie was crabby and Harold kept getting so drunk he had to fall asleep. Ron left and went back to Kamloops where Gunvor was sleeping off a two-day drinking binge.

After Ron left, Harold was ashamed. He got a job again and again, first as a contractor and then a salesman. He kept his jobs no longer than three months at a time. He started to manage his drinking better though. Marion would not give him money for booze anymore so the only time he drank he had a job.   The drinking caused him to lose the job and the cycle continued. He still had nightmares from the war. Harold never really knew how to reach out for help, not for his drinking and not for his trauma suffered during World War II. Harold was a drowning man.

Chapter Ten

Ron and Gunvor (1963 to 1968)

Gunvor and Ron's time on the river did not last long. By November Ron was behind on a month's rent and they received a month's notice to leave. Gwynne did not care. She was tired of using an outhouse. One night she was stuck out there for an hour with a bear sniffing around the door. They had to boil water just to wash. She was in grade nine and she had to wash, blow dry and curl her hair before school everyday. She hated the energy it took to be presentable with cold running water. When she came home from school mom had to open the oven door and let her put her feet on the oven door so she could warm up just a little. That is where she was sitting the day President John Kennedy was assassinated; home from school, feet stuck up on the oven door when he was shot in Dallas. An image she never forgot or where she was when it happened. Television was showing live events for the first time and it was changing the way people lived. Watching the Viet Nam War play out on television was creating a radical movement.

They moved into a two-bedroom prewar house by the railway tracks in Hope, just a block from the theatre and the library, Gwynne's favourite places. She became popular once they moved to town. She was on the grass hockey team, acting in plays and she seemed like just another cute, happy blonde to her fellow classmates. Her friends would have been surprised to know how passionate she was about the world and politics. Their teen lives were focused on buying forty-five records and lipstick at the drugstore afterschool.

Hope was a pretty town with a huge park in the centre where everyone gathered. The stores along the streets all faced the tree lined rectangular shaped park. At one end was the hotel at the other there was a hardware store. The teenagers in Hope gathered in the Park for everything. It was the place to be.

Ron was driving a bullet nose Studebaker that puffed smoke out the back and every time the car went around the corner the passenger door flew open. Gwynne dreaded the days dad decided to pick her up from school. A couple of the boys thought it was a cool car, but it was humiliating for Gwynne.

Even more embarrassing was the fact that Ron had a job as a Sheriff. It was a piecework job where he got paid for every subpoena he handed out. He was able to make a few hundred dollars a month while on Welfare. However, the job was not without danger. A lot of the men he had to serve were abusive ex-husbands or deadbeat dads. He came in one night after work puffing and out of breath. He told Gunvor and Gwynne he ran a block to get away from a deadbeat dad who was wielding a baseball bat. He clutched his chest as he sank onto the couch, "I'm too old for this shit."

He was not even sixty yet, but it had been a hard life of booze and drugs. Welfare visits were the worst. Gwynne was always worried that the worker would be one of her friend's moms. Twice, a snooty woman from the welfare office came snooping around. They had to hide the television as you were not allowed to have luxury items like that. Ron put it in the trunk of the Studebaker that was parked down the street.

They lived in a tiny house with hardly any furniture; a couch, a chair, a table, two beds and two dressers. Gwynne had a sewing machine in her room, an old treadle machine that she got second hand. When they were still in Kamloops, Ron had entered her name in a McGavin's Bread contest, and she won a bike. She had to go on television and be thankful she won. She was not thankful, she was shy. It was a nightmare for the shy girl. She rode the bike for about a year in Kamloops and learned to love the bike. When she moved to Hope she thought she was too old for a bike and sold it. Then she found out all her friends had bikes.

She bought the treadle machine which smelled of oil and caused her to cough. She had bronchitis twice that first winter. She never learned to sew. There were days when she regretted selling the bike because whenever the kids in town went out to the tunnels or the lake, they hopped on their bikes. She had to borrow one. Sometimes she would hitch a ride with one of the boys.

She was sort of dating a boy whose father was an RCMP Sergeant. They had a house attached to the jail and the station house. On Friday nights sometimes the kids went to the jail and they went into the cells to hand out bananas to the prisoners. So, her friends all knew what a joke job being the Sheriff was. A couple of the boys teased her about it at school. One guy yelled at her in the hall, "There is a new Sheriff in town, and he is dan-ger-ous."

But for the most part it was a happy time for the Robinsons. Bill, Marie's son dropped by for a visit and Ron's sister Freda moved back from California. She came to visit. Elna and Mike lived in town and there was always a lot of family stuff going on with the nieces and nephews. Elna had three girls and a boy. Gay often came from Kamloops to babysit and even got a job in town for awhile. Then she decided to get married. Everyone thought she was heading off to theatre school in Montreal because after summer school she got a grant for the fall Semester. She decided to marry Eugene who had been an on and off again boyfriend for awhile. She was working at a store in Hope but quit her job and went back to Kamloops so her Auntie Lottie could buy her a wedding dress. As usual Ron and Gunvor had no cash.

In fact, three days before the wedding Ron was charged with passing a forged cheque. In a small town this did not go unnoticed. Front page headlines. Gwynne was humiliated and Gay was furious. She and their cousin Sharon came back from Kamloops two days before the wedding and went to the jail. Gay begged them to let Ron out so he could walk his daughter down the aisle. The Sergeant knew who Ron was, knew who Gwynne was and that his son had a crush on her. He felt sorry for the distraught young woman in front of him and he let Ron out.

Gwynne discovered dad had been arrested because the Librarian's daughter invited her over and threw the newspaper on the table where they were about to have tea. Sheriff of Hope Arrested for Fraud. Gwynne ran from the house, burst through the door at home and screamed at Gunvor who was knitting, "Why did you not tell me he had been arrested?"

Gunvor quietly replied, "I thought it would blow over."

"What the hell happened?" the fifteen-year-old asked.

"Oh, you know," she said with a wave of her hand, "Harold owed him a hundred dollars and he sent dad a cheque he took out of Marion's purse and dad signed it and cashed it. That is the story, nothing else."

"This has just ruined my life. And what about Gay? She is getting married in two days."

"She is at the jail now getting him discharged until Monday when he has to go to Vancouver to go to court."

"Why Vancouver?"

"Because that was where the cheque was cashed on a Vancouver bank."

It was a good story, but it was not true. The cheque was for three hundred and four dollars and it was sent by Shell Canada to the Shell gas station owner in Hope whose name was Robert Robinson. The cheque made out to an R. Robinson was a refund on product. Nobody ever knew the truth about the cheque. Every family member had a different story. Gay heard that Harold did send a cheque to Ron. But that did not make sense as the cheque was cashed in Vancouver in February. Gunvor hated Harold so it was not odd she blamed it on him.

When he went to get gas in January, Ron saw the envelope on the counter and could see through the cellophane window it was made out to an R. Robinson. Before anyone came to take his money for gas, he scooped the envelope into his pocket. He did not know until he got home it was for over three hundred dollars. He did not tell anyone but in February he made a trip to Vancouver and got

Harold to take him to his bank where Harold knew everyone. Harold vouched for him and they cashed the cheque. Nobody knew how it was traced back to Ron being the R. who cashed the cheque. Ron did not believe Harold told on him. He would not do that. But he must have.

Gay succeeded in getting Ron out of jail for the weekend and on August 15, 1964 she wed Eugene Sundin. It was a marriage that had failure written all over it, but everyone acted happy. Except Gwynne who was wearing a ridiculous pink dress some cousin made for her that made her look fat. It was heavy material like the kind you would make a coat out of and had long sleeves. It was August. Lottie bought Gay a pretty, short, white wedding dress and Gay looked happy at least. The reception was at Elna and Mike's. Gwynne stayed in the bedroom and took care of the kids. None of them wanted to be in the living room with the drunks.

The guests were drinking moonshine that Mike made. He laughed and declared, "This'll make ya go blind."

They lined up and took their shots, even though a month earlier Mike had opened a bottle that had a dead mouse inside. He fished the rodent out of the bottle and drank the contents anyway. Gunvor did not drink that night. It had nothing to do with dead mice or moonshine. She was furious with Ron over the cheque forgery and she did not feel sociable. She made Ron take her home about nine when the rest of the crew was getting hammered. He was not unhappy about leaving. He was disappointed in Gay and her choice to marry a man he thought was lazy.

Gay was offered a scholarship to theatre school at McGill University. A paid scholarship for the first term. She would have to get a job to pay for lodging and food, but she would be able to do that. Ron had no idea why she threw that away to get married. Theatre was in their blood. Gay would not talk to him about it. Of course, it did not help that every time he tried to talk to her about it, he yelled at her. She did not like confrontation.

Gay knew why she did not go but she kept that secret for many years. She was not able to tell anyone that she did not feel worthy of the scholarship. She was, after all, a skinny girl from the wrong side of the tracks. She deserved nothing. She was so down on herself her favourite song came out earlier in 1964 called Ragdoll by the Four Seasons. The lyrics were about how a young girl went to school in hand me downs and people laughed at her when she came into town and called her ragdoll. When she and Gwynne sang it at the top of their lungs it made Gay cry and Gwynne laugh. Even though Gwynne had a lot of the same experiences she never felt down on herself like Gay did. It made her more rebellious as in 'I'll show you'.

While most family members were happy for Gay, nobody understood why she was getting married. But the good part was most everyone loved Eugene. He was a funny guy who told a lot of jokes. They seemed like they would make a good couple. The actual wedding was at the United Church in Hope and quite a nice affair. The reception was not.

Before the end of the night Mike and his pals took Eugene's little red Volkswagen and lifted it onto the roof of the shed so Gay and Eugene could not leave. Gay went into the bedroom where the kids were and cried until Gwynne went out and informed Elna, it was not a funny joke. Gay wanted to go. Elna convinced Mike and his pals to get the car off the roof and let them go on their way to their honeymoon. Not that there was a honeymoon. They drove less than a hundred miles to a hotel and spent the night. It was not an exciting beginning.

Gwynne stayed with the kids in their cramped bedroom and did not go home until dad left for the police station Monday morning for his escort to Court in Vancouver. She told mom when she got home that they were going to have to leave Hope. She could not go back to school in Hope to grade ten like nothing happened. She would be a laughing stock at the school. Gunvor said, "You don't need to worry about that. Dad wants to move back to Vancouver."

For all the upset it caused, the charges against Ron were dropped. Nobody talked about it. It was done. Ron went to Court and pleaded with the Judge to take into consideration his poor health, his daughter's wedding that had been overshadowed by the charges, his family who was starving and poor. He admitted he cashed the cheque as it was delivered to his house. He did not steal it. He was a Sheriff, an officer of the court. The cheque came in his mailbox, addressed to R. Robinson. He said he did not know it was not for him.

The Crown argued that he must have known it was not for him, but Ron refused to admit that. He answered, "A cheque comes through the mail slot. I have no money. I had to pay the rent. I swear I did not know it was not for me. I had some dealings with Shell awhile back. I had to go to Vancouver to see a heart specialist and I cashed the cheque. I figured if it caught up to me and it was not meant for me, all I would have to do is pay it back. I did not know I was breaking the law. Your honour, anyone living on such a small income would have done the same."

The Judge looked at the tired man in front of him. He did not, for one minute believe his story, but he felt empathy for the man. He discharged the case, ruling there was no evidence that Ron Robinson did anything illegal. It was a mistake. He was ordered to see the Court Clerk to plan for payments to Shell Canada. They had reissued a cheque months ago to Robert Robinson. Ron agreed to pay the Court twenty dollars a month for fifteen months. He never repaid a dime.

They left Hope two weeks later and moved to a dump on Kingsway Street in Vancouver. It was two doors down from a house Bill Dick rented to run a scam operation selling magazines. Even though The Vancouver Sun ran an article about his operation being a phoney a year earlier, he was successful. The Canadian National Institute for the Blind issued a warning not to buy subscriptions to Vision Magazine published by the Canadian Federation of the Blind which was a dummy non-profit set up by Bill. He says in the article that seventy percent of the money collected went to his workers and thirty percent to the CFB. He did not tell anyone he was the CFB.

Gay and Eugene moved into the ugly house on Kingsway that had a bedroom upstairs. She was pregnant and went to work for Bill selling four copies a year of Vision Magazine for two dollars. She made ten percent a sale. Gwynne wondered how blind people could read a magazine for and about them and when offered a chance to work in the phone room, she declined. Ron worked long hours as well in the phone room selling the magazines. Gwynne worked for Bill filing subscriptions in a huge filing cabinet he had set up in his motel room where he lived.

It seemed an odd place to do filing as he had a huge house as an office, but nobody realized that he was grooming Gwynne. He was forty-nine and she was fifteen. His marriage to Donna fell apart many years earlier and he had a mistress and several girlfriends he was cheating on her with, but he had his eye on the bubbly teen. She had no idea. She thought he was awesome. On Boxing Day after the worst Christmas, they had ever had, Bill took Gwynne shopping at The Bay.

She had spent Christmas Day crying in the one chair they owned in front of a television that barely worked. Ron was in the basement cutting up old tires to feed into the furnace to try and keep the drafty house warm. There was no tree, no gifts. Ron, Gunvor, and Gwynne ate two cans of spaghetti for Christmas dinner. Gay and Eugene went to Kamloops to spend the holidays with Eugene's mother. On Boxing Day Gwynne was praying for aliens to come and beam her up when Bill turned up. Bill was so handsome. He was wearing a red scarf and smelled like Old Spice. He offered to take Gwynne shopping. She thought it was an act of kindness. They jumped into his gold Cadillac and Gwynne felt special. He bought her a black sweater and black stretch pants that would have looked better on his mistress, but she did not care; they were new clothes. She had not had new clothes in over a year.

On the way home he proposed that he set her up in an apartment and he would pay for everything including sending her to university after she graduated. It did not take Gwynne long to figure out what he meant. She was horrified. She made him stop the car and she walked home in a pair of sling backs with her feet getting soaked in the wet snow. She avoided him after that, but she never told anyone. When she quit working for him her dad was mad, but she refused to tell him why. She figured dad would have killed Bill for suggesting a sexual relationship with his little girl.

In February they all moved out. Eugene had a job and he and Gay moved to Burnaby where she gave birth to a baby boy. Somehow Ron found a great up and down duplex on the good side of the tracks with a huge sun porch that Gunvor loved. She filled it with plants and the sun filled it with sunshine. Ron had prostate surgery in January and Gunvor had gallbladder surgery. It seemed they both wanted to live a better life than they had been living. Gunvor hardly drank anymore and when she did, she did not take to her bed for days after. Gwynne did the second half of grade eleven and the first half of grade twelve in that house with her best friend living in the down suite. It was the best times she had ever had in her life.

Gunvor spent most of her Sunday afternoons in her bedroom reading or knitting. Harold started coming over Sunday afternoons to sit at the table to drink whiskey with Ron. Usually, Gwynne avoided her parents when there was booze around but somehow with Ron and Harold it seemed fine. It was fun. She spent many afternoons laughing with them listening to their stories. They told her about stealing the piano from The Bay, about the con jobs and fake business cards for cleaning chimneys and construction work. Ron even gave her one of his Private Investigator cards. They told her about what a great piano player Harold was, and Ron said, "He could take a piano apart on Saturday night and put it back together to play it on Sunday morning."

Ron almost seemed a proud dad when he talked about Harold and how he was so smart he was borderline genius. Harold talked about Ron like he was the best guy in the world and his exploits were legendary. Gwynne always felt warm and fuzzy around the two of them. She did not know why but felt it was a special time for all three of them. Every time she tried to talk to her mom about them Gunvor would say something negative like, "Those two are a pair all right. A pair of idiots!"

Gwynne saw Harold give Ron some money one day and thought it was super nice that Harold was helping them out a bit. They seemed to have more money than usual in that duplex. Part of it was because she and her dad were working the carnivals spring and summer breaks at Playland. He always ran the Crown and Anchor, and she worked the Balloon Joint. She loved the carnivals and was a good hustler, just like her dad. Everyone said so. She loved the carnies and thought it cool that dad's nickname was Tiny. Even she called him Tiny on the fair grounds. She wanted a nickname and one of the toothless ride operators dubbed her Twinkle-Toes because she was always dancing to the music that blasted from the rides.

That summer she was sixteen her dad gave her a pink fuzzy teddy bear she called Rosebud. Tiny gave it to her in front of the Ferris Wheel one afternoon. She was walking back to the balloon booth to work and he came out of nowhere and threw the bear at her, yelling, "Happy Birthday kiddo!"

She waved at him and kept walking, "Thanks Tiny."

She did not want him to see that she was crying. It was the first gift she remembered him ever giving her besides the gold satin Chinese pajamas for Christmas the year before. It had been such a good year it was hard to remember how tough things had been. Gunvor was happy and mom was never happy. She started talking to Gwynne more than she ever had, about her life on the farm and for the first time she told her daughter about her seven dead babies.

Gunvor was happy. The mini farm she had growing on the front sun porch filled her heart. She felt like she was coming out of a fog. She had been drinking far too long. She was fifty-five the summer of 1965 and she had been in a dark place for about twenty years. Of course, there had been good memories and months of sobriety, but she had never felt happy before. Ron was nice to her. He did everything: cooking, cleaning, groceries. He was being honest and not stealing as far as she knew.

There was one day in May. They were at a huge grocery store and as they walked by some packages of seeds, she saw him slip three packs in the pocket of his suit coat. Just then the Manager walked up behind and asked, "Would you two please come with me?"

They crammed into his tiny office and he asked, "Sir, what do you have in your pockets?"

Ron grinned and produced the seeds, "Seeds. I'm buying them for my wife."

"Buying sir?" he asked, "or are you stealing them?"

"They are not considered stolen until I take them from the store. I put them in my pocket because they are small and fall out of the cart. I have every intention of paying for them."

The Manager smiled, "Ok, be sure you pay for them. I'd hate for your day to be ruined because I must call the police over a dollar's worth of seeds."

Gunvor was angry. She knew Ron was not planning to pay for them. They left the store after she made sure the seeds were on the counter and properly paid for and she told him in the car, "Don't ever do anything like that to me again. You were going to steal them."

"Who me?" He grinned and turned the car on for the cold and quiet drive home. Ron never stopped shoplifting. It was second nature. If he was in a store he was stealing. Not big items but screws, screw drivers and light bulbs from the hardware store. At the grocery store he took chocolate bars and apples. One afternoon at the Salvation Army he stole a pair of pajamas for Gwynne that looked like a clown suit. She came home and found them on her bed. They had a fight the day before because she stayed out too late and she thought it was a gift to say he was sorry. She could not believe it. Three gifts in one year.

Halfway through grade twelve they had to move. The beautiful duplex had been sold and they had to leave by the beginning of March. Ron had not been feeling exceptionally good and was not working very much. The only place they could find was a three-room apartment above a pizza joint in Little Italy. It was a dump and had weird mice with snouts. Gwynne hated it. After a year of having friends over she knew she would not be inviting anyone to the dump they moved into it. It depressed Gunvor too and she went on a long drunk.

After about three weeks she was bloated and sick, but she kept begging for more booze. One afternoon Ron just could not stand it anymore and he asked Gay if he could spend the night with her and Eugene and his grandson Mark. He broke down and cried. He told Gay he was too sick to take anymore. Gay said, "That's it dad. Tomorrow I will go over and sober her up."

Gwynne had to go to school in the morning, but dad had asked her if she could take care of mom for the night. He said there was a few ounces of whiskey in the cupboard beside the wood stove. He left. Gwynne did not know what to do. Mom was in the bedroom crying that she needed more booze. It was the first time that she realized what dad had been putting up with. She went into the bedroom and told her mother, "Mom, there is just a tiny bit of booze. Dad said I should save it until ten or eleven."

"Give it to me now," her mom screamed at her.

Gwynne got a cold cloth and tried to sit on the edge of the bed and cool her mother off. Gunvor was beet red and hot. There was no appeasing the woman who may or may not have been going through hallucinations. She was thrashing around, hitting Gwynne, and screaming for whiskey. Gwynne tried to calm her down and got shoved, then pushed off the bed. She struggled to her feet and caught her mom as she was trying to get out the door to find the bottle. They shoved each other and all Gwynne could think was, 'man she is strong'.

Gunvor slapped Gwynne and that was it for Gwynne's attempts at controlling her mother. She stomped into the kitchen and got the whiskey. She threw it on the bed next to her mom and said, "Here ya go. Drink it. That is all there is."

Gunvor drank it and Gwynne laid on the couch in the next room and cried. She felt so sad for her mom, her dad, and the mess they were in. She called Gay who would not let her talk to dad as he needed his rest. Gwynne was heartbroken, alone, and afraid. She knew it was going to be a long night and it was. Gunvor cried, yelled, and threw up. Gwynne tried everything to calm her. Eventually Gunvor went to sleep, drenched in sweat cursing at her daughter.

In the morning Gwynne went to sleep. After about two hours of rest Gay turned up with Mark in tow. Gwynne said, "You don't want him here."

Gay snapped at her, "What am I supposed to do with him? Eugene had to go to work and dad is sleeping."

Gay stayed for four days and 'dried mom out'. Gwynne went back after school that first day and took Mark home where she babysat while Eugene was at work. It was not new, her not going to school. Somehow, she managed to keep good grades and only attend school three or four days a week. After four days Gay's work was done. Gunvor never drank again.

If you were outside the small family circle you would not have known Gunvor had a problem.

Later that year Gwynne graduated from high school. She needed at least two hundred dollars for her gown and hairdo. Dad said not to worry, and he left the house coming back two hours later with two hundred dollars. Gwynne bought a beautiful blue dress with a train for eighty dollars. It cost thirty dollars to get an upsweep hairdo and another twenty dollars for elbow length gloves, and some pearls. She bought new make-up and a pair of white pumps. She proudly showed Ron her purchases and returned fifty dollars to him. Graduation night, he watched her walk across the stage. Gunvor stayed home.

A few days later Harold dropped by. He seemed extremely interested in what she wore, how her graduation was. She showed him pictures and then Ron said, "Give him one of the copies of you in the dress on the back porch."

Gwynne thought it odd that Harold would want a picture of her but gave the copy to him. He looked at it, smiled and said, "I opened a bank account today in your name."

"What?" she asked, "why would you do that?"

He was sitting beside her on the couch, and he leaned over and slapped the side of her leg and said, "Because I always liked you kid."

It was not creepy, like when other old men in the family touched her. After Harold left Gwynne asked Ron, "Why would Harold do that? Leave money in an account for me?"

Ron shrugged and looked away, then replied, "I don't know. But if he said he did, he did."

It was the first time that Gwynne wondered if the family gossip was true. She had heard that some guy named Bill Baldis was her real dad. She had seen pictures of Bill and his wife Sally but did not feel a connection. And deducted that Bill and Sally came into their lives after she was born. She had seen her mom with Gil Tymich a few times and thought there was something going on between them, like a secret language or something. Gil was always so thoughtful and nice to Gwynne. Then when she was fourteen, he blew his brains out with a shotgun. Gunvor had cried for days. Gwynne had silently wondered if he killed himself because he loved Gunvor, and he could not be with her and his daughter.

Nobody ever talked about it. Gwynne never asked her mom or dad or her sisters. But that day it crossed her mind that maybe Harold was her real dad. He always seemed to be around when she got extra money for things she needed. He gave her that expensive doll when she was seven.   Dad got two hundred dollars from somewhere when she needed it for grad. There were other times, she remembered. Once when she needed winter boots, Harold came to visit and later that day Ron gave her twenty dollars to go buy boots. The thought it was so absurd she forgot about it. Mom hated Harold.

Gunvor rarely spoke to Harold. But it was not because she hated him. She was hurt that he had not been man enough to stand up and be Gwynne's dad.   She had loved Harold and he disappointed her. Instead of being the man she thought he was, he got involved in petty crimes with Ron. She had her heart broken twice. Once with Harold and once when Alton, the man she loved more than any other man, left her and went to war. She could not forgive him for that.

However, the only man who stood by her and took care of her was Ron. He may have had his faults, but she knew one thing about Ron, he loved her like no other man ever had. He brought her coffee in bed every morning. He took care of her like a mother bird with a newly hatched chick. She was aware of his faults and he had been violent with her a couple of times. But she knew it was her fault. He tried to feed her when she was drunk once, and she spit the food all over the couch. He shoved the plate in her face, but she deserved it. Another time she was on the floor begging him for whiskey and he kicked his leg at her. She grabbed his leg and hung on as he tried to walk away. He kicked her but she deserved it.

By the time Gwynne left home the summer she graduated, Gunvor and Ron were closer than they had ever been. Without drinking they had lots of time to do things like go for rides to the beach, go to a deli for lunch and to watch television together. Gunvor was busier than she had been for many years, knitting, preserving pickles and baking. When the girls came to visit, they could not help but think that all these years this had been their mother, this calm, patient busy woman. She was sweet and if you could get her to laugh, it was the best sound in the world.

Chapter Eleven

Ron (1968 to 1973)

When Gunvor sobered up, life changed for Ron. A huge weight was lifted from his shoulders and he was able to sleep at night. They started to laugh again. The family seemed to come together. Gay had a couple of boys and they visited with her and Eugene quite a bit. They never babysat as Gunvor said she did not want to be responsible for taking care of any babies. It caused a problem between her and Gay. Gunvor did not feel comfortable being alone with babies. Seven of them had died in her arms.

Gwynne grew closer to her parents. She moved out when they went into subsidized housing. Gwynne had a good job at B.C. Hydro in accounts payable. She was making so much money she was able to help them out. But Ron had some concerns about her behavior. He knew she was drinking and maybe even smoking pot, but she had a nice boyfriend Dave, and Ron could see that maybe she would no longer be his responsibility. Not that she was any trouble. She was independent, a feminist and a freethinker.

She credited Ron for teaching her right from wrong. Even though he was often dishonest and a petty thief he instilled morals and integrity. He was not a chauvinist. Her boss was though and called her into his office to tell her she had to wear a bra to work. She felt her rights were violated and quit her job. Ron was upset she quit, but she explained that he taught her to stand up for herself. Was he not the same man who went to her school and convinced the Principal not to give her the strap? Gwynne hit a girl over the head with a bible off school grounds because she thought she was preachy. Did Ron not threaten to call the cops if the Principal punished her?

She reminded Ron that it was his belief that she could make up her own mind and that is why he never made her go to school. He let her stay out late and be responsible for herself. He had to agree he had been a liberal father, but he felt she should not quit her job. He said to her, "Wear a bra."

"No, dad," she said, "I will not bow down to the man. Besides, he also told me to go to church."

"Oh well then," he agreed, "I can understand why you quit."

Ron had his own issues with religion interfering with his life. He railed against the strict pious upbringing he had. He saw the hypocrisy of it all. Even though Ron did not freely admit to believing in anything, he did. He believed in God. He believed he would be judged for the things he had done. He believed in loyalty and country, England, and Canada. If Ron were sitting in a Royal Canadian Legion bar and God Save the Queen was played, he was the first man on his feet. Although he had been Dishonorably Discharged, he marched in every Remembrance Day parade, as proud as the rest of the soldiers for his contribution to the war effort. He always voted. It was his civic duty. If he ran into someone less fortunate than him, he helped in any way he could with money, food, clothing.

His rebellion came from a righteous place. He was asked by senior officers to find girls for the party where they were served alcohol. He did not, on his own, give the underage girls liquor. Several other men were charged along with him, but they were able to raise the money for the fine. Because he was poor, he went to jail for three months. He was well-aware of the inequity of the system and taught his daughters to stand up for themselves.

He had been strict with Gay and lax with Gwynne. Gay had to make good grades, she had to be the best. She was not allowed to skip school and she had to be on the Honour Role. The different treatment was not lost on his girls. Gay was jealous because

Gwynne had it easy. Gwynne was jealous because she felt Ron did not care about her as much as he cared about Gay. Truth was, Gay was his real daughter and Gwynne was not. He had expectations of Gay.

Gwynne went up north with a girlfriend to work at a hot spring's hotel as a front desk clerk. That is where Elna was living and Gwynne missed her sister. Not long after, Gay moved to Terrace as well but then Gwynne came back and took off to Los Angeles. Free spirit that she was, Ron agreed that she should go and have some fun. She went with a girlfriend. Two weeks later, he got a call asking for her birth certificate so she could marry some guy who had been married twice and been to Viet Nam three times. It seemed like a poor choice, but he sent the birth certificate. He started to get worried, but he need not have, as she found out the guy was gay and came home. Ron had a chuckle over that. Gunvor always said of her girl, 'we give her just enough rope but not enough to hang herself with'.

Ron could see that it was a whole new world and while it seemed crazy, he was proud of his outspoken daughter who was going to go her own way and do her thing, as she said over and over. When she returned from Los Angeles, they had about a week together alone. It was the best time the two of them had ever had together. Gunvor caught a train to Ontario to visit her mother and was going to be gone for two weeks. Gwynne and Ron spent the time playing the card game, Rummy. He realized it was the first time he had been alone with his daughter for more than a few hours at a time. It was a lot of fun, for them both.

They had always worked the carnivals together and she was the only one who would go on an afternoon raid with him. That was what he loved about her. When she was fifteen Ron took her to the West Hotel one afternoon to 'roll' one of Gunvor's uncles. They found him passed out and while he held the drunk man up, Gwynne found the wad of money they knew he had in his pocket. He figured she was a chip off the old block. Even though he was not her 'real Dad' he influenced her daily life. It just happened she had a similar personality. Even though she felt rolling Uncle was uncomfortable, she was willing to do it. What he did not understand was that it was one of the few bonding moments she had ever had with him. She would have robbed a bank with him if he had asked.

The time they were alone was full of laughter. One afternoon he told her about burlesque and dressing up as a woman on stage. He admitted he loved dressing in drag, all Englishmen loved drag he said.

Gwynne said, "Really dad?" and ran into the bedroom.

She came back with a black dress someone had given Gunvor for a funeral, one of her mom's purses, a pair of gloves and a hat.

"Here, dad," she said, "lets' see you in drag."

She did not expect him to put on the dress but got her camera ready just in case. He went into the bedroom and came back in the dress and they both laughed while she snapped pictures of him prancing around the living room. He figured Gunvor would be shocked. When she came back, but she just looked at the pictures and laughed, "Kind of like the old days, huh?"

Ron and Gunvor were getting along so well. He still took care of everything. He cooked, cleaned, did the laundry, the banking, the groceries. Often Gunvor went with him and just as often she stayed in the car. They visited a lot with his sister and her husband. They went on short trips to visit Lottie and Waldy in Chase, outside Kamloops. Ron and Gunvor lived in a new high-rise rent subsidized one bedroom and they loved it. They were on the eleventh floor and Ron had pair of pigeons he fed every day. He called them Bill and Coo. He also had a budgie named Peter.

Ron spent hours sitting on the small balcony looking at the parking lot below. His balcony was over the dumpster and he scored a lot of stuff out of it. One day he salvaged two chairs and redid the seats. He stripped and revarnished the wood. He found out from a friend at a secondhand store they were old chairs from City Hall. He gave one to each of his girls. He found an old radio cabinet, stripped it, and turned it into a glass door cabinet where Gunvor stored all her treasures.

When they lived in Kenora, Gay and Gwynne used to go to the five and dime and buy Gunvor matching china pieces; two fish, two whistling birds or two cats. Gunvor had a few old pieces her mother had given her as well. It was the nicest gift Ron had ever given her.   Her collectibles meant a lot to her, especially the matching figurines the girls had bought her.

Ron did not see much of Harold. He and Harold met at a bar a few times and raised a glass of beer. They always had a good time together. The memories of all their scams still made them laugh. Ron had promised Gunvor he would not bring Harold around to the apartment anymore. A few weeks after one of their pub visits, Harold set fire to the apartment he and Marion lived in. It was gutted. Harold called Ron from the hospital and said Marion had finally kicked him out.

"First, how are you and what are you going to do?"

Harold said, "You know me I always land on my feet."

Ron laughed, "And you never spill a drop."

"I blew it this time. I was passed out and if she had not come home, I would have burned up inside with all her belongings, my piano. . . but don't worry about me buddy. Marion said she could not take the drinking anymore."

"Why don't you slow down?" Ron advised.

"Ah, it's Ok though. I can get a room downtown somewhere," he ignored the question then carried on, " The burns on my face were not first degree. I look like hell, but the pain is not bad. I fell asleep with a cigarette in my mouth."

"Gheesh Harold, you could have been burned alive."

"My eyelashes will grow back," he laughed, "the apartment though suffered a ton of smoke damage and Marion lost almost everything she owned. She had renter's insurance. So that was good. But she isn't going to replace my piano. I got a disability pension now from the Army so I can live on my own and I don't have to work. You ever get your air force pension?"

"No," Ron replied, "I never got a damn thing after four years of service. You know I got that discharge? Look I have to go now."

Ron promised to look him up. Harold promised to call.
Neither one of them ever seemed to get around to it. Back in 1969
Gay and Eugene rented an apartment in the same complex Harold
and Marion were living in. They had their baby Mark and got reduced
rent for yard work. Harold was the manager of the building. It was
just another building he managed in the string of complexes he and
Marion had managed over the years.

Harold got drunk one night and went out on the stoop and
screamed insults at a German woman, calling her a Nazi. She lived
in the apartment above Gay. Gay heard the confrontation. When
the woman took Harold to court Gay was called to testify. Nothing
ever came of the defamation of character charges. Harold had a
lawyer who expressed what a war hero Harold was and how he
struggled with alcohol and should not be held accountable. Besides,
the lawyer pleaded, nobody but the woman and Gay heard the
insults. No harm, no foul. Harold evicted Gay and Eugene.

Ron found it hard to see Harold after that. He evicted his
daughter who was doing her duty. Maybe she should have taken
Harold's side but she didn't. Harold apologized but it seemed
empty. He argued with Ron that he had begged Gay not to go to
court and she would not listen to him. He asked Ron, "How could I
be her landlord after that?"

Ron heard his brother Fred was dying of throat cancer. They
had all been smokers, all the Robinsons. At one time everyone had
smoked. It was the cool thing to do. When they all started smoking
it was portrayed as glamorous and harmless. Ron had driven by
Fred's mansion in British Properties with Gwynne in the car in 1963.
He pulled over when he saw his brother get out of a Mercedes and
walk up their driveway to the house. Ron yelled, "Fred", from his
open window.

Fred looked and scowled. He went into the house. He did
not want to see his brother. There was no forgiveness for debts
owed and promises broken. Ron dropped his head in the car and
Gwynne asserted, "What an ass. That's your brother, then no
thanks!" she paused and looked with admiration at the beautiful
home and added, "nice house though."

Fred battled cancer for a few years and then ended up in hospital. Freda said he was not going to make it. Ron decided to go see Fred before he died. He figured his brother would not be able to talk due to tubes and surgery and he would get to say what he wanted. He went to the hospital and up to Fred's floor. He saw him through the glass window. He was alone. He put his hand on his frail brother who looked like a little boy bundled up on the bed. Fred looked up in panic and Ron said, "I'm not here to kill ya. I'm here to say I'm sorry. For all the crappy things I did to you."

Fred's eyes were cloudy, but Ron could tell he knew it was his brother and he knew he heard what he had to say. They stared at each other for so long Ron wondered if maybe Fred had died and then he felt it, the hand under his moved a tiny bit and Fred raised his hand up, put it on top of Ron's hand. Fred patted Ron's hand and the two men both let silent tears run down their faces, crying for time lost. Fred went to sleep after a bit and Ron left. For the first time in a long while he felt peace in his heart. He phoned Freda when he got home and told her about the visit and she said, "I'm glad you went. Fred died about an hour ago. You were the last person to see him. The nurse said he was gone minutes after you left the room."

His father gone, his mother gone and now his brother dead at the age of fifty-nine. Ron remembered the rain in Felling, the smell of the fields. He and Fred used to run in the fields and play marbles together even though Ron was five years older. He could feel the coal fire warmth of the drafty old houses they lived in. He remembered his mom making roast beef and Yorkshire pudding, his dad coming home smelling a bit like beer after winning a fight at the pub. Thomas used to box, a little. Ron told everyone his father was the lightweight champion in Northern England, but he was not. He was not the famous Kid Doyle that Ron bragged about. He was a tired old coal miner fighting in the pubs for a few quid to feed his family. Now Ron's younger brother was gone. It was 1971. Ron's heart was beating fast and he had to lie down and slip a pill under his tongue. They were heart pills.

The doctor had given him some other pills that make you relax. He told Gunvor one night when he was having heart pain,

"Look I'm not going to end up in hospital with tubes down my throat. When it gets too bad, I'm going to take those pills and do us all a favour."

"Oh Ron," she said, "you wouldn't do that."

But she was not sure. He was tired all the time. She knew his heart would just stop one day soon and she was not ready for that. They had been having the best years of their lives. She hid the pills in the cupboard above the stove. They had so much to look forward to. Lost years to make up for.

After that week Gwynne and Ron had together, she took off again, but this time with Dave. They hitchhiked across Canada and then went back to Terrace because she was pregnant. Her sisters jokingly had a shotgun wedding for her and stood up for her at City Hall. But Gwynne and Dave did not stay in Terrace long. They came back and moved into an upstairs suite in the West End. But times were tough, and they could not pay the rent after Christmas. Gwynne was six months pregnant and called her dad to come and help her move out while Dave was at work. The landlord had threatened to confiscate her belongings that day if she was not gone by five.

Ron had made both girls matching hope chests which amused them a lot. Gwynne said, "What is there to hope for? I got married because I was pregnant. I wanted to get a motorcycle and go to Mexico-yippee."

But she loved it. It was an old box with a padded seat covered in grey vinyl. Gay's was green. Gay was amused as well with the hope chest as she felt it was something every young girl received before she got married. She had been married five years and had two sons. The hope chest was Gwynne's concern that day. They did not have much in the apartment. There was an old mattress she did not care to take with her. Everything else was in bags or boxes and could be easily moved but the hope chest was heavy. So, she called her dad from the pay phone down the street.

He turned up the same time as the landlord who was twenty years younger and a foot taller than her dad. The two of them raced up the stairs. Ron clutched his chest as he slid through the door and Gwynne slammed it. The landlord pounded on the door yelling, "Get out now. I am going to change the locks and confiscate all your belongs."

Gwynne opened the door, "You said I had until five and it is only three."

Ron pushed the door open wider, "Stop threatening my daughter and get out of the way. We still have things to move out before five."

"Do you live here?"

"No, I don't," Ron answered.

The landlord argued, "Then stay out of it. She is not taking anything with her."

He must have thought she had an apartment full of furniture and it made Gwynne laugh, "I have a hope chest and some stuff in garbage bags. I have nothing of value."

"You are not taking anything," he shouted and shook his fist.

Ron stepped out of the apartment to the small landing at the top of the stairs and he hissed at the landlord, "She will take what she wants."

Then he pushed the landlord down the stairs. Gwynne gasped as the man tumbled and hit the bottom. She slammed the door shut, after she pulled her dad in behind her. They heard the last thump and then the landlord slowly walking back up the stairs. He was puffing and gasping. They were surprised he was not injured. Gwynne opened the door a crack and said, "I'm sorry he should not have done that."

"Get your stuff and get out," he said so quietly she barely heard him, "you have two hours."

He turned and left. Gwynne and her dad ran up and down the stairs loading as much as they could into Ron's 1954 beige Austin. If Gwynne had not been pregnant, she would have done it all but even she was getting out of breath. Ron was ash grey and struggling before they each got on one side of the hope chest. They struggled to get the heavy box down the stairs and into the car. Ron collapsed behind the wheel. He put a pill under his tongue that helped with the angina and Gwynne ran back upstairs one more time to get him water. She had left dishes on the counter, rinsed out a glass and filled it. She was running down when the landlord started to come up the stairs. She shoved by him and said yelled, "Out of my way you mother fucker."

He stepped aside and she got in the car with her dad. She usually never swore. It felt good to tell someone off. She handed the glass to her dad and he drank it, started the car and as they pulled away black smoke puffed out the back. She was not embarrassed or humiliated. She was proud of her dad. This was the same car he was driving the day they rolled Uncle at the West Hotel. He always stood up for his girls.

She and her sisters were trying to cross Hastings Street one day to go to the Pacific National Exhibition. They had eight children in tow. Elna had five of her own, Gay had two and Gwynne was pushing her baby girl in a carriage. Ron stepped out in front of traffic and held his arms out like a crossing guard. His parade of little ducklings crossed the road. He protected them. He always had.

After the baby girl was born Gwynne and Dave moved to Prince George but the plan was for Ron and Gunvor to join them. As part of the plan, they moved into a huge duplex with four bedrooms. It was three times bigger than any house Gwynne had ever lived in. It was new, clean and had two bathrooms. Dave had a good job; their daughter Kristen was two years old and they could not wait for Ron and Gunvor to join them.

Gunvor was excited to be moving. She felt that life would be easier for them with Gwynne and Dave to take care of them. Ron's health was not good. He could not work the carnivals at all. There was no extra money coming in, but he had turned sixty-five so got old age pension. Gunvor was only sixty-one but was able to get early old age pension with a disability pension at the age of sixty. They had more money than they had been used to. The benefits of subsidized housing had helped and people who worked at the community centre made the arrangements for her to get early pensions.

Ron was not sure he wanted to go north. He liked Vancouver. He liked that he could walk slowly to the bank, the pharmacy, and the corner store. He had established a close and loving relationship with his sister Freda once again. It was her who showed Ron the newspaper clipping in 1972 about Marie. He did not have to read the article to know that she was called the Big Boss of Powell Street, he had never stopped visiting her. He usually dropped in once every couple of months. They had a whiskey together and laughed about old times. Once Bill dropped by when he was there, but they did not have much to say to each other.

Bill had opened a restaurant on Victoria Drive and the last time Ron had gone out of his way to see Bill was the day Gwynne brought the baby home from the hospital in 1970. Dave had to work, so Ron went to the hospital to get Gwynne and her tiny daughter Kristen. On the spur of the moment as they went down Victoria, he said, "Let's go say hi to Billy."

Gwynne had not seen Bill since he propositioned her five years earlier. In a way she wanted to show him her beautiful child. But when they went in, he was rude and took one look at the baby and sniffed, "Barefoot and pregnant, hey? I guess you married a loser just like your sister Gay did?"

Even Ron was taken aback and offered, "Dave's a hell of a kid. Hard working. He's going places."

Bill pointed at Gwynne like she was not there, "What about her? Baby machine, nothing else."

Ron said, "She is a hell of a writer."

Gwynne had been surprised by the comment. Most of her writing she kept to herself, only sharing a few poems with him. She had written a book when she was fifteen and she guessed maybe her dad had read it. It was not hidden in her room but on her dresser for months. She had stayed home from school for three weeks to write it. It was supposed to be a funny look at the crazy life she had led with her family. In sharing it with friends she discovered it was not funny but more tragic. Several friends cried. She did not want that and threw the manuscript out. She figured he must have had time to read it before she tossed it.

In January of 1973 Ron and Gunvor were ready to go. Everything was packed except for day-to-day items they would need.

Ron had already paid February's rent as they were not going to remove any of the furniture. They would not get the damage deposit back, but the landlord knew that and agreed management would cart the old bed, table, chairs, and couch to the dump. All they were taking was the small stuff like the china cabinet he made for her, a lamp, and a small bookcase.

They had just finished a dinner of hash and mashed potatoes when there was a knock at the door. Gunvor went to the washroom as Ron went to answer the door. It was odd as people had to buzz to get into the building and the intercom was used to give advance warning of who was coming. Ron did not even think of that and opened the door wide to find a rough looking character in the hall. Ron took a step back. The guy was unkempt, wearing a frayed jean jacket and a toque over a mop of black hair. Ron glared at him, and asked, "What do you want?"

The guy advanced then and Ron could see he had a knife in his hand. Quietly the man threatened, "I want your money old man."

Ron's quick reaction was to slam the door, but it caught the guy's foot and left the thug on the outside with Ron trying to push his foot out with his foot. It was a struggle keeping the door closed as much as he could trying not to give an inch to the intruder. The guy was cursing. Ron could barely breathe as the push and shove went on for at least two minutes. His back and shoulders throbbed, he was sweating, and his heart pounded hard against the inside of his chest. All Ron could think of was that he had to protect Gunvor. He knew that men raped old women. They had heard of a woman on the seventh floor who had been raped at the age of eighty. Maybe the guy did want money but was high on drugs. Who knew? It was a bad area. Ron was not about to let him in and give him the last twelve dollars he had.

After the scuffle Ron was able to kick his foot out the door. He slammed it hard. He locked it. The guy started pounding with his fists as Gunvor came in from the bathroom. She saw Ron hunched over, clutching his chest, back against the door and thought he was dying. She grabbed the phone and called 911 and yelled into the phone, "Someone is trying to get in and my husband is going into cardiac arrest."

The would-be intruder heard her and fled down the stairs. Ron collapsed to the floor. He just slid down the door like every bone had dissolved. Gunvor bent down to him and held his hand. He was grey, breathing heavy and unable to speak. Gunvor rubbed the back of his hand and whispered, "It will be fine. I promise you. It will be fine."

They sat like that for about ten minutes until the paramedics arrived. When they banged on the door, she had to pull him away from the door, which was not easy, but Ron had enough left in him to help slide away so they could get in. The paramedics came in and gave him oxygen while he lay on the floor. Gunvor sat on the couch with her hands folded together patiently waiting for them to revive him. And they did. His heartbeat was erratic, so they gave him one of his pills and helped him to his bed. They left him even though Gunvor felt he was clinging to life.

He survived the night. The next morning Gwynne phoned to discuss final details of the move. Gunvor told her the moving truck was picking up their belongings on January thirty-first as planned and her and dad would be driving to Prince George. They would take it easy, she said, stop in Quesnel to visit relatives and be mindful of the icy roads. Before she hung up, she told Gwynne about the assault but assured her that dad would recover, and they would see her in about two weeks. It was a casual comment about the intruder as she did not want to worry Gwynne.

Ron did not recover the way they had hoped. He was short of breath and it took him awhile to do anything. Gunvor was worried the drive would be too hard on him. He told her that he was fine. They would take it easy. He laughed at her fears, "We are almost home-free. Once the truck gets here in the morning and we load up we will go to Lillooet to see Gay first. Maybe stay a few days. There is no rush. When the truck gets to Prince George Gwynne will take care of everything."

"Yes," Gunvor agreed, "Gwynne's already bought a bed, bedding and even a dresser. She has a big basement where she can store all of our stuff."

That week they relaxed as they were ready to go. Gunvor asked him to go see the doctor but he said he was fine. He seemed to be. Calm and peaceful and in good spirits. They watched a lot of television and he played solitaire while she did crosswords. On the night of January 30th, they went to bed early. The truck was going to be there in the morning, and they would begin their new adventure. For the first time in a long while Ron gave Gunvor a big kiss on the lips when he crawled into bed and said, "Well, sweetheart this is it. A new life awaits us."

She smiled at him, "I know I am excited about it but worried . . .you know, the drive."

"It will be fine," he said, "everything is going to be alright."

He rolled over and as was usual for him he was asleep within minutes. Gunvor tossed around and finally fell asleep about midnight. Then around two AM something woke her up. Not a sound. It was the lack of sound. Ron was not snoring. The room was quiet. She lay in the dark afraid to move, afraid to know, afraid to see. She started to cry. She knew. She asked quietly, "Ron are you alive?"

He did not answer. Ron had died shortly after midnight. It was January 31st, 1973. He was sixty-six years old. He would have been sixty-seven in two months. When Ron did not answer Gunvor got up and turned on the lights. She looked at him. He looked at peace. She thought it almost looked like he was grinning. She walked over to the bed and whispered, "Ron are you dead?"

She shook his shoulders, and he did not respond. She tapped him lightly on the cheek with her fingers. She held a mirror under his nose because she had heard if he was breathing the mirror would show the air. She put her head to his chest. Nothing. She lay down beside him. She did not know what to do. She felt a rage build up in her that had been still for so long; a rage that made her feel like her head was going to blow off. She was feeling panic build in her. She could not control her breathing or her thoughts.

She sat up. With a force she did not think she had, she slapped him hard across the face, and cried, "You sonofabitch! How dare you die and leave me here."

She left the room and sat on the couch in the living room. She was shaking, but not with sorrow or fear; she was mad. They were home free he had said. He was home free; she was stuck with a hell of a mess. She did not know what to do. Ron did everything. Did they even have money in the bank? Did he have money put away for a funeral? What would happen to her now? That damn moving truck was coming in just five or six hours. She did not cry. She stepped out on the balcony and the cold night air brought her back to reality. She called Freda and told her, "Your brother is dead. I don't know what to do."

Freda, no stranger to death with her mother, father, brother and one of her son's gone, told her to be calm. She would phone the coroner and she and her husband would get in the car and be at her apartment within the hour. Gunvor asked in a small girl voice, "What do I do for an hour?"

"You wait," Freda said sternly.

Gunvor held the phone in her hand on the couch and did not move until Freda buzzed from the lobby. Freda and her husband checked Ron out as soon as they arrived and needlessly pronounced him dead. It was four in the morning. A few minutes later the coroner arrived and pronounced him dead. The paramedics put him on a stretcher and carried him into the living room. Gunvor looked up as they were going through the door and at the last moment, she saw his body start to slide off the gurney. The paramedic caught him, and they went out. She never said goodbye. It was over. Ron was gone.

Chapter Twelve

Gunvor (1973 to 1983)

Gunvor made coffee. The moving truck arrived so Freda went down to the lobby and explained to them what happened. They said there would be a hundred-dollar cancellation fee. She wrote them a cheque on the spot and went back upstairs. Gunvor had showered and dressed. They had sent Freda's husband home, so it was just the two of them. They were calm and sat at the table and decided on a plan of action. Freda offered to call relatives but Gunvor said she could do it. When her kids arrived, they would take care of everything. Freda offered to book a time for a service at Boal Memorial, where her brother Fred had been cremated in North Vancouver. Freda left feeling she should be helping more but Gunvor seemed to want to be alone.

Gunvor called Elna and Elna said she would call the other girls. Elna hung up the phone and poured herself a tall glass of vodka on ice. Her oldest daughter Holly had lost her baby in December, a crib death, and now this? She felt sometimes that her life had been cursed since she got married. It seemed there was always a tragedy or a painful event. When her grandson was born, she had never been so happy. She had thought his birth might bring happier days. And then the little guy was gone. She had phoned Ron and told him. He called around to the other family members. She had not been able to do that. She had never been that fond of Ron, but he had been there for her on many occasions when she needed a dad. She sighed, drained the glass of vodka, and called Gay.

Gunvor called her sister Lottie and then went to lie down. She changed the sheets and made the bed first. For a bit she tossed around but then she slept for two hours. The phone was ringing. She knew better than to answer, so she just let it ring. Gunvor began a quiet time of no talking or thinking. She made lunch, she worked on a crossword. She would let her girls figure out what to do. Elna called back in the afternoon and told her mom, "Gay is getting on the train this afternoon and will be there by supper time. Eugene can't come until tomorrow. Mike and I are leaving first thing in the morning so we'll be there Saturday afternoon. It's a two-day drive from Terrace on icy roads, mom, but we will be there."

"What should I do?"

"Nothing mom we will figure it out, the funeral and all."

"He wanted to be cremated. Freda will call and make some arrangements before you arrive. Otherwise, we would not be able to do anything until Monday," Gunvor paused, then asked, "what about Gwynne and Dave? Are they coming?"

"Yes, I called Dave. Gwynne was at work at Woodward's, so I told him. He said they would be leaving around five so you can expect them in the middle of the night, mom. But Gay will be there before them."

For some reason Gunvor did not want to call Gwynne. They had been close, always close. She thought maybe if she talked to her, she would break down. She loved her dad so much. There was guilt there too for Gunvor. She always thought someday she would tell Gwynne that Harold was her dad. But not now. It was too late. Would it not be better to let the deception die with Ron's death? What good would it do to tell a twenty-four-year-old woman that the man who just died was not her real father? Gwynne was not the most stable woman; immature and reckless at times. She sat on the couch and waited for Gay to arrive and knew that seeing her would be difficult. Gay was dramatic, and this loss would be huge for her. Not only did she love her dad, but she worshipped him.

The next few days were a blur for Gunvor. Freda booked a time for cremation and a service on the Tuesday. The kids were going to have to get a payment to Boal Memorial by Monday. Gunvor was not worried. The rent had been paid for a month. She could just stay in the apartment. She would be fine. Maybe Gwynne would stay with little Kristen for a few days and help her get unpacked and settled. Her girls would take care of things.

Gunvor knew she should call Billy, Marie, and Harold. Maybe she should call some of his carnie friends? She decided not to let anyone know. They meant nothing to her and wasn't the point of a funeral to support the bereaved? She called Billy's ex-girlfriend Fran who she was friendly with and told her. If Fran wanted to tell Bill, she could. Gunvor did not feel any of them deserved to be notified. They had not been real friends for many years. She spoke to her sister Lottie for a long time and Lottie told her that her daughter Linda would drive her and Waldy on Monday for the Tuesday service. Gunvor had no idea what that would entail; or how much money it would cost.

Everyone arrived. It was chaos. People. Alcohol. Gunvor had not drank for five years and she was not going to start again but she could not tell them they could not sit at her table and drink. It was loud and they were all laughing too much. She had a quiet conversation with Gwynne, and she confided to her that she was afraid Ron might have taken some pills to 'go to sleep'. They searched and found the bottle empty. Gunvor had told the paramedics the same thing, but during the autopsy they ruled suicide out. There was no sign of drugs in his system. He just went to sleep, and his heart stopped. 'How lucky he was' she thought, 'it is how everyone hoped to go'.

The next few days were a blur. Cousins, aunts, uncles drifting in and out. Gunvor did not eat. Mike went to the bank and pretending to be Ron, took out every penny in the account. There was only three hundred and forty-two dollars. Mike gave it to Gunvor, joking, "Don't spend it all in one place mom."

Freda told them they needed to pay a thousand dollars on Monday for the cremation and the service. A Minister would say a few words. Everyone looked to Dave to figure it out. He had a boom box and lots of music he travelled with. He wrote a poem and a eulogy and took over as master of ceremonies. He went to the florist and got some flowers. Just a couple of bouquets of Lilly of the Valley. Freda told him he could plant a bush in honour of the deceased in the woods around the Crematorium, so Dave bought a Ponderosa Pine. His father-in-law loved Bonanza, the television show and the Ponderosa Ranch. Eugene signed the Death Certificate. Mike went to Household Finance and borrowed a thousand dollars.

Mike poured shots for the three of them; Eugene, Dave and himself and toasted, "To the old man. May the old bugger rest in peace. And you two, owe me three hundred and thirty-four dollars each to pay for this shindig."

Family slept where they could, and when they could. Gwynne, Gay and Elna organized what mom could take and what should be taken to the dump. Gay convinced Gunvor to go to Lillooet to be with her. They were going to load up Eugene's car, Mike's truck, and Ron's car and that is all the room she had. She could not keep anything that did not fit.

Gwynne was heartbroken over her dad's death and devastated that they steamrolled her mother into going to Lillooet. She had wanted to take dad's car, but she was still taking lessons for her driver's license. Gwynne had no way to get her mom to Prince George. Dave was driving a little Datsun. Elna was going to take Ron's car as far as Lillooet to drop off mom and her things then hop in the truck with Mike to head to Terrace. They all had to leave Tuesday right after the service. Everyone had bills to pay and jobs to go to. Elna was driving a school bus now and Mike worked out in the bush hauling logs. Nobody could afford time off.

Too soon Gunvor found herself bunking in with her grandkids in Gay and Eugene's trailer. There was a lot of drinking. Eugene worked in a liquor store and Gay worked in a bar. She wanted to go to Gwynne's. She had a bed and a room there. It took a couple of months but the two of them figured it out and by spring Gunvor was living with Gwynne and Dave in a huge duplex. Gwynne was not working so the two of them had lots of time to shop and enjoy the fireweed and tulips popping up in the backyard. Gunvor was as happy as she could be. But it did not last. Gunvor could not be happy. She was missing something in her life. It was obvious she was missing Ron, but she could not seem to voice that. She stayed with Gwynne for about three months and then she went to Elna's place, and then to stay with Lottie.

Gunvor bounced around for about a year and a half and then Gwynne and Dave bought a small house on an acre of land. She moved into a small bedroom with Kristen again. It was a crazy year and a half. The girls seemed to go nuts over their dad's death. Gay and Eugene split up and Gay ended up in Prince George as well. Gwynne had left Dave for six months and took Kristen to Vancouver where she got a job and lived with some guy she went to school with. Dave had a girlfriend. Gunvor often said to all her children, "I am fed up with the lot of ya."

Gwynne went home, and her and Dave were waiting for the birth of their second child. Gunvor was going to help but she did not see how that would happen. The baby could be with Gwynne in her room in a cradle for six months but after that he should be in with his sister. Gunvor would be moving on again. She decided she would live in Chase near Lottie and Waldy. Maybe she could finally unpack some of her dishes and personal belongings.

The baby was due in June, so she planned to leave for Chase in September. The baby boy was born with a lot of problems, club feet, stunted muscle growth, a hole in his palette and a hernia in his stomach. He was in casts from the time he was six weeks old. They called him Super-Scrap. Gunvor loved this baby so much, she cuddled him a lot. It seemed she was over her fear of babies, holding him more than she had held her other grandkids. Gwynne seemed to be in a good space. Gay had a boyfriend and was going to college.

Gunvor moved on. By 1975 she was taking care of herself. She had not done that since 1944 and it felt good. She lived in a small senior's complex She had a bank account. She was saving money. She was even able to help her girls out from time to time. Being on old age pension was the richest she could ever remember being. She knew the cheque would come every month and how much she was getting. She had a lot of time for reflection. She knew she missed Ron. She knew she loved Ron. But she did not cry for him. At times she felt a stirring of happiness at how normal life could be without living with a con man. She was mad at herself for letting him control her.

She had diabetes and had to go on the needle for that. She had some atrial fibulation. She had arthritis. But she was healthier than she had been for many years. Her children spoiled her. Her grandkids adored her. She forgave Ron for the things he had done to her. She felt a stirring of anger from time to time but Gunvor never dwelled on the past. Her father had died in 1971 and she was close to her mom, her sister, cousins, and many old friends from the past. With Ron gone friends who did not care for him now came around.

Gunvor ate well. She started eating food that she liked; macaroni and salt pork, pea soup and she baked coffee cakes. She had been eating English style cooking for so long she had forgotten how much she loved the Swedish food from her childhood. She kept herself busy with knitting, crosswords and reading. Gunvor loved the Harlequin Romance Novels. She watched television quite a bit, mostly the soap operas like As the World Turns. Ron used to call it As the Stomach Turns making her feel guilty for watching what he called 'crap'.

She loved her little apartment in Chase. It was a five-minute walk to Lottie's house. She saw more Swedish relatives in the year she lived there then she had since Eagle River. She really missed seeing her daughters and the grandkids. After a while she let Gwynne convince her to come live with her. Gwynne and Dave had left Prince George and were renting a duplex in Surrey with a basement suite. Kristen was in grade three and David was going to be five. They seemed to be in a good place. Gone were the photographs of them in hippy garb and instead they sent pictures of a television family. Dave in a suit, Gwynne in a dress with a jacket, the kids dressed to the nines.

It was a great apartment. She had her privacy, but she ate most of her meals upstairs, so she did not have to cook every day.

Berndt, her brother came to visit because their mom had died in 1977 and he was alone in Eagle River. He was thinking about moving to B.C. where his brother and sisters lived. The visit was fine for a couple of days and then Gwynne dragged them to a bar for supper. Gunvor did not want to go because she knew her brother did not handle drinking very well, but he also insisted. He got drunk and when they went home, he staggered up the stairs to sleep on Gwynne's couch.

Gunvor did not know anything had happened until the next day. She was drinking coffee at her table doing a crossword and Gwynne came storming down the stairs. She heard her yell at Kristen who was hanging out with Berndt in the bedroom, "Get upstairs now."

Then she came through the door her long hair flying all over as she had been brushing it. She still had the brush in her hand. Shaking the brush at her mother she hissed, "How could you let my daughter, your grandchild crawl under the cover with that pedophile?"

"I didn't know," she stammered, "but what are you talking about?"

"Oh mom, you know. I heard about the young girls in Eagle River he was taking care of, put them through college because they did favours for him. Well, he told me last night what those favours were," she spat the words out like rotten food from her mouth, "mom, he sexually abused those girls and then that bastard propositioned me and stuck his hands between my legs."

"Well, you were pretty drunk yourself."

Gwynne had started to turn around to leave when the words came out of her mother's mouth. She felt a blind rage for all the years her mom sat back and let uncles stick their whiskey drenched tongues down her throat. Gunvor had ignored the rumours about Elna's husband Mike and gave him free rein with her and Gay. When there was an incident, she asked for their silence to not tell their dad or he would kill Mike. She never protected them.

Gwynne had told mom she had some bad feelings about Uncle when she went to visit him when she was eight. She did not know how to explain it but told her mom sometimes Uncle had made her feel 'icky'.

Gunvor said, "If you don't do what he asks, he can get mean."

Gwynne said, "Mom, I did not do anything when I was a kid to make Uncle mad. I can assure you of that."

"Well, you must have," she insisted.

Gwynne remembered the two summers she spent at the farm when she was eight and nine. Sometimes Uncle was crabby, but it was not because she did anything wrong. She swept up the sawdust in the workshop. She brought lunch and drinks out to Uncle. She even swept up the hair from when he gave people haircuts. She laughed at all his corny jokes. And one day he hugged her and told her she could have the blue ukulele he made if she were a good girl. He promised her the blue ukulele he made. All summer he teased her with it.

When she left to go back to Kenora she asked for the blue ukulele and he told her she did not deserve it .   Gwynne remembered something happened, but she did not know what. She remembered an army blanket pulled tight over a cot in the workshop. That memory made her feel like puking. She remembered crying in the car all the way to Kenora wondering what she did to not deserve the blue ukulele. When she tucked Uncle in on the couch with a blanket the night before he asked her to come to Ontario with him and take care of him. She laughed, "Uncle I can't do that. I have a husband and children."

He grinned drunkenly up at her and slyly said, "I'll give you the blue ukulele."

Then he grabbed her between the legs. Gwynne had felt such revulsion and a rush of memories that were not quite there. She ran into the bathroom and slid down to the floor sobbing. She stayed in there for an hour, unable to see what she knew she should be able to see. Did he abuse her? The memory was like a shadow and she could not catch it. And now her mother was going to justify her baby girl curled up in bed with him? Rage, all she felt was rage. She threw the brush at her mom as hard as she could. The brush hit Gunvor on the cheek and fell onto the floor. Gwynne ran upstairs and cried in her room.

They barely spoke for the next few days and when Uncle left Gwynne gave him a hug like nothing was wrong. Later she went downstairs and told her mother she was sorry. Gunvor still had a little red mark on her cheek but she said, "It is fine. I understand. But you must believe Gwynne we all grew up with dirty uncles and men we could not trust. You just must learn to live with it and carry on. We all had to do that. Elna was raped when she was fourteen and you don't hear her crying about it."

Elna had told Gwynne about the rape but she did not call it that. She said one of the cousins had forced her to have sex. Gwynne told Elna, "That was rape. You were fourteen."

Elna replied, "Fourteen and not a virgin. I had Mike, remember. I got married at fifteen. I knew better."

"You said no didn't you?'

"Sometimes Gwynnie you are so naïve."

Conversations with family members about rape, sex, age of consent always went that way. It seemed if you were born female it was your responsibility to say 'no' even if you were three or four. Gwynne did not recognize the number of times she had been raped. She was drunk, passed out but knew she did not willingly submit. It did not seem uncommon for her relatives and friends grew up the same way. She loved her mom and knew she was a good woman who was abused. She did not want her child to join the club.

Dave and Gwynne bought a new house and Gunvor moved into the basement. Dave built her a room. She did not have to cook, clean, or do anything. Dave gave her insulin shots in her leg in the mornings and made her coffee. Gwynne cooked all the meals. When Gwynne worked Gunvor had her two grandkids to take care of her afterschool. Gunvor told Gwynne more than once that this was the happiest, she had ever been in her life. They took her to Disneyland, and it was the most fun Gunvor had ever had.   They took turns pushing her in a wheelchair. Her legs just did not hold her up too well anymore.

Gunvor even went on the Pirates of the Caribbean water ride and enjoyed It's a Small World. She told the grandkids she had never seen anything so wonderful. She was a little scared when they went to Universal Studios and they thought the train was going to collapse into the water and they would be eaten by the shark from Jaws. But even though it was fun Gwynne never felt she could please her mom. Gunvor complained about everything. Not long after the trip Gunvor decided to get her own apartment. It seemed silly to Gwynne, but she also understood that Gunvor had no privacy.

Gunvor loved the family but she could not stand the drinking. Dave and Gwynne partied a lot. After Gwynne had worked as assistant editor and publisher, she decided to start her own business. It was the early eighties. Singing telegrams, balloon deliveries, and strip o grams were big. You could not watch a sitcom on television without seeing some clown delivering a bouquet of balloons and singing. Gwynne's business Just Imagine Fantasy Company and later the Balloon Battalion became successful.

Gwynne and Dave were super busy. There were a lot of crazy performers in and out of the house. Dave worked as a lineman and made great money, but Gwynne had him running around in gorilla suits and superhero costumes on the weekends. Even Kristen and little David dressed up for parades, were Santa's helpers and joined the crazy circus. By the time Kristen was twelve she was doing clown parties for little kids. It was too much for Gunvor and she moved to Hope where Gay was living. She was able to get a small cottage there and be on her own.

The cottage gave her the privacy she craved. One afternoon she went through the tin box and threw out the nude photos and dirty greeting cards. She tossed the court case records Ron had hung onto for security. Nobody was going to come now and try to arrest him for perjury or bribery. Thinking back on their scams to help people get a divorce amused her. She could not believe she had been that woman, posing with drunk men in bed. It was not a bad time in her life although she regretted all the booze. Her and Ron had a lot of laughs. One thing she knew for sure was that Ron had loved her.

She just could not seem to cry about the loss. She cried in 1979 when she found out her first husband, Alton passed. Sobbed in fact. There had been so many deaths; her parents, aunts, uncles, Holly's baby, and Alton. She had cried when she heard Harold got burned in a fire and Marion kicked him out. She felt sad for him. Another lost life. But after thirty years with Ron, through good times and bad she had always loved him. And now he was gone, she sat in her cottage dry eyed and happy.

She felt an overwhelming sense of loss, missing him. She felt loneliness but tears for his death, no. She had a lot of time in her small place to reflect. She was alone a lot. She had Sunday dinners with Gay and family and her grandkids popped in after school. Gay had two boys and two girls. The last daughter was with Gay's boyfriend she had been living with for five years.   As close as they were, Gay and Gunvor were not seeing each other daily. Gwynne called every day. She was always mad at someone or something. But Gunvor did not feel worried about her girls.

No matter what happened to them, they bounced back, reinvented themselves, moved on. No, she did not worry about her girls. They were feminists. Women of Gunvor's generation did not have that luxury. She knew life was not perfect for any of them, but their lives were far better than anything she had lived through.

Gunvor had been having heart palpitations. The doctor sent her for tests, scans and told her she had suffered several minor heart attacks. She could not believe that. She never felt them. She had her diabetes under control and ate very carefully. She walked and was getting exercise. She could not knit anymore as her fingers were too crippled up from arthritis, but she was healthy, at least she felt like she was healthy. She found herself wanting to go home. The problem was Gunvor did not know where home was. Certainly not the cottage, no matter how cute it was.

One night she was getting ready for bed and she heard something at her window. She looked up and realized she had not closed her curtains and there in the window was a young man staring in at her, jerking off. Gunvor got off the bed as quick as she could pulling her nightie over her head and closed the curtains. She called Gay to come right away. She was shaking with fear. She could not understand what had just happened. How could a young man be getting off on her old saggy boobs? She remembered Gwynne telling her rape was not about beauty, age, or sex, it was about violence; this made her afraid.

It took Gay a long time to calm her down. They called the police and reported the Peeping Tom but Gunvor never felt safe in her place again. Like Ron had felt when the man with the knife attacked him at the door, she felt violated, indignant. Where was human decency and respect? She could not imagine anyone treating her father or mother that way. She believed the knife assault the week before Ron died was the cause of his death. In that moment, Ron gave up. He was too old to fight anymore. She felt that way. Despite loving daughters and grandkids, she felt alone and left by the side of the road, as she would say, 'like a pile of trash'. Gunvor was bitter.

A few days later she was talking to Gwynne and she told her how disgusted she was about the man at her window and Gwynne said, "Mom why don't you just come back and live with me? You said you were lonely even before this happened."

"I am lonely in a crowd," Gunvor said dramatically.

"Oh mom, I'm sorry."

"Not your problem," she said.

Gwynne said, "Mom, I quit drinking you know. I told you that. I have not had a drink for at least six months. And now that I have opened two stores, one in Surrey and one in New Westminster, there are no crazy people popping in and out of the house."

Gunvor joked, "Well, you and Dave still pop in and out don't ya? And that crazy cast of characters who live in your cul-de-sac?"

Gwynne admitted it was a busy place still. Everyone had moved in at the same time to the new houses forming what Gwynne recognized as an unhealthy bond. In fact, she had been thinking about moving. Gwynne hung up the phone and remembered the day not long before her mother moved when they had been driving down the road and a song came on, 'I can't live, if living is without you'.

Her mom had started to cry, and she said, "That is my song. That is how I feel without Ron."

It had been the first time she expressed that she missed him. The two of them had driven along listening to the song and crying. Each of them remembering the man who loomed so large in their lives, the man who loved them and took care of them for so many years. Gwynne had reconciled his death finally but never stopped missing him. She had been happy to realize that her mother did love him. It became a special shared moment in time between the two of them. She loved her mom and wanted her to come home, but she knew Gunvor wanted her own space.

That Christmas was the first one that Gunvor had not been with Gwynne and Dave. Nothing made her happy. Gay called and confided to Gwynne that 'mom was grumpy'. They both tried hard to please their mother, but it seemed nothing did. They pitched in and bought her a grandmother clock. Gwynne had also bought a rocking chair and drove it up to Hope on Christmas Eve. They had sipped hot chocolate while mom rocked in her chair. Gwynne drove back to Surrey with an odd feeling in her chest.

But the holidays came and went, nobody died. On the tenth anniversary of Ron's death, January 31 Gwynne went to Hope to be with Gay and her mom. They went to the Hope Hotel Café for lunch and mom had the liver and onions like she always did. They went shopping at some of the little stores in Hope and when Gwynne dropped mom off, they hugged a long time. Not one of them mentioned that Ron had died ten years earlier even though that is all they carried in their hearts.

In the beginning of February Gunvor just felt exhausted, listless, and tired. She finally made a doctor's appointment because Gay told her she had to go get her heart tested. On the morning of the ninth Gay was supposed to take her to the doctor at ten in the morning but she did not show up. It was Gay's birthday and she had been celebrating after work the night before. She slept in. Gunvor was furious and she called a cab. She took the cab to Gay's house and she told the cab driver to wait, she would just be a minute. That was all it took to rush into the house, go to Gay's bedroom door and yell at her, "Thanks a lot. You were supposed to take me to the doctor."

Gay rolled over and looked at the clock. It was almost ten. She sat up and mumbled, "I'm sorry mom. I can get dressed really quick."

"Don't bother," Gunvor snapped and walked out to the cab. She went to the doctor. She never wished Gay 'happy birthday'.

At the doctor's office he told her he did not like the way her arrhythmia was and admitted her to the hospital. He called Gay and told her that her mother was in hospital. Gay ran up to the hospital and all she could think was that it was her fault. She expected her mom to still be angry but when she got there, Gunvor patted her hand and said, "I was just anxious but now I am fine. I never said Happy Birthday."

She reached into the purse on her hospital bed and handed Gay a card with money inside. She seemed to be fine. They doctor was going to run a few tests and she would be home the next day. The next day they took Gunvor to Vancouver General Hospital to the cardiac wing by ambulance. She was not fine. Her lungs were filling up, she had pneumonia, and her heart was bouncing around. Gunvor had never been in an ambulance. When her appendix burst, she walked to the highway in Eagle River with Elna and hitched a ride to emergency. Alton had been too drunk to take her. When she went into labour ten times she always had a ride to emergency. They did not turn the siren on so that made her feel a bit better.

Gwynne met her at the hospital in Vancouver and stayed with her until it started to get dark. Gwynne went home and called her sisters and assured them that mom was fine. She was fine. The next day Gwynne went to the hospital with photo albums of their trip to Disneyland. She thought mom would be cheered up with the snapshots of a happier time. She was and told Gwynne, "Thank God for that trip. It was the best thing that ever happened to me."

It was the first time Gunvor had ever seemed grateful for anything. They had a great visit and just when Gwynne was relaxing her mom suffered a small heart attack and they asked her to leave the room. When she came back, they had intubated her mom to help her breathe. Gunvor looked up at her with tears running down her cheeks. Gwynne did what we all do when someone is slipping away and said, "You will be OK mom. Everything will be fine."

Gunvor shook her head violently from side to side and tried to pull at the tube down her throat. The nurse gave her something to calm her down and when she walked Gwynne out to the hall she said, "If you have family to call, you better call them. She does not have much time left."

Gwynne barely remembered the drive home. She called her sisters and told them to come right away. Gay drove from Hope the next morning and Dave went to the airport to get Elna and Mike. Then the three sisters went to see mom, praying she had gotten better through the night. But she had not. She lay on the bed, alert, frightened and crying, pulling at the tube down her throat. Elna asked if it could be removed but was told 'no'. They also told her that Gunvor had signed a 'do not resuscitate' order.

The three sisters stayed all day taking turns holding her hand, crying with her, and begging the doctors to take the tube out. They said they could not, or she would die. They argued that she had a DNR order, so she had made her decision. All three of them could not believe their mom had gone from smiling and not feeling too bad to fighting to breathe. It did not seem right. Nothing seemed right. About five o'clock Elna and Gay wanted a smoke, so they kissed her and went outside. Gwynne had quit smoking, but went with them.

Once outside the three girls laughed and joked around like they did when they were kids. They did not talk about their mother dying. They did not believe she would. But she did while they were gone. She tried to rip the tube out, clawing at it like a mad woman until they helped her by disconnecting the tube. She blinked her tear-filled eyes at the nurses with gratitude, and she asked her girls to forgive her, but she had to go. She did not want to see their faces again. It was making dying too hard to bear. She knew her girls would be fine. Her beautiful grandkids would grow up better than they had, she knew that. She may not have been the best mother but her legacy was one of love. She did not want to live and suffer everyday with pain, or with fear. She felt peace enter her heart. She could go and life would take care of itself. She was not afraid. She wanted to be free. She let go.

When Gwynne, Gay and Elna got off the elevator holding hands and giggling the nurse stopped them and said, "Your mother is gone."

The sisters went to the door of the room. Elna and Gay went in and stood on either side of the bed holding her hands and crying. Gwynne stood in the door arms defensively tight around her body. She felt her soul leave her body and fly to the top of the room where she felt her mother was. The two of them looked down on the room. There was no feeling. There was no sadness. There was calm, peace and serenity. Then Gwynne felt her mom move up and away from her. She felt her hand slip through her hand and Gwynne's hand felt a rush of air. She felt heavy and not light anymore and with a thud she was back in her body. She saw her sisters on either side of the bed. She felt she was being supported by the door frame. It was hard. She could feel tension and pain in her body. It felt like she could be swallowed up by the harsh lights in the room. It was so bright and cold. It was reality. It was filled with pain.

Chapter Thirteen

Harold (1973 to 1983)

Harold did not know for over a year what had happened to his friend Ronald Robinson. He tried his number. It was disconnected. He tried phoning people he knew were close to Ron and could not get any answers. Finally, in late 1974 he went to Marie's place at 358 Powell Street. It was a short walk from where he was living. She was there with her yappy little chihuahuas, but only two as one had died. She was not friendly at first, as in 'what do you want' kind of unfriendly.

She always made him nervous, but he cleared his throat and asked, "Seen Tiny around?"

"No", she answered.

"He doesn't answer his phone. In fact, it has been disconnected. And I don't really know where he was living. In a project off Hastings, maybe?"

"There aren't any phones where Ron is. He's dead. He died last year."

Harold felt his heart start to pound fast, "What? Why didn't anyone tell me? I'm easy to find."

She did not answer. She just stood at the door with her arms wrapped tight hugging an old grey sweater to her chest. She was quiet then finally said, "Do you want to come in?"

"I would like to know what happened to Ron, and Gunvor."

They settled at her table in the dusty kitchen. She offered him a whiskey, but he said no he had a bleeding ulcer but could handle a beer. She got him one out of her fridge and sat down.

"Nobody told me either, Harold. Ron died in January last year and he was cremated. Bill's old girlfriend Francis told him a few months later. Gunvor moved out of town in a few days. Not one of his kids, not his sister or Gunvor thought to call me. Or Billy."

Harold replied, "Someone should have called me."

"They didn't even put an obituary in the paper. I found out because Francis heard from Gunvor when she moved to Prince George this summer to be with her daughter Gwynne when she gave birth."

Harold said, "I knew she got married. Ron told me. You know, I am her dad, not Ron."

"I've known that for years. Ron didn't keep secrets from me. Gwynne has two kids. She has a girl who is at least four and now a son who is a few months old," she paused, "I always knew Gwynne was your daughter. Ron felt she was his own, just like the oldest one. He loved all his girls."

"Yeah, I guess he told you everything. He was a good dad. What happened . . .to Ron?"

She took a swig of whiskey, "He died."

"How?"

She sneered at him, "Like we all do. Old age. Well, he wasn't that old, sixty-seven but he had a hard life. Drugs, booze."

"I am trying to slow down on the hard stuff."

"You know he had a bad heart?"

"Yeah. I know. This is terrible news. I loved that man. He was like one of my brothers."

"I know." she said, "I loved that man too."

They clinked their glasses together, her shot glass of whiskey and his mug of beer.

He did not stay long. They had never really liked each other. He walked slowly back to his hotel. Someone had donated a piano a long time ago to the residents. He liked to think it was the one he and Ron stole and donated to the cop shop so many years ago. He sat down at the piano and he started to play. He played and played, one song after the other. He could feel the tears run down his face. He was oblivious to the small group who had gathered to sit quietly on chairs and watch him mourn. They all knew him. This group of misfit men who lived at the Hotel. It was kind of the last stop for old soldiers. Most of these guys had fought during World War II and had battle fatigue. Most were alcoholics.

When Harold had fallen asleep a few years earlier with a cigarette in his hand he burned his face. He had burn scars around his chin and it took a while for his eyebrows and eyelashes to grow back but he suffered no long-term loss from the fire. Except Marion. She kicked him out after years of trying to rehabilitate him. He still saw her occasionally but only for short visits. She brought him food and sometimes clothes she found at the second-hand store. He was only fifty-eight, but he felt a lot older. His life had slowed down a lot.

Harold was able to get on a disability pension from the war. The armed services had begun to recognize the wreckage that was left for some of the men. It was enough money to keep Harold from the streets. The Hotel was not an official home for lost soldiers, but it turned out that way. They drifted in. The joke around the place was that you only drifted out feet first, dead, in a body bag. That was why the beds were all placed so your feet would face the door. Easier to carry you out. These days most of the guys were drifting out, not in. There were a few hippies taking up lodging now.

Harold ate around the corner at the Blue Bird Café. A waitress there liked him and gave him free coffee. On the days his stomach was too bad for coffee she gave him decaf tea. He was not drinking as much as people thought. He did drink everyday but sometimes it was only one or two beer.

Both his brothers Burge and Vernon dropped in from time to time. They brought news from home. Harold had not been back to Standard since the late sixties around 1969. He'd gone to Vernon's house, swarming with kids. He had an old friend with him, and they were drunk. They asked him to leave. It was so upsetting he did not even go back to visit his family when the dad died in 1973. His mom had already moved into a senior complex in Calgary.

He did phone his mom though. They got along well because they only talked about the past, on the farm. Harold had gone to the Vancouver Public Library one day and found a book written about his mom's great uncle Neils Hansen, the uncle who was the explorer on the Rasmussen side of the family: her side. It was a university textbook students studied from called, To Plant the Prairies and the Plains. The Life and Work of Neils Ebessen Hansen. He loved the payoff from sharing stuff like that with her. It kept them talking for hours.

She told him the family story about how her Uncle was in China in the late 1800s along the Yellow River when he came across a slave market. He could not stand to see the auction and the people being sold to the highest bidder. For ten dollars he bought all of them and set the slaves free. He so angered the locals he had to leave the small community by the Yangtze River. She told him about the blue glass brick he had collected that had belonged to Pharaohs and stories about the thirties during the four years he was in Russia; how Stalin had sealed off large areas of the Ukraine and the people were starving because he had stolen all their grain.

When Harold moved into the Arno Rooms at 42 East Cordova it was a skid row area. As he was living there, the neighbourhood changed from derelict drunks sleeping on the streets to tourists rushing to see the beautiful Gastown, the steam clock and the statue of Gassy Jack. The hippy stores were vacated, and trendy new shops were opening. His rooming house was now called the Central Hotel and work was underway to connect the building next door. The building was to become a subsidized rental for people like him. At least the top three floors. The income from renting by the night hotel rooms was just too good so the bottom three floors were for tourists.

It was an odd mix. There were a bunch of old men who had been in the war on the top floors. On the bottom were people from Germany, Japan, and England. Harold loved it. It made life going to the bars at night interesting. He no longer had to only drink with old men but spent evenings chatting with young men who worked in the stock market and women who owned boutique shops. It could still be a rough place at night, but Harold never stayed out past nine anymore. He was just getting too old.

His daughter Marlene came to visit a couple of times. They always met at a restaurant close by. She would pick the place and he would turn up in one of his rumpled suits, hat perched on his now almost bald head. She shuddered when she saw him lurch down the street. It was his unmistakable stride, and he was taller than most, so he stood out. They were short visits. They made her uncomfortable. They made him uncomfortable too. He felt inadequate and at a loss for words. He did not like the visits as much as he should have. He loved her but they had nothing in common.

He thought a couple of times about trying to reach out to his other daughter Gwynne. Marie seemed to know where she was living most of the time. In 1980 she was in Surrey about two blocks from his old friend Bill who stole his wife from him. His first wife, Pearl. He never did marry Marion but considered her his second wife. Pearl was in a home in Terrace. Marion was still working and still dropping by. But what would he say to Gwynne, "Hey remember me? Your dad's old friend? We had some great times together didn't we kid, sitting around the table drinking whiskey. Ha-ha, well you were not drinking whiskey but man you sure loved our stories."

He remembered when she graduated from high school he helped with some dress or something and he had seen her around that time and told her he opened a bank account in her name. He had. But it was gone. He drank that money up a long time ago. What would he say to her? Sorry I never told you I was your dad? Sorry I was never there for you? Sorry I am a failure? Ron was a good dad to her and a good friend. He missed Ron more than anyone else he had lost. Harold spent a lot of time in reflection and sadness. He knew he had not lived up to his potential as a man, a husband, or a father. He did not live up to his musical talent, his quick mind, or his potential. Thinking about it just made him drink more.

He was only five blocks from Marie and he often walked over and stood at her fence while she watered her flowers in the big wine barrels. They chatted easily about Ron and old times. Everyone called her the Big Boss of Powell Street. She was not the boss of much anymore, but he got a kick out of her. She had more stories to tell than Ron did. In the Spring of 1980, he walked to 358 Powell Street and saw the house where she lived was empty. The rooming house across the alley was busy with a Chinese restaurant, a shoe store and a boutique and he noticed a For Sale sign in one of the second-floor windows. He went into the Chop Suey House and ordered some hot and sour soup. He knew it was going to kill his stomach ulcer later, but it had been a long time. The waitress came over and he said, "The Big Boss not around?"

She looked at him and raised an eyebrow, "You mean the cook? He is in the back cooking."

"No, I mean Marie, Marie Robinson, the Big Boss of Powell Street."

She swiped a damp cloth across the table and said, "Sorry fella she died just after New Year's Day."

"What happened?", he asked.

"She was old man, like over eighty. Her son put the building up for sale so I don't know what will happen to us. We were operating without a lease. Marie was not too fussy on the legal stuff. But Bill, he wants us out I think."

"Well, he is selling it. What does he care?"

"I guess he got what he always wanted. To be a rich man from selling this joint."

Harold finished his soup and on the way out he told the waitress he wished her luck with a new landlord. He went across the alley and stood at Marie's gate. He took off his hat and bowed his head and from somewhere a prayer came out of him. He prayed for Marie and Ron and then he prayed for his mother and Gunvor and Pearl and Marion and Marlene and his grandsons and Gwynne and her children. Harold prayed like he had not done for thirty years. He went home and did not even go to the pub that night. He sat at his window overlooking the busy street and felt a huge loss and mourning fill up inside him.

The next couple of years drifted by for Harold. Burge came to visit and then Vernon. Marion quit coming around. He heard she moved out to the Fraser Valley when she retired from the Hospital. He got Christmas and Birthday cards from Marlene. He talked to his mom a couple of times a month. Harold was sick a lot. He had gastric ulcers that caused him to cough up blood. His stomach hurt all the time. He quit drinking in 1982 but he still went down to the lobby to play piano once in a while. He always drew a crowd. His heart was not good. He had hardening of the arteries and he opted not to seek medical help.

On September 18, 1983 Harold died in his room. Alone. He was sixty-six just like Ron had been. One of the residents had not seen him in that day and he always went out to eat so he alerted the management to go check out his room. Harold had been sicker than usual. The clerk and the old friend walked in together and found Harold on the bed. He was dead. He was already cold. They called the Coroner and when the paramedics came, they asked the old friend if there were any people to call. He said, "Not that I know of. He had an ex-wife. I think her name was Marion, but no next of kin."

"Do you know her last name?"

"No sir," he said, "I do not. He had a couple of daughters and family from back east, Alberta, I think. No, he was a lone, man. It was just us old guys he hung out with."

The put Harold on a gurney and took him out of the room, feet first. Harold was Dead on Arrival to Vancouver General Hospital. If Marion had still been working, there maybe she would have heard about his death. They brought him to the morgue. They tagged his toe just like Harold had done to so many people so many years ago. His friend from the Hotel said he was a veteran, so they called The Last Post, an agency that arranged for cremations and burials for veteran's who did not have any family. There were no family contacts and no last wishes, so his body was sent to the Vancouver Crematorium to be cremated. That's where Harold's ashes were when an uncle on his mother's side of the family, Elmer Rasmussen came to town. He decided to drop in on Harold.

The guys hanging around the lobby told Elmer abut The Last Post fund and Elmer tracked down the ashes. Elmer took the cardboard box with him back to Standard, Alberta. Harold's brother Vernon then took the ashes to Calgary to where Harold's mom was living. They did not understand why he had no contact information in case of emergency. It seemed he wanted to be left alone. Or maybe, his mom thought, he did not feel important. Vernon's son David who had become a minister said a eulogy for Harold. Not many of the family were there. But his mother Katherine sat in the front and wept for the son she remembered as her first born, her strength, her beautiful boy.

INDEX

TIMELINE

AND

NEWS CLIPPINGS

Research-Facts and Reality
Chapter One   Ron, Marie 1928-1931

Mike Pilawski Found Lying Beside Railway Tracks; Badly Battered

Arrested in a Winnipeg hotel, Friday afternoon, Roland Robinson and Maria Hoick, formerly of Saskatoon, are being held by city police for questioning in connection with the mysterious death at Saskatoon, on Oct. 9, of Mike Pilawski, or Harrison, whose battered body was found lying beside the C.P.R. tracks outside that city.

The couple, who are well known to police here, the latter under the soubriquet of "Bohunk" Marie, are described in a circular issued by Saskatchewan headquarters of the Royal North West Mounted police as persons who can throw considerable light on the circumstances surrounding Pilawski's death.

Was Murdered

A coroner's jury declared Pilawski had been murdered. He had evidently been brutally treated. His head was gashed, and, when the body was found, the head was pillowed on a bloodstained pile of newspapers.

Shortly before his death Pilawski had possessed $400. No trace of this money has been found by the police. Marie Hoick is known to have been with him the night before his death, when he was involved in a drunken brawl. Robinson, it is believed, was one of the last persons to see him.

Three other persons beside Robinson and Hoick were mentioned in the Mounted Police circular, but most importance was placed on the two now in custody. Sergeant Brown, of the Mounted Police, left Regina Friday night on receipt of word of the arrests, and will interview the prisoners today.

(The Winnipeg Tribune, November 3. 1928)

SUSPECTS IN M. PILAWSKI CASE FREED

Man and Woman Held in Winnipeg Released After Paying Fine

DETECTIVE BROWN RETURNS TO CITY

SAYS HE PICKED UP SOME VALUABLE INFORMATION WHILE IN MANITOBA

Ronald Robinson and Marie Hoick, alias Dyck, alias "Bohunk Marie," held at Winnipeg since Friday awaiting questioning by Detective Sergeant Brown of Saskatoon, concerning their knowledge of Mike Pilawski, who was murdered here on October 9, were released today.

FINED $10 EACH

This morning the two appeared before a magistrate in Winnipeg city police court and were fined $10 each for registering at a hotel as man and wife.

Detective Sergeant Brown, of the R.C.M.P., returned to the city late last night and stated this morning that he had obtained some information which should prove of great benefit in inquiring into the mystery.

He declined to state the nature of his information but said it fitted in closely with police theories concerning the manner of the murder and admitted that it made things look black for one or two

The Star Phoenix, November 6, 1928

Released By Police

WINNIPEG, Nov. 6.—Ronald Robinson and Maria Hoick, alias Dyck, who have been detained since Friday by police for questioning in connection with the recent mysterious death near Saskatoon of Mike Pelawsky, today were given their release, police officials announced.

Edmonton Journal, November 6, 1928

Chapter Two   Ron, Marie (1932-1940)

(Leader-Post Special Press Bureau)
PERDUE, Sask., Sept. 6.—Following a daring robbery here Sunday afternoon when a woman walked into the kitchen of the King George restaurant and picked the pocket of the Chinese cook, obtaining $27, and her companion, another woman, robbed the local garage, Mrs. Marie Robinson and Mrs. Grant Boyer appeared before Justices of the Peace George Saunders and W. Taylor here Monday night.

Mrs. Robinson pleaded guilty to theft from the garage and was fined $5 and costs, and Mrs. Boyer, pleading not guilty to the charge of theft from the Chinese, was found guilty and fined $10 and costs or 30 days in jail.

The two women were arrested in company with their husbands

September 1932 The Leader Post

Mark Sue Kowk a Ronald Robinson Sentenced

Six months in Fort Saskatche
jail each was the sentence imp
on Mark Sue Kowk, Chinese,
Ronald Robinson, who were fo
guilty of vagrancy charges by M
istrate Primrose in police court S
urday.

Two joint charges of retail
possession of stolen property w
dropped against the accused by
crown when insufficient evide
was produced to prove that a qu
tity of goods found in their roon
10802 98 st. was actually in t
possession. Both accused swore t
did not know the articles were h
den in the cupboard.

"I may soy you are two pro
vagrants and if I could give yo
longer sentence I would," the
remarked.

When it was revealed the S
vation Army had arranged for a
in Cherhill for Leo Mattern,
was discharged from a vagra
count.

July 21, 1934, The Edmonton Journal

Ronald Robinson, pleading guilty
) a vagrancy charge, was remand-
1 to Thursday.

   *   *   *

IMPRISONED FOR THEFT

For the theft of three sets of driving lines, worth $12.60, from the T. Eaton company's mail order warehouse, Ronald Robinson was sentenced by Mr. Justice Tweedie in supreme court Tuesday to six months' imprisonment at Fort Saskatchewan. He was defended by W. G. K. Bloor.

October 2, 1935 Edmonton Journal

Chapter Four   Ron, Marie, Gunvor (1940-1948)

Mr. Murdock is a member of
ne 2nd Bn., Irish Fusiliers (VR),
RF), while Ted Gordon, another
'ancouver barrister who had
een associated with Mr. Mur-
ock, is serving overseas with
 Canadian unit.
Ronald Robinson, a former
nember of the staff, is an AC 1
ttached to RCAF headquarters
t Jericho Air Station and Oliver
Vilson . is with the RCAF in
;astern Canada.

May 1941, The Vancouver Sun

Other decrees went to:
Marie Robinson, 358 Powell, mar-
ried in 1928 to Ronald Robinson,
Kamloops.

May 1947, The Vancouver Sun

Five-Year Sentence in Drug Case

One of Western Canada's largest drug cases closed in police court Tuesday when William Dick, 32, was sentenced to five years.

Dick was convicted by Magistrate W. W. B. McInnes on a charge of possession of $76,000 worth (black market price) of brown heroin. His Worship directed that Dick also pay a $500 fine or serve an additional three months.

Dick's conviction came as a sequel to the conviction Monday of John Serniuk, 31, who was charged with the illegal transportation of the drug.

Serniuk was sentenced to seven years, plus a $1000 fine or an additional six months.

The drug was intercepted by officers aboard a CPR train. It was in a suitcase which watching officers said was claimed by Dick two days after its arrival here.

Dick denied any knowledge that the suitcase contained drugs.

RCMP officers told of following Dick's car through town and finally stopping him in Stanley Park, where an officer confronted him with a drawn gun.

June 1947, The Vancouver Sun

Court Confirms
Drug Conviction

Conviction of John Cerniuk, for shipping $70,000 worth of morphine from Toronto to Vancouver, was confirmed today by Court of Appeal.

Cerniuk will appeal Monday from a sentence of seven years and a fine of $1000 or another six months, imposed by Magistrate W. W. B. McInnes.

Appellate Court today also refused to interfere with the magistrate's penalty of five years and $500 or three months given to William Dick, 358 Powell, for possession of morphine. Dick was found guilty after the suitcase, checked in Toronto with the morphine in it, had been claimed by him in Vancouver.

December 9, 1947, The Vancouver Sun

Chapter Five   Harold   (1940-1948)

A purse with $25 was taken from Miss Pearl Larsen, 1395 West Twelfth, at Second Beach Sunday.

Three and a half yards of cloth valued at about $20 were taken from the room of J. D. McDon-

May 1947, The Vancouver Sun

Chapter Six Harold, Ron, Gunvor, Marie (1948-1952)

BYE-BYE MALE: BYE-BYE BAIL

Because James Budd departed for parts unknown, Marie Robinson, 358 Powell, is out $1,000.

That is the amount of bail the woman put up for Budd who was charged with retaining stolen goods.

County Court Judge C. J. Lennox made the order forfeiting bail Friday after Budd failed to appear in Police Court.

January 1950, The Vancouver Sun

CUT MOUTH

R. J. Boond, 60, of 140 North Delta, Burnaby, who suffered a cut mouth in a two-car crash in the 3600 block East Hastings. Harold J. Larsen, 34, of 755 West Broadway, who received a bruised head and leg in a mishap in the 1100 block East Hastings. Kathleen M. Lastik, 23, of 3417 Worthington, and Mrs. Ada C. Morash, of 931 Frederick, who were injured in a two-car mishap at Kingsway and Gladstone.

September 25, 1950 The Vancouver Sun

Warrant Issued for Drug Case Accused

A bench warrant was issued by Mr. Justice Clyne for the arrest of the Mallock brothers of Winnipeg, George and John, when they failed to appear in Assize Court today for trial on drug charges.

An application is being heard by His Lordship this afternoon for forfeiture of $40,000 bail posted for the Winnipeg brothers.

Bonds of $10,000 each were put up by Stella Cushman, 2026 Cornwall; Annie Emily Rice, 1750 Kingsway; Marie Robinson, 358 Powell, and Harry Eriikson, 1376 Adanac.

CARTER APPEARS

A third man, accused with the Mallocks, of conspiring last summer to sell heroin to Henry Giordano, U.S. narcotic bureau supervisor, is William Carter, who is on $10,000 bail.

Carter appeared for his trial and pleaded not guilty.

The case is proceeding, in Assize Court with Paul B. Paine defending.

D. McK. Brown is conducting the prosecution.

HEART ATTACK REPORTED

As counsel for the Mallocks, T. A. Dohm told the court Monday he had been advised by telegram that George had had a heart attack, but that they would be leaving Winnipeg by air Monday night, to stand their trial in Vancouver.

Mr. Dohm stated today that he had received no further word from his clients and had been unable to find any record of any reservation on the plane having been made by them.

Incoming planes were checked by RCMP officers, who reported that the Mallocks did not arrive at Vancouver Airport.

Lytton Blacked Out As Generator Fails

Special to The Vancouver Sun

LYTTON, Jan. 30.—Failure of the newly-opened B.C. Electric power plant here plunged this Fraser Canyon centre into darkness at 6 p.m. Monday and left it without power in 15 below zero weather today.

Officials said that a generator had burned out. It was not known how long replacement would take.

...MES

...eliveries ...aily Basis

more calls and deliver 50 percent more letters.

Postal officials acknowledged the cut on service to residential areas would work a hardship on suburban businesses.

Letter carriers are paid an average of $175 a month, he said. The staff reduction, therefore, would save the Vancouver Post offfice $20,000 a month or $240,000 annually.

Fifteen thousand business mail calls will not be affected by the

January 30, 1951, Vancouver Sun

Crown Won't Take Bondsmen's Homes

The four Vancouver residents who forfeited $40,000 bail when George and John Mallock failed to appear in court Monday on drug charges will not immediately lose the homes they put up as sureties.

The four confiscated $10,000 bonds will become a registered charge, in effect like a mortgage, against each of the four properties, as provided for in Section 169 of the Land Registry Act.

After the Crown charge is registered against each property, there need be no hurry about further action to cash the bail bonds, Douglas McK. Brown, Crown prosecutor, said today.

Mr. Brown got a court order Wednesday confiscating the bail bonds.

The four bondsmen are Marie Robinson, 358 Powell; Harry Erickson, 1376 Adanac; Stella Cushman, 2026 Cornwall, and Annie Emily Rice, 1750 Kingsway.

February 2, 1951, The Vancouver Sun

Collusion Claimed In Divorce Trial

A daughter of Lady Cornwall of Ashcroft and the late Duke of Cornwall, is in Supreme Court here seeking a divorce.

She is Lavender Millicent Dyson, New Westminster, and she was married 12 years ago to Alvin Lester Dyson who was released recently from Oakalla Prison farm where he was sentenced to one year for theft.

Mr. Justice Whittaker is hearing her petition, which is defended by Dyson on the ground that he was "framed" and that the case is collusive.

Dyson has not yet given evidence, but in his reply he claimed he was offered money while he was in Oakalla by his wife's lawyer to give her her freedom.

This was vigorously denied in court today by the Kamloops counsel who was acting for Mrs. Dyson.

"That's too ridiculous even to consider. It is the last thing in the world I would suggest," said the lawyer when asked about Dyson's allegation that he had been requested to sign a confession to facilitate a divorce.

The judge heard evidence of an

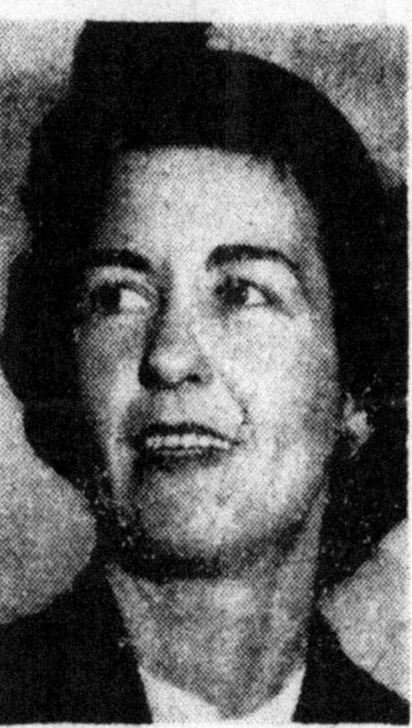

MRS. LAVENDER DYSON
... duke's daughter

investigator concerning Dyson and a Kamloops woman in the fair grounds at Kamloops three summers ago. The trial is proceeding this afternoon.

May 1951, The Vancouver Sun

Alleged Frame In Divorce Case Probed

A divorce action in which Alvin Lester Dyson claimed he had been "framed" was referred by Mr. Justice Whittaker to the attorney general Monday.

An adjournment for an indefinite period came after D. A. Sturdy withdrew as counsel for the petitioner, Lavender Millicent Dyson, New Westminster.

Mr. Sturdy took over the case for J. O. C. Kirby, Kamloops lawyer who was acting for Mrs. Dyson when her husband alleged that he had been framed.

Last week, the judge heard evidence by Ronald Robinson, Kamloops investigator, who said he had followed Dyson and a woman into a stable at Kamloops fair grounds three summers ago.

His evidence was followed by testimony by the woman, a quarter breed Indian, that Dyson forced his attentions on her.

Kirby then took the stand to deny, as Robinson had done, that any suggestion was made by either of them to Dyson during a visit to him at Oakalla Prison Farm last spring, to make a divorce deal with him.

December. 1951, the Vancouver Sun

Chapter Seven Marie (1950-1954)

Court Hopes to See Bail-Jumping Pair

The old adage, "absence makes the heart grow fonder," is working in reverse for bail jumpers John and George Mallock.

The former Winnipeg brothers skipped $40,000 bail here in the spring of 1951 and their case has been postponed from one Assizes to the next ever since.

The latest postponent came Wednesday afternoon when Mr. Justice Manson was told that the police are scouring North America for the pair.

"Their absence doesn't make our hearts grow any fonder," commented His Lordship.

"I have every confidence they will be picked up sooner or later."

An order was made at the Spring Assizes, 1951, when the Mallocks failed to appear for trial on a charge of conspiring to sell narcotics, for the forfeiting of the bail.

No steps apparently have been taken as yet to collect from the bondsmen, who put up property valued at $40,000 for the brothers.

They are Mrs. Stella Cushman, 2026 Cornwall; Mrs. Annie Emily Rice, 1750 Kingsway; Marie Robinson, 358 Powell, and Harry Erickson, 1376 Adanac, who posted $10,000 each for John and George respectively.

At the request of Prosecutor Wilfried H. Heffernan, Mr. Justice Manson on Wednesday adjourned until November 24 the Crown's application to enforce the forfeiture order.

November 13, 1952, The Vancouver Sun

Move to Sell Bail Forfeited Property

Proceedings to collect $40,000 bail posted for the missing George and John Mallock nearly two years ago were referred today by Mr. Justice Manson to Mr. Justice Clyne.

On Friday, D. McK. Brown will apply to Mr. Justice Clyne at New Westminster Assizes for authority to sell the property posted by Mrs. Stella Cushman, 2026 Cornwall; Mrs. Annie Emily Rice, 1750 Kingsway, and Mrs. Marie Robinson, 358 Powell, who put up a total of $30,000 for the Mallocks.

The fourth bondsman was Harry Erickson, 1376 Adanac, who posted the remainder of the $40,000 bail.

The Mallock brothers jumped bail before they were scheduled to appear in Vancouver Assize Court in January, 1951, on a charge of conspiring to sell narcotics.

Mr. Justice Manson said today he wanted to see the Crown proceed with the forfeiture proceedings against the bonds people.

D. A. Sturdy is expected to attack the validity of the proceedings on behalf of the three bondswomen when the case comes up on Friday.

November 24, 1952, The Vancouver Sun

**AR ATHLETE
'53 SOUGHT**

ho was B.C.'s finest
ie — professional or
teur — male or female
1953?

ancouver Sun readers,
d by an 11-man panel
ports experts, will have
opportunity to select
star of stars for the
ted "B.C. Athlete of the
r" award made annually
The Sun.
or details see Pages 16
18.

50,000
an Asked
r Pool

tish Empire Games So-
wallowing in financial
les, has asked the city for
-interest loan of up to
000.

e society is offering as
eral anticipated gate re-
s at the 1954 Games of
000.

e loan is needed to enable
to proceed with construc-
of the Little Mountain
iming pool.

easurer W. H. Raikes has
en City Council explaining
the society will not be able
aise sufficient funds to
r all commitments before
games next year.

e wants City Council to ad-
e the money and take re-
nent from the gate receipts
uarantee a bank loan.

e request goes before the
s finance committee on
day, and it may be headed
trouble.

dermen have already made
lain that no contracts will
igned until the BEG can
v it has money on hand to
r commitments.

ty has already put up $200,-
in four annual payments
of revenue to aid the BEG.

ratepayers last December
roved a $750,000 stadium by-

n additional $71,000 will be
ided to help meet the ex-
stadium costs, and a second
iey bylaw will be put up
year to cover enclosure of
swimming pool.

'anada Out

Powell Street
Tenement Gutted

A pre-dawn fire raced through a Powell Street tenement building today killing three people and driving 29
to the street in night clothes.

A second early blaze at White Rock killed a 16-
month-old girl who died while her parents fought the
flames with buckets of water. (See story below.)

Left dead in charred ruins of
the downtown Vancouver frame
building, which District Fire
Chief J. E. Shaw described as
a "terrible trap," were:

Valentino Coccenic, 74.

Jack Roberts, 73.

Helen Haden, 48.

The two men, both ill, were
overcome by smoke and died
trying to escape from their
small rooms. The woman died
from burns in her room where
the fire apparently started.

DOGS SAVE LIVES

Three small Chihuahua dogs
prevented the death toll from
soaring much higher in the terrible fire.

Owner of the building, the
Marine Rooms, 358 Powell. Mrs.
Marie Robinson, said the barking of the tiny dogs awoke her
as smoke started seeping into
her downstairs suite.

"I knew something was
wrong even before I heard the
roar and crackle that seemed
to be coming from the walls,"
she said.

ESCAPES "NIGHTMARE"

Those who survived the fire
described the 10 minutes of
frantic escape from the building as a nightmare.

Said George Maisuradze, 74,
who awoke to find the thin
walls of his room bulging from
the heat: "The smoke made
everything so dark I couldn't
see the light burning in the
centre of my room.

"I could hear cries up and
down the halls and the building
alarm was ringing. Then it
would stop and start again."

PARTIALLY BLIND

Henry Hiebert, 76, another
old aged pensioner and partially blind, heard that halting
alarm bell.

"There were two ways out—
the back and down the front
stairs," he said. "I couldn't see
but the heat I felt coming from
the back hallway stopped me
before I had gone 10 steps. I
turned and went down the
front."

Brooder
Fire Takes
Baby's Life

WHITE ROCK, Sept. 12.—An
overheated chick brooder in a
baby's bedroom was blamed for
an early-morning fire that
claimed the life of 16-months-
old Margaret Burns here.

Fire Chief C. W. Pollard of
White Rock Department said
an electric light bulb used in
the brooder was the likely
source of the blaze.

One room of the tiny two-
room frame dwelling housed
the brooder and the baby's crib
while her parents, William and
Winnifred Burns, slept in the
second room.

Smoke and gasses overcame
the child before flames en-
veloped the crib, Chief Pollard
said.

Next door neighbor George
Stanworth said afterward he
was awakened by Mrs. Burns
pounding and screaming at his
door.

"I didn't know what it was
until I heard her yelling fire,"
he said. "First thing I did was
try to use my garden hose on
the flames but it was too short
so I grabbed a couple of.
buckets.

"Then they told me the baby
was inside but it was too late
to try to get in."

TCA Inaugurates
Link to Mexico

MONTREAL, Sept. 12 —
(BUP)—Trans-Canada Airlines
announces it will inaugurate a
once-weekly service between
Montreal and Mexico City
October 31, almost the same
time that Canadian Pacific Air-
lines plans to start flying io
South America from Vancouver.
President Gordon R. Mc-

September 12, 1953, The Vancouver Sun

September 12, 1953, The Vancouver Sun

Fire Second Costly Blow

Today's tenement fire at 358 Powell that took three lives was the second financial blow to Mrs. Marie Robinson in the past two years.

Mrs. Robinson, who said she would lose heavily, is the same woman who put up $10,000 of the $40,000 bail bond for John and George Mallock. They jumped bail while waiting to face narcotics charges.

Mrs. Robinson wept in court as her $10,000 was confiscated.

September 12, 1953, The Vancouver Sun

Vancouver Woman Loses $10,000 to Bail Jumper

VANCOUVER (CP) — A woman who posted and lost a $10,000 bail bond watched bleakly Thursday as the trial of bail jumper George Mallock opened here.

"I'd like to scratch the man's eyes out," exclaimed Mrs. Marie Robinson as the heavily-manacled Mallock was taken into court to face three narcotic charges. She was one of four people who put up $40,0000 bail for Mallock and his brother John when they were arrected in 1950. Both Mallocks jumped bail and the bond money was estreated.

Mrs. Robinson said she put up the bail money because her children went to school with the Ballock brothers in Winnipeg. George was arrested in New York last December. His brother is still at large.

Henry Giordano of Kansas City, a United States narcotic bureau undercover agent and first witness, testified that Mallock and William Carter agreed to deliver more than $2,500 worth of heroin to him here in 1950.

Carter now is serving a seven-year term in B.C. penitentiary for a narcotic offense.

The trial is continuing.

Bush Jackson Charged With Beating Wife

TORONTO (BUP) — Harvey (Busher) Jackson, a member of the Toronto Maple Leaf hockey teams' famous "kid line," was arrested today on a charge of giving his wife a black eye.

Jackson was released on $1,000 property bail.

1954, The Vancouver Sun

DICK—HUMPHREYS—On November 26, 1954, William Dick, son of Mrs. Marie Dick, of 358 Powell St., to Donna Humphreys, daughter of Mr. and Mrs. Jack Humphreys of Vancouver, B.C.

October 1954, The Vancouver Sun

Chapter Nine Harold (1953 to 1961)

Unscheduled Stop For CNR Express

HOPE (CP)—The Super-Continental Express of Canadian National Railways made an unscheduled stop here Friday because of a troublesome drunk. The conductor told the police the man claimed he was a private detective and tried to arrest the dining-car cook. RCMP said Harold John Larsen, 36, of Vancouver was charged with causing a disturbance.

February 17, 1958, Nanaimo Daily News

Train Drunk Fined

HOPE — A man taker police from a transcontine passenger train Friday fined $20 for creating a turbance by being d r u Harold John Larsen, 36, o West Broadway, Vancou was also ordered to pay in costs.

February 1958, The Vancouver Sun

Five Motorists Face Charges

Five motorists were charged with impaired driving during the past 24 hours by Vancouver police.

They are Ralph Sullivan, 43, of 4150 Blenheim; Herber Fleck, 42, of 5563 Columbia Myril Clifford Olsen, 43, o 2043 Stainsbury; Harold Lar sen, 43, of 827 West Broadway and Arthur Percy Holland, 61 of 2743 West Sixteenth.

October 1959, The Vancouver Sun

Men jailed over liquor

Harold Larsen, 43, of 827 West Broadway, was jailed Tuesday for three months for impaired driving.

His licence was suspended for two years.

Chapter Ten   Ron, Gunvor (1963 to 1968)

SHERIFF CHARGED

Vancouver police have charged Hope sheriff Ronald Robinson with passing a forged $304 cheque.

Robinson, 58, was remanded to Aug. 19 and released on his own recognizance when he appeared in magistrate's court today.

The charge against Robinson alleges a $304 cheque made out by an oil firm to R. W. Robinson, a former Hope service station operator, was forged and passed in Vancouver last Feb. 7.

August 12, 1964, The Vancouver Sun

Charge Dismissed Against Officer

Magistrate Bernard Isman dismissed a forgery charge against a Hope sheriff's officer.

Ronald Robinson, 58, was charged Aug. 12 with passing a forged $304 cheque in Vancouver on Feb. 7.

August 1964, The Vancouver Sun

Institute Warns of Phonies

The Canadian National Institute for the Blind has issued a public statement emphasizing that it is not making any separate appeal for funds at this time.

Capt. M. C. Robinson, national director of the CNIB for Western Canada, said it is a member of the Community Chest, receiving public donations through the Red Feather United Appeal.

"We urge the public to make full inquiries before contributing to any appeal on behalf of the blind," he said.

Capt. Robinson said the CNIB has received a large number of inquiries about the sales of the magazine The Vision published by the rival Canadian Federation of the Blind.

Local federation representative William Dick later said subscriptions to The Vision sell for four copies for $2 a year, with 70 per cent of the money going to the people who sell the magazine, and 30 per cent going to the federation.

Dick said the federation hopes to realize more money when the magazine's circulation, now at about 40,000, reaches 100,000 and it will carry national advertising.

September 26, 1963, The Vancouver Sun

Ronald Robinson

28 Mar 1906
Woodbury, East Devon District,
Devon, England
31 Jan 1973
Vancouver,
Greater Vancouver Regional District,
British Columbia, Canada
North Shore Crematorium
North Vancouver,
Greater Vancouver Regional
District, British Columbia, Canada

Gunvor Robinson (Berglund,Weberg)

4 Aug 1910
Sweden
12 Feb 1984
Vancouver,
Greater Vancouver Regional District,
British Columbia, Canada
North Shore Crematorium
North Vancouver,
Greater Vancouver Regional District,
British Columbia, Canada

020 Deaths

LARSEN — Harold Johannes, passed away at Vancouver, B.C., September, 18, 1983, at the age of 67 years. He leaves to mourn, his loving daughter, Marlene and husband, Ken McLeod; three grandsons of Kitimat, B.C.; his mother, Katherine Larsen of Bethany Care Centre, Calgary; one sister, Leona Christensen, Calgary; two brothers, Burge and Vernon, Standard, and numerous nieces and nephews. A Memorial Service was held on Saturday, September 24 at Bethany Care Centre. Interment, Mountain View Gardens.

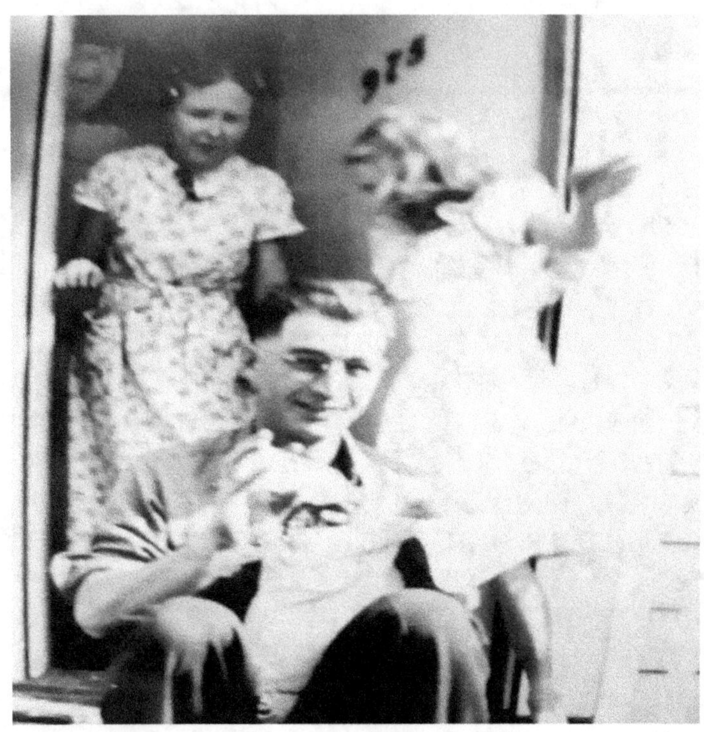

Gunvor, Elna, Harold and Gwynne (baby), 1949 Kamloops

Author Profile

Gwynne has been writing all her life. A poet, a playwright, a novelist, she has written, directed and produced over thirty of her own plays. She wrote four books, hundreds of poems, radio plays and monlogues. Social injustice is the theme of her work and her life and she has taken a lot of her work to the stage doing performance art for over thirty years. A long-time advocate for giving people a voice she has mentored and taught children, teens, people with brain injuries, and aspiring writers. Working with non-profits, Gwynne has raised thousands of dollars to help end violence against women and girls producing Even Ensler's The Vagina Monologues and supported women in crisis through healing workshops. Giving voice to those without a voice has been her life's work and this latest book Through My Lens gives voice to the past, to her parents-her mother, father and stepfather.